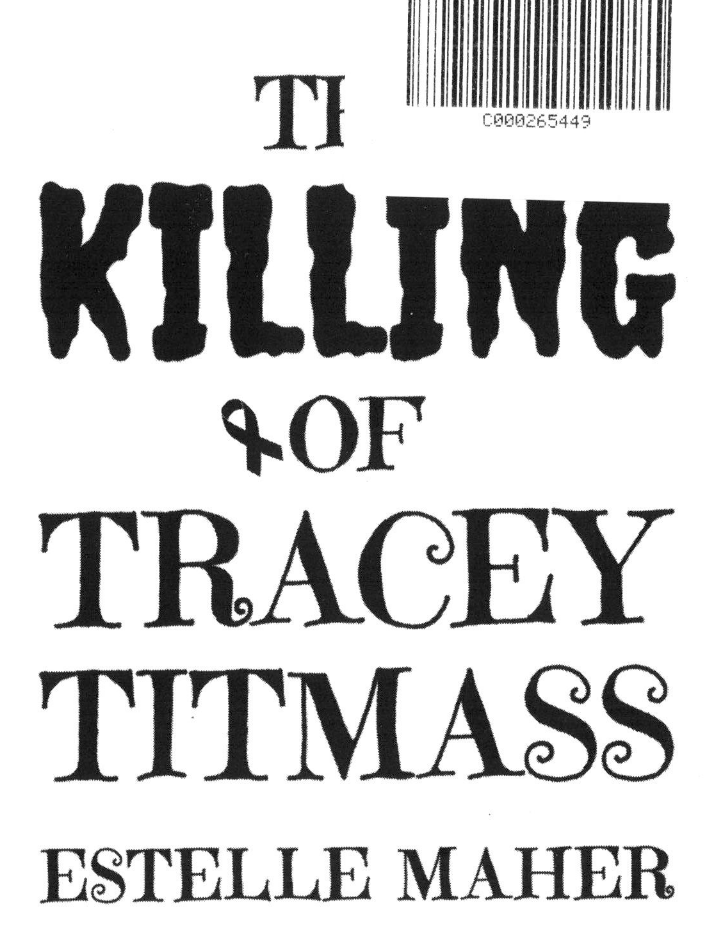

Beaten Track
www.beatentrackpublishing.com

The Killing of Tracey Titmass

Published 2020 by Beaten Track Publishing

Paperback ISBN: 978 1 78645 465 2
eBook ISBN: 978 1 78645 466 9

Cover Design:
Estelle Maher & Debbie McGowan

Beaten Track Publishing,
Burscough, Lancashire.
www.beatentrackpublishing.com

For the scarred.

Acknowledgements

First, I want to thank my publisher Debbie McGowan from Beaten Track Publishing. Thank you for editing my ramblings and making sure I've spelt Pinot Grigio correctly. I would have just said wine, but I wanted the readers to think I was sophisticated. She is someone I am yet to have a drink with, but I fear if she does, she will ask me to get her a Curacao—a word I can spell but not say. It's bad enough being judged on the former.

I want to thank my beta readers. First, Bob Stone, the bookshop owner who became my friend and supported me not only with the book but also during my recovery. When he's not swilling wine or listening to Ian McNabb, he is organising charity walks. Crowley's Crusaders would not be here without you, and only for you did half of Crosby charity walk wearing angel wings.

I'd also like to thank Jeanette Moore. After beta-reading the page where I insult vegans, she confessed to being one herself. But only on days when she doesn't fancy meat but sometimes fish, but only with bacon. But not real bacon, the pretend bacon for vegans made from turkey.

Thanks to Jude Lennon for her encouraging feedback. I would also like to apologise to her for putting up with my constant heckling during her writer's retreats. I think if the teacher in you could, you would give me detention and send me home with a note. However, you inspire me to write more and to drink less. (The last bit is a lie, but you taught me to write creatively not convincingly.)

Thanks to my third beta reader, Lesley Rawlinson. A fellow survivor whose feedback meant the most to me. Us girls gotta stick together!

Thanks to Lorna McCann PR for making me look good. Not an easy task!

Thanks to all my beautiful friends. I can't mention you all, but you know who you are. Without you, I would have been more sober fighting Tracey, so thank you for holding my hand during the haziness.

Thank you to Katherine Gillard. If it wasn't for you, I would have turned into a complete basket case.

In fact, I want to thank most people who have made me smile this last year, including the postman who didn't say a word when I opened the door in my bra. Was it the cancer treatment? Or have I always had a secret crush on the courier? Find out in my next book, *The Man from DPD and Me – A Health & Safety Nightmare*.

I would not be here if it wasn't for the staff at Clatterbridge Cancer Centre. Saying thank you isn't enough when people save your life, is it? But thank you.

My biggest thanks, of course, go to my family. My children, Chloé and Zack, made me smile every day, never left my side and still treated me like Mum, which was the most important thing.

And finally, Pete, my Mr. M…for everything.

Once you make peace with the path that you're on then the journey is easier.

Especially if you dance now and again.

Estelle Maher

Prologue

He didn't mean to pry. He very rarely went through her drawers. He was simply looking for a pair of scissors. He wanted to cut the label off the new shirt he had bought for tomorrow. When he thought of the following day, his nerves gripped him, sometimes rooting him to the spot. He had to do it, though. He wanted to do it. He had to be there for her, for his Jo.

He didn't find the scissors in the drawer—in her drawer. He found her sleeping tablets, her lavender pillow spray and a peach-coloured notebook with a gold J adorning the cover. He didn't deliberate much. Maybe it was the glint of the initial, but like a magpie, he reached for the small yet surprisingly weighty book.

As he sat on her side of the bed, a faint waft of her Jo Malone perfume laced with her pillow spray caressed his nostrils and brought him comfort. It was some time before he questioned whether he should be reading her diary. On every page were her hidden thoughts, her deepest feelings, the rockface of positivity that she clung to every day and above all else, her constant and familiar humour.

She had never told him she kept a diary. She had never told him lots of the things each page revealed to him. He questioned why she never said more—why she felt she had to be strong all the time. Whether he did enough for her.

It was hours later when he finished. It was hours later when he realised just how much she had been through. It was hours later when he cried for her. He thought about what she would say if she could see him crying. She'd tell him off, swear at him, then call him a name to make him laugh. Because that's how she coped—by making herself laugh and wanting others to join in.

Cancer invaded so much, but she never allowed it to possess her humour.

Tuesday, 1st January 2019

So, my first entry in the diary bought for me by my friend Lucy. She thinks that because I write a lot at work, I may find keeping a diary enjoyable. I apologise in advance, Diary; I am not known for my long-term commitments. I stayed in Brownies until I had the uniform, as that was the only thing I wanted. I wasn't arsed about camping or selling cakes. I only stayed in various school clubs long enough to receive a badge of recognition of some sort, and I only became a library monitor as I hated the playground. In my later years, this was replaced with detention from me constantly being caught smoking on school grounds. I'll try my best, dear Diary, but you may be used at a later date for phone numbers and odd notes about what to buy when I next go shopping. You will no doubt have numerous pages ripped out by the end of your short life, which, according to your front, is a standard twelve months.

I'm hungover today. It was my friend Mia's wedding yesterday. A typical affair of a cold church and manor house reception. Mark, my boyfriend, was my plus-one. Well, to be fair, he was actually on the invite, seeing as Mark and I have been together for seven years. The church was freezing, and Mark reckoned the priest probably didn't think it was worth heating the whole building for a twenty-minute exchange of vows. I didn't know anyone there, as most of them were family, and I was one of the few that Mia had invited from work. She looked pretty, of course, as most brides do, but I couldn't help but notice the corned-beef effect on her upper arms from the minus-four temperature in Christ the King Church.

The manor was charming until Mark started moaning about the price of the beer behind the bar. Judging by my pounding head, it didn't slow us down. I only drank more because the wedding, at the end of the day, was a grim affair. The meal was nice, but we were on a table with a lady who had gone to school with Mia and looked a lot older than thirty-five. Maybe she was in the sixth form while Mia was in year seven. Unsurprisingly, judging by her appearance and demeanour, she had come with her mother. You could tell this girl had no friends and her mother was her whole world. They whispered between themselves about the quality of the meat, and eventually, the mother insisted she needed to go home and settle down for the night. It was only half past three at this point. The girl, who I think was called Shelley, returned and recognised me being from her dining table and thought it automatically made us friends. Mark made an excuse to leave the company and left me with maybe-called-Shelley, who I vaguely remember collaring me in a corner.

"Do you think I should join a dating website?"

"Maybe."

"Should I tell the truth about my life on the dating website?"

I was struggling with what the details were and if she had a life. I was also struggling to remain upright. "It's an idea," I said, too pissed to care.

"Should I tell my mother?"

I can't remember my answer, but Mark recalls me saying something about, "Fuck your mother, or better still, fuck the best man." How that was received…I won't know until I next see Mia, I suppose.

Mark is downstairs, making me a strong coffee. He's a good bloke, and I'll probably spend the rest of my life with him. Judging by the ferocity of this hangover, the end could be somewhere between *Hollyoaks* and *News at Ten* tonight. Mia and her husband, Rob, were badgering about us being next. To be honest, Mia and Rob have only been together for a couple of years and were talking last night about starting a family straight away. They met at a networking event where a bunch of IT people went, discussed the latest digital solutions for local newspapers and ate cake. Mia and Rob took the mingling to the extreme. Neither returned to the office after the networking event, and they exchanged more than business cards by the end of the day. They have been inseparable ever since.

Mark and I don't even live together, and that suits us fine. Before I met Mark, I was with Stu for a whole twelve years. I thought we were happy until I found out he had been with Zoe for the last three of them. When I did find out, he left me the following day. Within six months, I sold the house and all of the furniture and moved into a flat on my own. I couldn't wait to leave the house that we had saved hard for. The couple who bought it were hard bargainers.

"Will you be leaving the carpets?" she asked.

"I'm sure we can come to an agreement," I said.

"Will you be cleaning them before you leave?" The hall carpet had visible footprints from Stu's muddy work boots. "I mean, there are dirty footprints all over the place."

"Yes," I said. "My boyfriend walked all over the carpet and then walked all over me." I gave her the carpets for free. What was I going to do with unfitted fitted carpets?

I met Mark two years later. I was in a club with my friend Charlotte, celebrating my thirty-sixth birthday, when he came over and asked if he could buy me a drink. I immediately fell in love with his accent, which I thought was American. He took great pleasure in correcting me and telling me he was Canadian. I liked that about him. I liked the fact he was proud of where he came from and gave an air that Americans were inferior to Canadians when anyone mistook him for one. His job brought him to the UK, and even though he misses his family, he admits that it's me who keeps him here.

After saying that, however, I cannot see us living together anytime soon. Even if we did, I would hardly see him as he works away a lot. Plus, with me moving into my new house, we just haven't got time to live together and make joint decisions and think about compromising and finding time for consideration. No, we're fine as we are, and I will be able to do up my house the way I want. If it were up to Mark, the whole place would be decked out with IKEA furniture, chunky plates and a ninety-inch telly to watch the footy match on. Sod that! This house will be all about me. Even the annexe on the side is being turned into a pottery studio. When I told Mark, he sniffed at the idea and said it would be better used as a party room. He forgets he's forty-four; he thinks he's still twenty, and I'm concerned about how much *Love Island* affects his personality. As soon as the new season starts, he feels the need to make his presence known at the gym and buys *GQ* magazine. He permanently carries a sports bottle, as if walking around his two-bed flat could induce dehydration and not give him enough warning to walk to a tap and the glass cupboard. However, he's kind-hearted, he has a decent job and the most incredible mouth, and he loves me, which I know sometimes is hard. I'm not the easiest person to be around. I drink too much, I'm very opinionated, and I swear like a sailor. But some people say those are my best qualities, so there you go.

I've decided that today I am going to venture to the sofa, watch some telly and catch the adverts that now revolve around booking summer holidays and buying sofas. I'll tell Mark to go home after he has fed me and then have a bath and back to bed. A perfect start to the New Year.

Wednesday, 2nd January 2019

I feel a lot better today. To be honest, I felt a lot better after Mark cooked lasagne. It's about the only thing he can cook well, and it did the trick for me. He didn't argue too much when I asked him to go home as I wanted an early night.

Today is my last day off before I am back in the office tomorrow, and I want to unpack some more boxes. I have been in this house for nearly six weeks, and I still haven't managed to unpack everything. Who am I trying to kid, Diary? I brought some boxes to this new house from my old flat that had never been unpacked since the last move. I moved one labelled 'Kitchen' that I found in the back bedroom of the flat, so I want to open that first, as it took me by surprise—I didn't realise I was missing anything. I'm also wondering, why did I put a box labelled 'Kitchen' in a bedroom all those years ago? I feel like it's another Christmas Day and I still have a present to unwrap. A crap version of Christmas, admittedly, but I'm excited, nonetheless.

I think my house might be haunted, though. I had an experience while I was in the bathroom—well, two, actually. First, I was in the bath and found a lump in my boob. It'll be nothing, I know. I had one of these a few years back, and

I had written my whole funeral service, the songs I wanted and who I was leaving my crap jewellery collection to. It turned out to be a cyst, and thank God it did! I'm sure I asked for 'Tragedy' by Steps to be played as they brought me into the church. I was quite dramatic in my thirties, looking back. This will be the same, no doubt.

But back to the haunting—all I can say is that when I was rummaging around feeling for more lumps, I swear I saw a dark shadow blocking the streetlight through my bedroom window. When I sat up in the bath, it had gone, and I didn't see it again. Aren't house sellers supposed to disclose if you're buying a haunted house, or is that only in America? *This house comes with three reception rooms, a splendid Spanish-style kitchen and a ghost that is particularly fond of playing pre-wartime tunes, wearing white nighties and turning the heating down. Viewing by appointment only.*

I'm not sure how I'd feel if this house is haunted. My aunt lived in a haunted house for years. Her ghost liked to steal things. CDs from boxes, half of a suit and shoes, to name a few. I lived with her for a few months while I was waiting for the sale of my last flat to go through. Her poltergeist, in the short time that I lived there, helped itself to a pair of trousers from a grey silk suit I had only worn once, my Gucci sunglasses (why?), a pair of black suede heels and my Norah Jones CD—not the case, just the disc itself. I had visions of the quite stylish ghost waiting for us to go to bed before she could swoon around the house singing 'Come Away with Me in the Night'.

The day before I left, I shouted to her to return my things as she'd had them long enough, and sure enough, they were all returned to the places last seen before the van moved me to the flat. The ghost was a kleptomaniac but was obviously pretty decent and had had her fun. Or she became fed up of Norah Jones, which happens to us all, apparently, even when you're dead.

I've not said anything to Mark about the lump. I'll keep an eye on it and see how it goes. I probably won't tell my friends either. It will just be a cyst. They say as you get older, you develop lumps in your boobs anyway. This is what age does to you; I'm developing porridge tits. Well, at least they'll match my cottage cheese arse. I've been dry-skin-brushing my arse for about six months now. The cellulite is still there, but I've got to admit the skin has never felt so peachy. Not that Mark has noticed. He's more of a boob man, but then most men are. Well, from my experience anyway. And why do they favour one more than the other during sex? Mark gravitates towards my left one more than my right, and of the two, it's the smaller one. Sometimes I feel a little sorry for the right one and give it an encouraging push in Mark's direction like it's a child with social anxiety issues. Give Mark his due, it's usually these occasions where he plays nice, while I lie back and enjoy the experience or plan the following day.

Don't get me wrong, Diary, it's not like I don't enjoy sex; I do. But I find there are moments when I start thinking about what's in the freezer and will I have time to go to the dry cleaner's during my lunch hour? I'm a busy girl, and I sometimes take multitasking to a level that I'm not sure other women or even men do. It's not like I'm hurting anyone with my silent mental efficiency.

I'm dreading going back to work tomorrow. I've been off for over two weeks. My job is pretty dull, to say the least. I spend most of my time editing other people's work before the population consumes it in their local newspaper. Unless there's a controversial traffic light erection or a bad frost resulting in deepening potholes or another local drug 'lord' has been arrested, then we struggle for stories. I use the word lord loosely, as in most places across the country, the word is applied to an individual with an extensive network of dealers, an international supply chain and a penchant for the latest firearms. Where I live, the label can apply to anyone who grows a supply in their nan's loft or has upgraded their Honda Civic with blacked-out windows.

To keep me sane, I have become a lover of pottery. Not buying it, you understand. Making it. I've been attending pottery classes for nearly two years. Not that they're teaching me anything anymore, but I still go so I have access to the kiln and can catch up with Johnny, who runs the workshops. The main reason I bought this house is because there is an annexe attached—a bit more substantial than a conservatory. I plan to put my own kiln in there and use it for my pottery. I have a little dream that people will seek out a piece by Jo Kearns. They will commission me to do a piece that will take pride of place on the large round table in the vast hall in their big house, and people will gasp as they walk in and enquire if it is a Jo Kearns. The collector will look as smug as I do every time I have that little daydream. But until then, I will have to sign off and iron some shirts for the rest of the week.

Thursday, 3rd January 2019

Being in work today was a drag. There was hardly anyone in, and I wondered if it was worth it. We don't print a newspaper for two weeks over the Christmas period. No one wants to work, no one wants to advertise, and no one wants to deliver the things. Any other time of year, we have a list of kids who are eager to take on the job of delivering the free weekly newspaper. But that list is quickly devoured when they realise what the sheer weight of a hundred papers is and that not every Wednesday—delivery day—is dry and sunny. By December, the list is exhausted, and we are relying on retired members of the community or children from strict parents, and the last time I saw one of those kids they were riding a BMX bike with their mullet blowing in the wind.

Most of the chat today was about Mia's wedding. Some were a little put out that they didn't get an invite. Apparently, working with someone for over five years qualifies you for an invitation, even though they never interact outside of the office, take lunch together or know where each other even live. You don't have to know my life story to be my friend, but some of the basics you should know are as follows:

1. The area I live in. You don't have to know my address—a point in the general direction is enough for me.

2. My attitude to marriage and children. That's a no to both.

3. My propensity for a drink. I like to drink. I make no apologies for my consumption.

4. My attitude towards salad. It's not a meal.

5. My attitude to Frankie Boyle. He's not funny.

6. My attitude towards hot tubs. It's simply having a bath with your mates. People think the fact that you have a bottle of fizz and do it in the hotel car park makes it acceptable. It's not.

If you know most of the above about me, then you're likely to be my mate, and if I ever get married, then you're in with a high chance of a wedding invitation.

Friday, 4th January 2019

I finished work early today and said I had a meeting with a local business about an advertising opportunity. I didn't and went straight home to start getting ready to go out. I'm out with the girls tonight. It's not a mad one, just a meal and a catch-up about how everyone's Christmas and New Year went.

The local restaurant, The Lobby, was pretty quiet most of the night. Everyone is either skint from all the festivities or still too hungover from all of the celebrating. Saskia, Lucy, Charlotte, Kelly and her partner Anne came. Anne is pretty much part of the group now anyway, and I would hope that if Kelly could not make a night out that Anne would still feel she could come.

Kelly and Anne have been together longer than they let on. Anne is at least fifteen years older than Kelly, and she was the headmistress in the school where Kelly still works, hence the secrecy. It was a good year after Anne retired from the school that they finally 'came out'. One of the reporters at my paper thought it would make a juicy story until I told him a better one of him attending the local strip club every week while his kids were in school.

The story never made it, and neither did the guy's marriage, according to Sam in Accounts.

I began to tell the tale of Mia's wedding. They have only met her once, and I keep trying to integrate her in my little gang, as I know she would get on with them all. Mia left yesterday for her honeymoon in Jamaica, and I will admit to being insanely jealous.

"I heard you're not allowed to leave the hotel," said Saskia during the first course.

"Who told you that? Some insipid white girl who has never been further than Cleethorpes?" said Anne. Her Lancashire accent makes me laugh, and I can see why Kelly finds her attractive. She makes us all laugh.

"Well, can you leave?" asked Saskia.

"'Course ya can. I went a decade ago and walked around the streets, jumped on buses and talked to the people. What's the bloody point of going on holiday if you just stay in the hotel and look at the pool? You've got to absorb these cultures and breathe the air around you. But not too much on the bus, mind. That's full of BO and weed, and you might miss your stop."

We were laughing, but she never laughs. She knows she's being funny and enjoys pretending that she doesn't get the joke.

"I didn't know you went to Jamaica," said Kelly.

"Oh, aye. I went a few times. Had a little holiday romance on one of my trips with a woman from Hull called Gail.

It was lovely while we were on holiday, but when I came back and went to visit her, I realised she had a look of John Craven about her. Jamaican rum has a lot to answer for."

Lucy was more quiet than usual, and when we quizzed her, she just kept saying she was fine. Then I noticed Charlotte give me the eyes. The eyes that say *I know what's up and leave her alone. I'll tell you later.* I never did find out what was up, but I'm sure if it was anything important, Charlotte would have encouraged me to go to the toilet with her.

Sunday, 6th January 2019

Mark stayed over last night. We went for a quick meal and a couple of wines and then decided to come home by ten p.m. to watch a film. He stayed in bed most of the morning while I unpacked a couple more boxes and rearranged the kitchen cupboards and drawers. I know it will annoy Mark, as he was the one who arranged it originally. But it's getting to the point now that every time I make a cup of tea I clock up five thousand steps, as the kettle, the cups and the teaspoons are at the furthest points away from each other. Making a brew is like joining in a line dance, and I'm in no mood for it at seven in the morning.

When I sat down to watch some telly, an advert came on about breast cancer, and I gave my boob a little squeeze. The cyst is still there, and I think so is my ghost. It slammed the annexe door in the kitchen while I was in full-on grope mode. Maybe it thinks I was enjoying it. Trust me to buy a house with a prude ghost. Actually, that could be a way of exorcising the ghost. I could leave *Sex and the City* on while I'm in work, and the presence will leave in disgust by the end of season one. It's probably all my imagination anyway. New houses make strange noises, and I just need to get used to it.

Friday, 11th January 2019

I'm having my hair done today, a prospect I do not enjoy. I hate salons, even for the fact they are called salons. All the people who work in them are far too pretty. I want someone who does my hair to spend most of their time looking at my hair and not themselves in the mirror. I also hate the way they serve 'fizz' while you're getting your hair done. Diary, we all know that the fizz is Asti Spumante from the local Costco and putting it in a cheap flute glass is only kidding the kids. No, I have a mobile hairdresser that uses my water, my shampoo, my conditioner and my towels, and I save myself at least a hundred quid. I always want a lot of body in my fine, frizzy hair, but she never can quite manage anything beyond the Pocahontas Blow-Dry. As soon as she's left, I'm re-blowing my hair and will not stop adding waves to my barnet until I look at it and feel seasick. Then, and only then, do I know it's curly enough.

I'm out tonight for Saskia's birthday. She's hired a local wine bar—not the whole bar, just the top floor. Mark is joining me, as most of our friends are mutual now. If we ever did split up, I wonder who would get custody of them. Probably him, as he lives handier to all the local pubs. In fact, the bar is nearer Mark's flat than my house, so I'm staying at his, and tomorrow, we plan to look at some weekends away. He wants to become all cultured and go somewhere like Rome, but I'm feeling Amsterdam. We've been before, and from what I can remember, we had fun. This time, I would like to go back and try and remember the stuff we visited while we're there.

I do like our weekends away. We always go for two weeks in the summer, but we also try to squeeze in two or three weekend breaks during the year. I look forward to these times, but I admit, dear Diary, I leave all the planning to Mark. He enjoys it too much to take it away from him. Well, that's what I tell myself. He missed his calling as a travel agent or a tourist board information clerk. While the rest of us admire celebrities or royalty, Mark is in awe of anyone who works on a Hop On Hop Off Bus. He is always the most attentive passenger and is ready to headlock anyone who dares to talk over the commentary. There could be a number of nationalities on the top deck, and Mark can make himself understood by all if they dare to offer an opinion on the local landmarks before the tour guide has finished his delivery. I pretend to Mark that I'm just as interested, but in fact, I see the buses as cheap taxis with the added bonus of a free poncho, which was a blessing on a recent and very damp trip to Paris. In the monsoon-type conditions, we walked around the sights like a couple of members of the Viet Cong. I'm sure only for the colossal double-decker bus painted on the back of the ponchos did everyone feel more comfortable around the Eiffel Tower. Anyway, whatever he picks, I will nod in all the right places, say how wonderful he is for finding whatever it is he finds, and then pack accordingly.

He is talking about getting away for Valentine's Day. I told Saskia and Kelly, and they're convinced Mark will propose. I hope not. I do want to stay with him, but I'm not ready to make that next step just yet. Maybe once the house is done, I might feel different.

Tonight, I'm wearing a red dress with black shoes and bag. I was going to wear my low-cut black dress, but have recently noticed a blue vein on the boob where I found the lump last month. It hasn't gone away, and I'm not sure the vein was there before. I don't have one on the other breast, so I think I should get it checked sooner rather than later now. The vein is probably not that noticeable, but the dress is cut so your boobs are giving a fine Anne Boleyn impression. I would be self-conscious if someone thought I'd marked it with a biro and not quite managed to wash it off. The red dress is cut a little higher and makes my boobs look a little more twentieth century. I've still not told anyone about the lump, and it's not like you can see it when you look at it, so it's probably all fine. I may just have a varicose vein. Can you get varicose veins in your boobs? I'll Google it later.

Monday, 14th January 2019

I had my smear today, which I should have had about six months ago, but with looking for houses, I forgot all about it. I know no one likes to go for a smear, but it's all the prep work you have to do before that annoys me more. I'm a Hollywood kind of gal down there, as that's how Mark likes it. But I will admit every now and again, especially if he is working away, I'll let it embrace the fashion of the 1970s. Mark once saw it in its natural state and compared it to the beard of Brian Blessed, which I was not best pleased about. Apart from the hair issue on my undercarriage, the legs also need a polish. So by the time I've finished with myself from the waist down, I'm fit to star in a porn movie and ready for my close-up.

The anticipation is always far worse than the actual procedure. Except for the one time the nurse took no notice of my warning that I have a tilted pelvis. She was in there longer than a Chilean miner, and by the time she finished, I wanted to call Mark and announce my celibacy. Today's nurse was exceptional, and she was in and out with the skill of a musketeer. I'm getting a bit older now, so with each smear I do worry a bit more. I just think the law of averages says by the time you have had as many smears as I've had, one of them is bound to come back abnormal. This could be the one. I don't know for sure how they treat abnormalities. A friend once told me that lasers were involved, and since then I haven't been able to shake the James Bond scene where Sean Connery is strapped to a table, and a laser is creeping up towards his bollocks, burning the table along the way.

I also had an NHS check, which essentially is like an MOT for humans. She took a barrel of blood, gave me a look that I didn't care for when she asked about my weight, followed by the standard lecture on drinking too much. All the time she was talking, I could smell last night's wine on her. Hypocritical cow! After I walked out, I realised I hadn't asked the nurse to check out my biro boob vein. It's not changed, so I'll leave it until next time I go.

Friday, 18th January 2019

The house is finally unpacked. I took the day off, as the weekends fly by too fast for me. It could be that I prioritise the things that involve drink or lipstick. I promise myself every weekend that I will be more domesticated, but it doesn't happen. I enjoy cooking, but that's about it when it comes to household chores. Mark is the one who likes to hoover and wash everything and arrange stuff. But he started to nag me about when was I going to finish unpacking, and surely I must need whatever was in the boxes. I didn't admit to him about bringing boxes to this house that were still sealed from my last move. Things like that make him sweat.

The annexe is the only room that is still empty apart from an old settee. I'm not sure if I will even have the space for it once I get all my pottery equipment in there, but it can stay for now. I get a strange feeling when I go in there. I'm not sure if it's because there are so many windows and I feel the room is exposed—which it's not—or if it just needs a bit of TLC. I'm sure it's the latter, and once I have some more of my crap in there, I'll feel right at home.

I'm heading to Mark's flat tonight. After all the unpacking and sorting, I said he can wait on me and cook my tea tonight. He suggested a takeaway or going out. Eating a home-cooked meal on a Friday turns Mark into Marty McFly and throws all his timing off for the rest of the weekend, as he doesn't know what day it is. He spends the weekend wandering around in a fog and eventually will lose his temper if he misses *Match of the Day*. Colonel Sanders underestimated his influence over time and relativity with my fella.

Wednesday, 23rd January 2019

Well, I found out tonight what has been happening with Lucy. Charlotte met me for tea after work to regale me with all the details. It turns out she has been having an affair with a married man. He also works at the Post Office with Lucy. Not sure if he's a postman, though.

"Wouldn't it be funny if his name was Pat! Oh, that would be hilarious!" laughed Charlotte.

"What about his wife?" I asked.

"I'm not sure what her name is."

"No, I mean what's the score with the wife? Does she know?"

"Oh, God, no!"

"How long has this been going on?"

"With the wife?"

"No! With Lucy!"

"I don't know! She only told me because I tried to hook her up with some guy. She looked really miserable, and I just figured she could do with a good time, if you get my drift."

"And then she just told you?"

"Well, not straight away. But I eventually got it out of her. It was when I said she had to dust herself off *down there* that she told me. She practically bit my head off!"

I'm surprised Lucy even told Charlotte in the first place. To call Charlotte promiscuous is like saying the pope likes to pray a bit. Whereas Lucy…well, some of us were starting to suspect she was still a virgin until now.

"You didn't upset her, did you?"

"Oh, she's fine. I told her that if she was happy just being his bit on the side, then that was up to her."

"She won't like living like that."

"I'm trying to explain her sad face. Are you keeping up? This is the omnibus edition as well."

We ordered another bottle of wine. One bottle between us was not enough for a conversation like this.

"So what's she going to do?" I asked.

"She said if she gives him an ultimatum, he'll pick his wife, and she'll lose him forever. But if she accepts things the way they are, she'll just end up falling for him even more, and where does that leave her in the long term? I told her to go and speak to you."

"Me? Why?!"

"Because you're good at this stuff. All I hear when people talk about men is dick, dick, dick. You can do feelings so much better than me. She can't go to Saskia because, let's face it, she can be a little judgemental. So that only leaves Kelly and Anne. Seriously, Kelly and Anne! It has to be you."

"What the hell am I supposed to say? 'I hear you've been getting a little more pushed through your slot lately'?"

"That's an icebreaker."

My friends always do this to me. When they need the sensible friend, they roll me out. Most of the time, I'm the support act, but when it comes to applying for jobs, how to cook risotto and now, apparently, how to find happy-ever-after with someone who might not be a postman, then I'm your man.

The second bottle only lasted a little longer than the first, and I told Charlotte I had to go. Drinking three bottles on a school night is not a good idea, even for me. When we went into the toilet together, I remembered my cyst and toyed with the idea of letting her have a feel to see if it felt odd to her. But then I dismissed it. I knew what she would say, so there was no point.

Sunday, 27th January 2019

Lucy and I went for Sunday lunch today in a lovely country pub. She seemed to be back to her usual self until I asked her what was happening with her love life. The mood changed rapidly.

"Charlotte's told you." She looked disappointed.

"Charlotte's told me what?"

She knew I was lying, but she went along with it and acted as though I didn't know a thing.

"I've been seeing someone."

"Oh, how exciting! When can we meet him?" This threw her off. Why would I be encouraging her to bring a married man into the fold if I knew he was married? I'm good at this.

"It's a little complicated," she said. I stayed quiet. "I met him at work."

"Love across the mailbags, eh? Sounds like a song from an old Elvis movie." I crack jokes when I'm nervous, and

I was starting to get nervous because I realised I had not practised my non-judgmental face enough.

"He's married," she blurted out.

Here goes.

"Oh." Weak, I know.

"It was all shit before I came on the scene."

"So he was going to leave her anyway?"

"Leave her?"

"Well, when it's shit, you either split up or sort it. Which one is he doing?"

"Like I said, it's complicated."

"Do you love him?"

"I adore him." She kind of took my breath away when she said that. I expected her to say she liked him or maybe she wasn't sure.

"Does he have kids?"

"No."

"Well, that's something, I suppose."

"I'm a shitbag, aren't I?"

"No, you're not. I can't even say he is, even though he's married. No one knows really what state that marriage is in, only them. And sometimes even the people in the marriage don't know how crap it is until it's too late."

"I don't know what to do."

"You sound like you're in deep with him, so all I will say is you need to start having some serious conversations with him. You don't want to end up like Angie Benson."

Angie Benson was a friend from years ago who got mixed up with a married man. He left his wife, she sold her flat, they went to Sydney to live, and three months later, he was on the wife's doorstep begging for forgiveness. Angie was now in a foreign country with no man and a shitty reputation back home. We all felt sorry for her, of course. But I'll admit I did judge her. Now I'm older and realise you cannot help the way you feel, so I'm not as judgemental as I used to be. Maybe if we had been better friends, we could have warned her.

"Do you ever hear from her?" asked Lucy.

"I only keep track of her through Facebook now. She looks happy, to be fair, but what she went through, Lucy... I don't want that happening to you."

"What? Move to Sydney and leave all this?" She smirked.

She then showed me some photographs on her phone of him. Some clearly had been taken after amorous events. Why do people do that? When Mark and I have finished fooling around, I never think to take a picture of us. When Mark takes me to bed, I look like me, Jo Kearns, but by the time we've finished, I look more like Joe Pesci! In her photos, she looked happy—she looked like a different Lucy, to be honest. He was cute, and in some of the shots, he seemed quite besotted with her. But I suppose he would look like that. He's hardly going to be snarling at her, is he?

By the end of the night, Lucy said she felt better for talking to me about it and made me promise not to mention it to the others. I didn't like to tell her that Charlotte might have already told them all by now. Mind you, if she had, Saskia would have been on the phone telling me what an awful girl Lucy is, and even though she would say nothing to her face, she would say plenty behind her back. Saskia is fab when it comes to being the sensible friend. She's the one you go to when you want something organising or need a favour. She doesn't mind getting her hands dirty and will rearrange your whole CD collection while you're making her a cup of peppermint tea. She hasn't touched carbs since Band-Aid 30 released their charity single, so watching *MasterChef* or *Great British Bake Off* with her is a nightmare.

Oh, and Lucy's married man isn't called Pat. His name's Dave. Yeah, I was disappointed too.

Saturday, 2nd February 2019

Mark has dragged me around IKEA for most of the day and made me buy crap 'I didn't know I needed', apparently. I only went in for a cupboard for the bathroom because I'm sick of his stuff cluttering up the side of the sink. I don't mind paraphernalia being on display if it's serving a daily purpose, but I cannot cope with looking at a used razor, shaving cream and face wash when they're only being used the odd time he stays at mine.

To stop him from calling me weird all the time, I accepted his offer of a run to IKEA to buy a cabinet to hide the offending articles.

"Do you want this cupboard?" Mark asked.

"Okay." The cupboard was a penny short of fifty pounds.

"Do you want this new dinner service?"

"Okay." We continued to follow the stick-on floor arrows.

"Do you want some of these glass bottles?"

"Why?"

"They have lids on like old Grolsch bottles."

"Okay."

By the time I reached the big industrial tills that look like car washes, I had managed to spend six times more than the price of the cupboard I was originally buying. How I was rinsed is only known to the Swedes and their stick-on floor arrows that make everyone walk around the store like *Night of the Living Dead.* I didn't know I needed a large chunky chopping board that's as thick as a Nissan Micra, a bag of tea lights so large I may never have an electric bill again, and an array of frames, plant pots and small lamps to cover every horizontal surface of my home—except the one reserved for the Nissan chopping board, of course.

We went home with the back of the car so weighed down it created sparks every time we went over a bump. Mark had found a home for all the items before I'd taken my coat off and the kettle had boiled. He should be an ambassador for the shop. The way he smiled and groped his way through the rug section left me feeling a bit dirty, I don't mind saying.

Andy, Saskia's brother, came around yesterday and gave me a price for decorating various rooms in the house. He was pretty cheap, so I've decided he can do all of downstairs from next week. He's okay when it comes to any jobs that require the first aisles in B&Q, but once you start heading south towards power tools and bits of wood that need cutting to fit, you're out of Andy's league. He wouldn't tell you that, but his sister would, and the quality of some of the work in her house will tell you even more.

"I've got a shelf that flaps in the draught if you open the bathroom window and a skirting board in the dining room so wonky that I walk in like Groucho Marx. It's very disorientating."

I've asked Andy to paint the lounge through to the dining room in pale grey-brown. It's called 'Elephant's Breath' by Farrow & Ball. I know it's pretentious, but it's just the right shade and finish. He'll paint the kitchen in a darker tone called 'London Clay'. Where do they get these names from? They must have a guy in the back room who's not quite got over an acid rave in the nineties. He comes up with these names, and the people in the marketing department, who don't know of his existence, swoon at all of the suggestions they think have been made at director level. Whatever happened to royal blue, pillar-box red and brilliant white?

Mark wants to go out tonight, but his creepy paedo smile from the rug section is still lingering in the air, so I've told him I'm meeting the girls for a drink instead. When I suggested he book something for Valentine's weekend, as it's around both our birthdays, and it was entirely his choice, he cheered up and said he'd compile a list that we could decide on. While he wittered on about destinations and talked himself into going back to Amsterdam, I texted Charlotte, who eagerly agreed to meet in Archie's Wine Bar at eight o'clock. Charlotte mentioned in passing that she and Gary have split up, so it should be an interesting night. I also texted Mia to see if she fancied joining us, and to my surprise, she said she would. I haven't seen much of her since the wedding.

Just to keep you up to speed, dear Diary, Charlotte has been with Gary for three months, and in all that time, he's taken her out twice. She said it's because he's shy, but we're all convinced it's because he's tight and bone idle. He works for the local council, and as far as we can all calculate, he hasn't worked a full month since Charlotte met him. Absences include 'flu', of course, which was a simple cold, a nasty skin infection, which turned out to be impetigo, and so many reasons for his bad back that we wonder how he isn't in a wheelchair. We figured his hands are okay, though, from the endless hours spent on the PlayStation and lengthy masturbating sessions, according to a disappointed Charlotte, who went through his search history. The guy is a tool, and I have every intention of telling her so she won't make the same mistake again. But she will. Charlotte can sniff out a grub within a ten-mile radius. Oh yes, he'd be charming at first. Some of them I've even fancied myself. But by the third date, we (I say 'we'; I mean 'I') find out what it is that's wrong with him. She only lasted two weeks with the Johnny Depp lookalike when he argued that all men have a secret drawer with women's underwear in—a detail I discovered when he asked how we felt about the new Victoria's Secret store opening up in town. Which reminds me, I need to pop in and get some decent underwear for our weekend away—nothing blue, though. The biro line on my boob is becoming more prominent. I think the cold could be accountable.

The wine bar was quite busy, even for a Sunday. Charlotte was already getting a drink when I walked in, and Mia was on her way, according to a text.

"So, you and Gary have split up. What happened?" I tried to sound sympathetic.

"I asked him what he had planned for Valentine's Day, knowing he had nothing planned, but I just wanted to see his face. He started bleating on about gross commercialism and how it's all a con, and why are we being sucked into a marketeers' paradise?"

"What did you say?"

"What could I say? I lied! I told him I was relieved he had nothing planned, as I was going away for the weekend with a man called Rick…who worked in marketing."

I couldn't stop laughing. The thing is, Charlotte probably will have a man by Valentine's Day.

"I had to end it, Jo. He used kitchen roll in the bathroom. Who does that? Have you tried to flush kitchen roll? The fuckin' stuff won't go down."

"You only need one sheet for one *sheet*," I said in a Spanish accent.

"That's the good stuff. Don't kid yourself. The only things he doesn't mind spending money on are Domino's pizza, beer and condoms. Whatever did I see in the guy?"

"His huge dick," I reminded her.

"Well, there was that. But after a while, you kind of get used to it, don't you?"

It was at that point Mia walked in. She looked slightly pissed off but insisted she was okay. After a brief introduction, Mia kissed Charlotte like she had known her all her life and shouted at the barman to bring the cocktail menu while she took her coat off.

"I like your friend a lot," giggled Charlotte at Mia's swiftness and decisiveness.

I explained for Mia's benefit, "Charlotte has just been telling us about her split with Gormless Gary. He took her out twice in three months but was hung like a Peruvian donkey."

"Well, at least they're bigger than the Venezuelan ones," Mia quipped.

We ordered cocktails—lots of them, as there was an offer on and it seemed rude to ignore the generosity of the bar—and as the night got hazier, Mia became a little looser with her tongue. With Charlotte's skilful questioning, which doesn't feel like you're being questioned, we got all the details out of Mia for why she was so gloomy.

"I spent two weeks with him in Jamaica, and all he talked about was him, his family and how much marriage will change him. By the end of the holiday, I felt like shoving that Piz Buin where the sun doesn't shine."

"Maybe he knows everything about you," suggested Charlotte.

"But does he? We came away from the honeymoon, and all he learned about me was I like piña coladas and I'm not too bad at the limbo dance."

"Well, that tells me volumes, honey," laughed Charlotte. Mia laughed as well.

"You have the rest of your lives to find stuff out," I said. "Why does he need to know everything now?"

Charlotte nodded in agreement. "Believe me, Mia, if he knows everything about you now, it's sure going to be dull in a year's time. And of course marriage is going to change him! He can't buy the car he wants anymore or stay out drinking until all hours. He has to come home at a respectable hour so he can get up early and wash his Zafira."

"He drives an Audi," said Mia.

"The point is, it doesn't matter as long as he pays the mortgage, keeps the fridge full and doesn't fool around with anyone else!"

Whether it was the martinis or the salty advice, Mia went home in a better mood than she'd arrived. She promised she would come next time we were out as a gang and meet the rest of the girls.

Wednesday, 6th February 2019

I'm still convinced that my house is haunted, and the ghost only pops up when I am in the bathroom. I was having a bath and talking to Mark on the phone when again I saw a black shadow. I can see my bedroom from the bath, and there, bold as brass, was a human shape in front of the window—if I wasn't mistaken, it was a woman. The only reason I'm saying this is it had a bun on top of its head—not like an iced bun, a hair bun.

I was feeling my breast and was just about to tell Mark about the lump that still hadn't gone away when I saw it. I screamed, and it disappeared. Bless Mark. He said I should go straight to his flat and stay there. I don't mind telling you, dear Diary, I did think of it for a short while, but I've not spent a small fortune on Farrow & Ball and the Swedes to be driven out of my house.

Next time I pass a church, I'll invest in some holy water. I'm not sure what I'm supposed to do with it. Do I drink it every morning and night for protection? Or do I just bless myself with it? Maybe I could put it in the iron and use the spritz button and blitz the house. A blessing and a workout at the same time—my iron is as heavy as a well-fed toddler.

Another purchase by Mark, who insists irons should weigh as much as Pavarotti to ensure a decent finish. However, my ironing board disagrees and has developed a distinct lean in the last couple of weeks.

Maybe simply having holy water in the house will be threatening enough to banish away any dark forces. Mia became quite friendly with Father Kinley from Christ the King Church—I might ask her to call him and see what I'm supposed to do with it. In the meantime, I'm heading off to TJ Hughes to buy an iron that won't give me arms like Popeye.

Wednesday, 13th February 2019

Today is Mark's forty-fifth birthday. He treated it like any other day and went to work. He doesn't like fuss on his birthday. I'm not sure if that's because his family isn't here or because he's Canadian or because he's a man. I suspect all three play their part.

He unwrapped a Ralph Lauren jumper he had spied a couple of weeks ago and a bottle of his favourite aftershave before he left. He was happy with both, and we made a promise to celebrate it properly when we go to Amsterdam.

Thursday, 14th February 2019

Mark and I flew to Amsterdam today. Even though the flight was short, I still filled my mouth with enough Valium to knock out the population of Newport. It was all washed down with a bottle of wine while Mark told me how impressed he was with all the checks the airport staff had given our plane, even going as far as to say they had been extra thorough. I snapped at him, telling him I was stoned, not stupid.

We were only in the air for an hour. I spent longer in Superdrug finding toiletries small enough for the trip. This stupid airport policy of not being able to take any liquids over 100ml in a single bottle defies me. Surely, if you need to make a bomb and need 125ml of VO5 volumising hairspray and 200ml of Aussie conditioner, you would just buy two bottles of each. A tenacious bomber will not be deterred by having to open a couple more bottles. After all the time I spent in there and becoming thoroughly fed up with not finding what I wanted in 'Ryanair size', I remembered I was not going to a Third World country and could simply buy soap when I got there. That would give me more room in my case for clothes and ugly shoes.

The last time we went to Amsterdam, Mark berated me for my choice of footwear. I had worn simple black boots with beautiful stiletto heels. Within hours of arriving, he had dragged me to a shoe shop, stoned out of his mind, telling the assistant to find me a pair of shoes that were flat and could cope with cobbles, trams, cyclists and weed. The assistant studied me—I swear she tutted at my beautiful boots—and then produced a pair of shoes that were last seen in public in a window display from Freeman, Hardy and Willis. I took them only because I was desperate for a drink. The weed was wearing off, and my mouth felt like I had eaten a whole box of Viennese whirls in one go.

The shoes are now back on my feet as I walk around Holland. They may make me look like a religious fundamentalist, but no one knows me here, and it keeps Mark happy. We decided on the first day that we would take it easy and go for a walk as soon as we arrived so we could get our bearings and have a coffee somewhere sophisticated. The hotel is smart, and once we had sussed out the in-room safe, we were walking back out of the hotel and on the hunt for culture and fun.

We'd only walked about two hundred yards when we found a bar overlooking the square. There were lots of people sitting outside already in scarves and sunglasses, smoking Marlborough and looking sophisticated. We decided to join them and see if we could get away with looking stylish too. I think we were doing okay, even with my foul footwear, until we pulled out the map the surly hotel receptionist had given us half an hour before.

After a few sips of my wine, I recognised where we were from our last visit.

"That nice coffee shop where we can buy decent weed is that way." I pointed. "And the gay area is that way." These were the two places we wanted to go back to, as they hadn't ripped us for drugs or drink.

Mark was chuffed and impressed I knew where everything was, as last time we were here, I wasn't sure whether my surname went before or after 'Jo'. Mark has always been impressed with my navigation skills. I'm not that good, but Mark is terrible and can only find his way around places that have arrow stickers on the floor.

I shoved the map in my handbag, knowing that it would stay there for at least three months, at which point it would be thrown away with an old lip gloss and a mint from an Indian restaurant.

We spent the rest of the afternoon and most of the evening celebrating Mark's birthday by drinking, smoking and taking a river cruise. We laughed a lot. That could have been the booze or the weed, but we didn't care. We laughed, proper belly-laughed, and took the piss out of each other.

"So much for us taking it easy," Mark shouted in a cake shop as I banged on the display glass like a desperate prisoner, pointing at various coloured macarons.

Friday, 15th February 2019

Can you believe we were up bright and early today, dear Diary? We went for breakfast and managed to piece together about eighty per cent of the day before.

"Do you have any bruises?" Mark asked. I didn't. "Well, we haven't woken up in a police cell, so I would say the going is good." He concluded we needn't worry about the missing twenty per cent.

I did toy with the idea of staying in bed until mid-afternoon, but I had to shower and go a-hunting to feed my addiction to caffeine. In the shower, I felt the lump again; the vein looks a little more obvious now. I've decided I've put it off long enough, and I should make an appointment to see the doctor. I know what he is going to say; I just need it confirmed that it is a cyst, and he can tell me what this vein is all about.

I wasn't sure when I would tell Mark, but then he started talking about someone in his office—

"You know Jamie in work? Well, his wife has found out she has cancer of the liver."

"Oh God, she can't be that old."

"She's thirty-six. Apparently, they can operate and she will be fine, but even still."

"Is Jamie okay?"

"He seems to be. He's still in work and won't be off until she has her surgery."

This was my chance.

"Mark, to be honest with you, I've found a lump." As soon as I said it, I regretted it. He looked a little dumbstruck as he tried to process what I'd said. "Look, I'm sure it's nothing. It'll be like last time. Remember when I had that cyst, and we worried, and it was all for nothing? Well, this will be the same. It'll just be a cyst, I'm sure." I noticed at that point I was babbling. I'm not sure how long for or if I have ever babbled before, but I certainly was this time.

"Does it feel like a cyst?" he asked.

I can't remember what the last one felt like, so how would I know? Surely, if a woman could tell if it was a cyst, then she wouldn't need to go to the doctor!

"It does a bit," I lied.

"So when is your appointment?"

"I've not called the doctor yet. I will on Monday, though, I promise."

Mark sipped his beer quietly, and I began to feel really stupid. He tried his best not to react, especially when I said I had found it a few weeks ago.

"I'll come with you."

"There's no need. I—"

"I'm coming," he interrupted. "I'm sure you're right, and it will be like last time."

"I just have porridge tit," I joked.

"Well, you are getting on a bit."

"Darling, no matter how old I get, I will never be as old as you," I said, pointing out the one-year age gap.

I was glad we were laughing in the end at the onset of porridge tit. He looked worried, though. For a moment, I caught the panic behind his beautiful blue eyes and the look of sorrow when I said it was in my left breast. I thought he would chastise me, and I would have taken the telling-off, as when I'd said I found the lump all that time ago and not done anything about it, I realised how neglectful I'd been.

The last time this had happened, Mark had been there for me, and the radiographer had sent us away with a smile because the lump was harmless. This time would be no different; I just needed it confirmed so I could stop worrying.

We didn't talk about it for the rest of the day, which I was relieved about. Instead, we went to the Sex Museum, and I can honestly say I will never be the same again. Mark thought it was hilarious and had a small but intense laughing fit at a photograph of a woman being fisted; the man delivering the fisting was clearly wearing a Casio watch.

"I hope that's waterproof," Mark roared all over the museum.

I am glad to say, dear Diary, that my lump has not put Mark off me, and we ended the night with both boobs joining in. Well, after all, it is Valentine's weekend.

Saturday, 16th February 2019

Today, we went to a coffee shop, got to a certain level of being stoned, and then went to Madame Tussaud's Waxwork Museum. I'm not sure if it was a good idea, as I thought every white waxwork looked like Pierce Brosnan and all the black waxworks looked like Daley Thompson. When I asked someone who the waxwork was supposed to be, Mark informed me I'd just asked a waxwork of the Dalai Lama who Nelson Mandela was. It was at that moment we realised we might have smoked too much.

We took a multitude of silly pictures in silly poses, which, to be fair, were copied by the people behind us. It's these kinds of things that make Mark and me feel quite smug in our artiness. Or it could simply be that people were going to pose like that anyway; they were just as stoned as us.

The rest of the day consisted of drinking, walking along the canals, wondering if we could ever live in Amsterdam, and eating macarons.

We didn't mention the lump. In fact, I hardly thought about it all day. I'm not sure if that was because I was too distracted or too stoned or because 'a problem shared' and all that. It could have been all three, but I only thought about it when we went to bed. It was then I wondered if Mark had been thinking about it. At one point, during sex, I wondered if he even remembered. Maybe he was so stoned when I told him that he has no recollection of it whatsoever. I guess the next couple of days will enlighten me to that dilemma. It's not like I'm going to bring it up again, is it? That's a conversation with a guarantee for one of us feeling stupid.

Sunday, 17th February 2019

I woke feeling a little sad because we are going home today. I could stay a few more days and not because of the macarons. Mark and I are finding our stride, our mojo. It always takes us a few days to find our level with each other, a state I suppose most married couples are in permanently. When I'm there with him, it's really comfy, and I start to think we should live together. But to be honest, I'm not sure how Mark feels about it anymore.

I bought my new house, and he made no hint of maybe us doing it together. Not that I wanted him to, but I do wonder if he ever thought about it, or have I knocked him back so much now that he's given up?

After packing, which took all of five minutes, we smoked the last joint and went for a walk to kill time before heading to the airport. I wonder how many people turn up at the airport stoned to fly back to the UK. Judging by the way the stewardess was ringing up the Pringles from the snack cart on the flight, I'm surmising quite a few.

Mark was very quiet on the road back home.

"I'll stay at yours tonight, if that's okay?" he asked.

"I'm okay."

"I know you are. I want to see your ghost."

I'm sure he just wants to make sure I make the doctor's appointment tomorrow. Yes, dear Diary, he remembered the lump. When I came out of the shower this morning, he asked if he could touch it and did it hurt? He looked a little shocked when he said he could feel it. I'm not sure why he was shocked. Maybe he thought it would be like when new parents show you their first scan picture and you say you can see the baby, but you can't. My lump is obvious, and it feels like a small kidney bean.

I've had to promise him that I will call the GP. I now feel I'm only making the appointment and getting it all checked to keep him happy. But this was the kick up the arse I needed. I insisted he should go home and I would see him tomorrow at some point.

"I'll call you as soon as I have the details of the doctor's appointment. But knowing my doctor's, they won't give me an appointment this week. The only time you get to see someone straight away is if you have something hanging off or if something is wet."

When I stepped in the house, I was scared in case someone was behind the door ready to whisper, *get out*. But there wasn't. The house was nice and warm, and I enjoyed a bath while I watched Friday night's *EastEnders* on the iPad.

Monday, 18th February 2019

I have spent most of the night groping myself for more lumps and bumps. I cannot find any more, and bizarrely, I'm glad the lump I have found is still there: at least I have evidence to take to the doctor's.

I always feel like a charlatan when I see my GP. As sure as day turns to night, my crippling symptoms have disappeared on the day of the appointment as if Jesus of Nazareth stood at the end of my bed during the night and performed a stunning miracle. I've also been known to roll around on the carpet, literally willing to sell my soul to make the pain stop in my mouth from teeth that are hanging by a thread, only to walk into the dentist the next day and as soon as he says, "Open wide!" I reveal a set of pearly-white gnashers like Simon Cowell's.

Surprisingly, the receptionist offered me an appointment at half nine today. I called Mark, who met me at the surgery. He obviously hadn't shaved and didn't look like he had slept much either. Maybe after the weekend we've just had, he struggled to sleep without the aid of a dried-out plant.

I went into the GP's room on my own when my name was called. My usual doctor is on holiday, so I was greeted by a very frail-looking lady who looked like she would struggle to find her own pulse, never mind my lump. Without asking where it was, she asked me to strip off and lie on the cold plastic bed that I remembered from my smear last month. I forgot to tell you, dear Diary, that was all clear. So my coo-coo-cachoo can breathe a sigh of relief for another three years.

Dr. Frail found my lump straight away, and I'm not sure how to feel about that. Is it good that she found it? That means it's not my imagination, and I'm not wasting her time. Or is it bad that she found it? Is it that obvious that something is wrong? She asked me to wave my arms in the air, and after I'd done my 'YMCA' dance routine, she said she wanted to refer me to the local hospital for further tests.

"I think we should fast-track you as well." She tapped away on her computer.

"Why?!"

"Simply because there is a definite lump there."

A *definite lump*? As opposed to what? If you can't feel a lump, then surely you don't get referred. What's the in-between bit where you get referred but you just simply have to wait your turn? Is that a lump that comes and goes? A shy lump? An indecisive lump?

Mark said it was a good thing I was being seen quickly, and I shouldn't be surprised I was being referred, as that was what happened last time with my harmless cyst. It's not like the GP has the equipment to tell me there and then, is it? I'm supposed to get an appointment in the next two weeks.

"I hope they send an appointment when I'm in the area. Amara wants me to do a few things for her down south."

"Are you serious, Jo? You go when you get called, and fuck Amara!"

"Hey! Don't be like that!" I snapped. "I will go when it's convenient for me. Waiting an extra day or two isn't going to make that much difference." Awful, I know, but I have a lot of work commitments.

Mark hates worrying, that's all it is, and he ends up being grumpy and snarly and takes it out on me. Well, he could be taking it out on other people, but I'm not there to see that. I should take him to IKEA and let him lose himself in the linen department as a form of therapy. Then we could go for some cocktails and laugh about how much of a pessimist he is.

Friday, 22nd February 2019

It's my forty-fourth birthday today, and I don't feel at all excited. I'm not bothered about my age anymore. I think once you're past the stage of saying 'and a half' when you tell people how old you are, the excitement has gone.

Mark bought me a framed picture that I fell in love with one weekend we went to London. It's a painting of a small village, and in the sky, you can make out a blurry image of an angel watching over it. I'm going to hang it in the living room, of course.

As a bit of a mini celebration, me and all the girls went around to Charlotte's tonight. We're all a bit skint, so we bought cheap booze and a pizza. Sometimes I prefer those nights more than going out to the wine bars. Mia came along to this one, because it's my birthday, and she met all of the gang properly. Charlotte carried on like they were old friends, which in some respects was kind of nice.

"So, Mia, what do you do in Jo's office?" asked Anne.

"I sort the IT. It's dead boring, but the people are all right, and the money's not bad."

"Oooh, IT? I've got one of those fit watches, and when I check my steps, it says I'm walking over fifty miles a day. I know I have a long hall, but it's not the length of Gatwick's runway! Could you have a look at it for me?"

Mia looked a little uncomfortable. "It's not really my area. I deal with computers, that kind of thing. Maybe take it back to the shop you bought it from?"

Anne was clearly unimpressed so changed the subject slightly. "It's a shame so many people do jobs that they just fall into and not the job they should be doing."

"What would you have done then, Anne?" I asked. "I thought being a teacher was vocational."

"I was the first in my family to go to university, and back then, teaching was a well-respected job. But being a lesbian in an all-girls' school caused certain issues."

"What?! Did you fancy one of the students?" asked Kelly.

"Don't be so disgusting! No, I did not! It was the bloody parents that caused trouble. I was the hot topic at every governors' meeting during the nineties. Now they would think I'm cool and call me gender liquid."

"Gender fluid," Kelly corrected.

"Whatever. They're swinging all over the show now, even in the language departments—especially German."

Mia looked at me for a reaction to this comment. I just shrugged.

"I once wore my sleeves up on a checked gingham blouse back in ninety-six, and they had an emergency PTA meeting about me being obvious. You couldn't get away with it now!"

"Here you go, Calamity Jane." Charlotte passed Anne a drink in the hope it would lighten her up.

It was later on in the night, when I felt everyone was suitably pissed, that I told them about my lump. They took it all in their stride, and each regaled me with a story of a personal experience or something that their mum, aunt or sister had been through, and it all turned out to be completely harmless. I'm glad I've told them. Mark is making me fret a little, and the girls brought it all into perspective, reminding me it isn't that bad and there's nothing to worry about.

By the end of the night, we moved on to talking about ghosts. I didn't tell them about my haunted house, though. I felt the spotlight had been on me enough for one night.

Thursday, 28th February 2019

I had to chase the doctors today, as I have still not heard anything about my appointment. A rather snotty lady on the end of the line said an appointment had been made for me the day before, which I had apparently decided not to attend. I pointed out to Snotty Lady that a decision could only be made once one was informed of the facts, and the only fact which was true was that I had no knowledge of the appointment. I was informed by Snotty Lady to go back to my GP and ask for another two-week referral, as the first one had run out. Like the referral is cheese and has a short shelf life! I called the surgery and told the receptionist, who apologised on behalf of the whole of the NHS and promised to send another cheese referral.

Mark was not impressed when I told him, and he raised the subject of going private. I pointed out that getting an appointment at the local BUPA hospital would mean two weeks' wait anyway, except I would have a massive bill at the end of it, and I'm saving my money to convert the annexe into a pottery studio. He rolled his eyes when I said this. He thought having a potter's wheel in the house would be sexy like a scene from *Ghost*, but he once picked me up from class and saw a very different side to the life of a potter. Shabby, encrusted overalls, dirty fingernails and a recently singed eyebrow from the kiln killed his fantasy of clay-writhing sex in the suburbs.

Monday, 4th March 2019

I finally received the letter from the hospital today. I am to attend the breast clinic, and I'm relieved to see it's the same place as last time when I had my cyst. Maybe that's a good sign. Last time I was there, it was lucky for me, and hopefully, this time will be no different. The appointment is set for a week from today, so I've booked the day off with work. I've only told a few work colleagues, and like me, they insist it will be a cyst. I have to admit, dear Diary, I do get a little annoyed with the people who become a qualified GP as soon as they hear your news.

"Oh, that's a cyst. Nothing more. Especially at your age."

"You're too young for cancer."

"Does your mother have it? No? Well, you haven't got it either."

"If you had cancer, you would be sick."

"If you had cancer, it would be sore."

"If you had cancer, you would be able to see it."

"No one who looks as good as you has cancer, so stop worrying!"

I wasn't worried until I spoke to that lot. Some people haven't got a clue. I know I haven't got cancer, but I also know their reasons for me not having it are imbecilic. I wish in a lot of ways I had not told anyone, including Mark. I wish I could just go to the clinic, get the all-clear, and no one would be any the wiser.

Tuesday, 5th March 2019

Had lunch with Amara, my boss, today. We were having a loose meeting about the staff, which ended up with us talking about various concerts we had attended since the age of twelve. Hers were top drawer, including Tina Turner and the Rolling Stones. I wanted to run into the main road with shame when I could only admit to Deacon Blue and Kajagoogoo. She laughed, but I couldn't tell if it was polite or sympathetic.

I told her about my appointment at the breast clinic for next week.

"When did you find it?"

"A couple of months ago."

She didn't hide her shock. She then tutted and took my hand. "I had breast cancer a few years ago."

I wasn't sure what to say. I find it hard to be sympathetic about something that has already happened, and judging by her attitude, she had come to terms with it. But it was not lost on me that I had taken her breath away with my revelation.

"Oh, I'm sorry. Are you okay now, though?"

"I'm still on a lot of medication, which causes some issues, but the main thing is I'm cancer-free." She smiled but was still clutching my hand. I told her I would be fine, I would keep her up to date, and I bought her a large wine, hoping it would lighten the mood, which it did.

On the way home, I thought about her story and started to see her in a different light. I've always liked Amara but have only ever seen her as my manager, and she's been a supportive one at that. But whether it was the fact that we shared a bottle of wine or that she shared a very personal story with me, I felt our relationship changed today.

I went home and called Mark and told him all about it. He has never met Amara, but he concluded she sounded like a nice woman and it was great she had been so understanding about my upcoming appointment. I put the phone down, knowing Mark was putting me in the same camp as Amara. What Amara had gone through was horrendous. She'd had cancer. She'd had a mastectomy. I simply have a lump, a cyst at most. Why is everyone being dramatic about this? I have enough to contend with, with my job, the house, various nights out, a ghost and Mark. Also, I'm not even that old, for fuck's sake.

Monday, 11th March 2019

I went to the breast clinic today. Mark came with me, and we sat in a waiting room full of nervous women next to nervous partners, husbands or friends. It reminded me of the couch outside the lingerie changing room in Marks and Spencer's.

The receptionist warned us that we could be there for a while, as there was the potential of having three tests if they needed to keep investigating. She was very friendly and explained that most women leave after the first examination, as most lumps are harmless.

Mark was in his suit, as he was planning to go to the office once I was done. I was planning to go straight home and work from there. Dear Diary, I felt a little nervous when I started to scan the informative posters on the walls, talking of various cancers that I've never heard of. There were also posters promoting clinical trials and lots of information with statistics; nestled among them all was the flyer informing people that the café was open until four p.m.

There was a massive pile of magazines that looked like the pages had been turned a lot by people probably as nervous as me. The waiting room also had a huge television on the wall, and Mark and I managed to giggle through *Homes Under the Hammer*. The only reason we enjoy it is the soundtrack they select when showing a montage of a property. People were staring at us when we laughed at a segment that showed a terrace property that had lost its boundary wall and was reduced to a small pile of rubble and a larger pile of dust. The song choice? The Style Council's 'Walls Come Tumbling Down', of course.

I have to say I was pleased Mark had come. A woman called my name, and I told Mark he could stay in the waiting room. The woman took me to a room that only had a bed, a desk and four chairs. She pointed to a clean gown and asked me to strip from the waist up and pop the gown on.

Once I was done, a stout lady entered the room and introduced herself as Mary Callum. She was a consultant at the clinic and wanted to give me a physical examination. With me lying on the bed, she kneaded my breast and then gave the other one a go for good measure. She reminded me of one of the Two Fat Lady chefs, but I can't remember which one. Next, she got me doing the now-familiar 'YMCA' routine, but this one had a bit of sass to it with bending forwards. It was then she told me to get dressed and return to the waiting room.

"Why?"

"I need you to have a mammogram. I'll come back and see you later."

I wanted to tell her that I wasn't over fifty, but I figured a woman of her qualifications probably knew that, so I silently put my clothes on and went back to Mark.

"I've got to have a mammogram."

"Well, that's okay. At least they're being thorough," he said.

I knew that, but I quietly sat and thought about a mammogram. I'd heard they could hurt, and I'm not that good with pain. What if I couldn't stand the agony of my breast being squished flat? It's not like I had a lot of flesh to stick in the machine anyway. I'm only a B cup. I was quietly hoping they would see my fried eggs and tell me the device was not built for my tiny offerings. I considered asking Mark to get me some water, thinking it might help, but then realised it only helps if you're pregnant and having an ultrasound.

I watched Mark answering emails on his phone. He was probably telling his office I was taking longer than expected, and I started to get wound up. I told him he could go, and he looked shocked at the suggestion. While I was explaining why, a different lady called my name and took me to a different room, which was freezing. The last time I had seen a room like that was in the opening credits of *The Incredible Hulk*. The mammogram machine looked like it would GIVE me cancer, never mind detect it.

There was no gown offered in this room. I was simply told to strip and stand on the mark on the floor, which was a crude cross made out of insulation tape. The lady, who was also nice, headed towards me with very red fingers to position my breast on the machine. When she touched me, it made sense why her fingers were so red. She was perished to the bone. If the NHS was in such dire straits that they couldn't afford to put the heating on, you'd think the staff in a breast clinic would be given hand warmers as a standard work requirement. I also wondered why she smelled of vodka and then realised it was the antibacterial gel she had slathered all over her hands.

She explained that there would be a lot of instructions to get me in the right position for the machine. Was that because my boobs were small and I'm deemed more of a challenge? She warned me it would be a little uncomfortable, and I could hear an old friend's voice echoing from the past about it feeling like she had been put through a mangle. According to her, it took over a month for her boob to regain its original shape.

The lady pushed and pulled various arms on the machine, and I eventually felt my boob being squashed into a shape that I knew it had never been in before. The nurse then scurried to the other side of the room and clicked a few buttons, and after a whirr from the machine, I knew the picture had been taken. I have to say though, Diary, maybe I'm hard as nails, but it wasn't that bad. I was in there for about ten minutes, and I was impressed that they chucked the other boob in the machine as well, probably because there was so much room to spare. At least I would know if there were any cysts in that one and I could ignore them in future.

The freezing nurse told me I had to go back to the waiting room—they were sending me for a scan. Why? Surely by now, they could see that all this fuss was unnecessary.

I had to go home and log on. I would have a hundred emails by now, and what would Amara think?

When I walked back into the room, Mark stood up, ready to go. I told him I had to wait for an ultrasound and that I really did not mind if he wanted to leave. Bless him, he stayed with me and grabbed my hand as we distracted ourselves with the now fully refurbished terraced house on *Homes Under the Hammer*.

Another nurse came and collected me and took me to a room that had subdued lighting like an expensive restaurant. There were a lot of machines and shiny, silver instruments around. I was passed a gown, similar to the one I had worn before, and was grateful that this room was warmer than all the others. Another lady walked in, the radiographer, who had a severely cut black bob and extremely lined skin that had either seen a lot of sun or a lot of laughter. With the restaurant lighting, it was hard for me to judge which it was.

She pulled down the front of my gown and squeezed a huge amount of sticky, odourless gel onto my breast. I wanted to say that I was only a B cup and they had wasted an awful lot of gel on there, but I didn't. I was told to lie on my right side, facing her and the machine, and raise my left arm over my head. As she started to push the scanner along my chest, I watched her face. I also noticed that her arm smelled of roses, which was nice—the flowers not the chocolates. Her face was giving nothing away.

I began to think about how much time I was wasting. All these tests. Surely one of these machines had already told them it was only a harmless lump.

"Can you tell that it's a cyst?"

"It's not a cyst," she said flatly and carried on staring at the small screen like Carol-Anne in the film *Poltergeist*.

"Excuse me?"

"It looks a little suspicious to me."

If it wasn't a cyst, then what the fuck was it? I was lying there, with an arm over my head like an orangutan, not sure how to react. How do you react when you look like you should be singing 'I Wanna Be Like You'?

I smiled weakly and became aware that the jelly she was continuing to smear all over my breast was now dribbling down my neck. I wasn't sure if it was an appropriate time to ask for a tissue or if I should think more about what could be in my boob.

She pulled her scanner away, and bizarrely, I wanted to smile because it looked like an old-fashioned price gun from the days when things were 'something and a half p'. I was grateful the mauling was over, and now seemed like a good time to request a Kleenex.

"I need to do a biopsy on you. Just stay in that position for me."

I lay there with my arm still over my head, tempted to ask her if I sang 'King Louis' whether she'd join in, just to lighten the mood. But my humour dived for cover when she produced an instrument that looked like it could jack up a four-by-four. She saw my face and said she would numb me up. I could've done with a general anaesthetic or at least a decent punch before she came near me.

To be fair, she had the skill of Eric Bristow, and she threw that needle into the bullseye before I drew breath. I then saw handfuls of metal and knew they were heading my way. So as I stared at the wall, I let Edward Scissorhands pierce, prod, poke and push. She gave it a 'snip'—three times as I recall. And with the last attempt, she clipped 'it'. A titanium clip is now buried in there like a little *Blue Peter* badge. I wondered if it had puffed itself up with pride at its new addition.

The nurse who had called my name in the waiting room appeared from the darkened corner and slapped on a plaster that I felt was far too small after the mauling I had received. Surely, a wheelchair and a gypsy cream were not too much to ask for. I was offered a smile and ANOTHER mammogram. I wanted to smile back; I really did. But forgive me, after what had just happened, I did not relish the thought of my now punctured boob being squeezed into the machine again. An image came to mind of *The Great British Bake Off* when they laminate pastry with a rolling pin, and I winced.

By the time I had headed back to the waiting room, the patients I had started the morning with had left with a smile and a cyst. I never thought a cyst could offer a positive emotion, but I'm sure all women who have ever been invited to a breast clinic have been grateful to leave with a cyst in their party bags.

I was the only one left.

Last time I felt like this, I was fourteen and sheepish, waiting to be picked for the netball team in a PE lesson. I was never chosen, and as I got older, I would spend each lesson waiting for the burly-looking, probably lesbian PE teacher to come in and tell me I was excused, even though it was my fourth period that month.

But there was no PE teacher this time. Just young nurses with perky tits ushering me from room to room.

The final room, the same as the first, felt ominous, and Mark came in with me. There was no machinery, car jacks or even the pricing gun. There was the familiar desk, four chairs, hand sanitiser and a box of tissues. I was delivered the news by the consultant, Mary Callum, and a Macmillan nurse named Abi, and when Mark and I were done in there, the only thing I hadn't used was the hand sanitiser. I left red-eyed with germ-ridden hands to digest the news. They can't confirm it until the biopsy results are back, which will be a couple of weeks, but they are sure that I have cancer.

Mark and I sat in the hospital car park for a while. My thoughts kept straying to having one boob and what that would look like. I had seen some pictures on the internet of women with one boob, and I could feel the lump rising in my throat. How can people be that brave? I am not one of those people. I started to pray that I could keep my manky boob, even though it was still sticky and the insufficient plaster was catching on my lacy bra. I then imagined being bald and promised myself there and then that I would become a hermit and spend my days in a wedding dress like Miss Haversham from *Great Expectations*.

"Pub?" asked Mark. I couldn't speak, but he knew.

Mark and I drove in silence straight to a pub. Within half an hour of being delivered the news, I was clutching a wine. I'm panicking now whether I should be drinking, and will that make my cancer grow? What am I supposed to do in the meantime? Mark's positivity was obviously still in the hospital, watching *Homes Under the Hammer*, as the Mark in front of me in the pub looked anything but.

"They don't bring in a Macmillan nurse if things are okay, do they?"

He simply nodded and agreed with me. He just kept telling me that things would be fine and we would sort it.

I'm staying at Mark's flat tonight. I don't want to go home just yet. If I'm on my own, I will think about it. I can't think about it; it's too scary. I just want to be distracted. I want to talk about anything apart from lumps, cysts and most of all, fucking cancer!

Tuesday, 12th March 2019

I stayed in Mark's flat again today. I am not going to work. I have decided I'm going to watch a lot of Netflix and be totally selfish. If I can't have a day or two to digest this news, then I'll be handing in my notice. I know for a fact that when Margi Newton in Classifieds was off for two weeks with 'kidney stones', she was actually getting her tits enhanced in Manchester. So they can all swing! Mine aren't getting enhanced. They are getting unenhanced. Disenhanced? You know what I mean, Diary.

I told the girls, who all want to see me, but I'm keeping them at arm's length for now. I'm not a victim yet. I still have the biopsy results to come back, and they may still say it's a cyst. I doubt it, but you never know.

I have decided to call the lump Tracey. Mark and I just keep saying that Tracey is a cow and she needs to learn her place. We imagine her a bit chavvy and common and laugh that I am too nice for her and far too sophisticated to be associated with a chav called Tracey.

But the main reason is that since we have named it, it doesn't seem as scary when we talk about it. But I will admit, dear Diary, I think Tracey may be a little hard and have a bit of attitude, and I'm scared. Hopefully, the biopsy will tell me she is nothing more than a simple bully.

Wednesday, 13th March 2019

I came home today. I wasn't looking forward to it, but when I walked through the door, I realised how much I missed the place, and it is my home after all.

It's feeling more like home since Andy has decorated all of the downstairs. He might have eaten all the biscuits in the house and drunk all of my milk with the thirst of a blood-starved vampire, but he did do a nice, clean job. I've told him he can do my bedroom next and have decided he can do it sooner rather than later, just in case. If I am to lie in bed all day like Yoko Ono, then I want the walls to be a nice, calming colour. I'll dig out the Farrow & Ball colour card and see if they have one called 'Kill Cancer' or 'You Still Have Two Tits'.

I called Amara, and she wants to see me as soon as possible. I don't know what to say to her. What if she starts talking and thinks I can relate to what she's been through? I can't relate to it, and even if I could, I couldn't do it with the positivity that she does. I'll have to play that one by ear for now. The girls keep texting, wanting to see me, but they are now taking the hint and laying off a bit. I will talk to them when I know what the hell Tracey is.

Thursday, 18th March 2019

I went to the hospital today. It's confirmed. I have cancer. Fuck!

Friday, 19th March 2019

I spent most of last night awake, of course. I'm not sure how to feel if I'm honest. Mary, the consultant, said I was pretty stoic when she confirmed the news to me. Is that a compliment? I'm not sure how I should have reacted, but looking back, I think I reacted more when they cancelled *Brookside*. Was my lack of reaction because, deep down, I knew this was coming anyway? Bringing Abi into the last meeting was a gentle giveaway, a hint of things to come. Like I said, I was awake for most of the night. I wasn't crying, and I don't feel scared either. They said they can sort it, and they will. I hope.

I put a post on Facebook last night telling people to check their boobs, as I have found cancer. I tried to make the post as upbeat as possible, but it was one of the hardest things I have ever had to write. I wrestled with the decision of even putting anything on social media in the first place, but Mark said it was the quickest way to tell everyone because I underestimate the number of people I know. He said to tell all the important people first, like my siblings, but then do one big announcement instead of hundreds of texts.

He was right. As soon as the post went on, I felt like my world went crazy. I told everyone that my tumour is called Tracey, and I don't know if that made it easier for people to talk to me and post messages, send texts, send emails and phone. There were so many, and after a couple of hours, they became blurry. I need to get back to so many people, but to be honest, the only one I wanted to talk to was Amara.

I called her this evening, and she listened to me, and then I started to cry. It came from nowhere. Well, actually that's a lie. It came from a bottle of Chenin Blanc! Drunk crying is the worst. The poor person you are talking to cannot understand a word you're saying, as you sound like you are drowning with a severe cold. Throw in a couple of 'why me's and it's hard for anyone to be sympathetic.

"Tell me again, Jo. Just take your time." Amara was trying to tell me to get a grip.

"I have to have a lumpectomy. Then they will blast my boob every day for three weeks, and then after that, they will look at therapy for me." I sniffed.

"Chemo?"

"They're not sure yet. But definitely some kind of hormone therapy, as Tracey is estrogen receptor positive. Christ, Amara, I smoked for years, and it's hormones that end up trying to kill me!"

"Why didn't you ask them about a mastectomy?"

I was shocked at the suggestion. Why in the hell would I want my breast removed if they can cure me by just taking the tumour out? They said my breast would be smaller, and radiotherapy might not help with size difference afterwards, but even still. I could maybe get the smaller boob looked at, at a later date—at least I would always have something, and what I had would still be mine.

"I'm happy to go ahead with the lumpectomy, to be honest."

"Well, whatever you think is best, and I'm sure the consultants have the best treatment plan for you. When is your surgery? I would like to see you before then."

I told her my surgery is planned for 9th April, and we have promised to meet before then. Even though what she went through was more devastating than anything I will go through, I like talking to her, as she talks plainly without sympathy. It's nice to have people feel a little sorry for you, but I need some balance as well, and I need the friends who say, "So what if you have cancer? You're not the first, and you won't be the last. Snap out of it." Amara is my Cher from *Moonstruck*.

I've started to look for distractions so I'm not thinking about it all the time. I called Andy today to ask him to paint my bedroom and to have a look at the annexe for me. There is a strange smell in there, and I don't know where it's coming from. If I didn't know any better, I would say that it's cigarette smoke, but it can't be. I don't smoke, and I know the neighbours don't either. Even if they did, I haven't opened any of the windows. There are, however, a few cracks in various places. Hopefully, when he fills them in and paints, it will feel more inviting in there. At the moment, the room is creeping me out. A bit like when I walk through the organic section of Sainsbury's. I feel that the area is for vegans or the middle class only. I am neither.

Saturday, 20th March 2019

I found myself sitting in front of my dressing room mirror today. I kept staring at my reflection and wondering why I didn't look ill. I keep trying to convince myself that I have cancer, but I don't look like I have cancer. I don't look sick in any way. I'm not even sure what to say to people.

"Hey, I've got cancer."

"Hi. My name is Jo, and my tests showed cancer."

"Hey, I have cancer, and I've called it Tracey. Aren't I hysterical? Aren't I funny? Don't you wish you were me with my witty sense of humour and cancerous breast? No? Shame! Maybe next time."

It wasn't until I was desperate for a glass of wine that I realised I had been sitting in front of the mirror for nearly two hours and it was still only 1:30 p.m. Yes, I know it's early to start drinking, but who cares? Really? Does anyone give a hoot? I doubt it.

I brought the bottle and the glass up to my bedroom and sat in the silence and drank the bottle in less than an hour. The glass was still clean when I had finished the wine.

No one was watching me drink from the bottle. If ever there was a moment to drink straight from the bottle, then it was today. I now feel scared. I now feel alone. And I want to feel drunk.

I found the film *Stella*, starring Bette Midler, on the laptop and settled down to watch, even though half of it was hazy with drunk fuzziness and crying. I needed to cry, but it just felt so raw on my own.

My phone was constantly dinging, and I turned it off in the end. I know people will worry, but tough. I'm not here to look after them. I don't want to talk to anyone, but I don't want to feel like this either. How do I make it stop?!

Please, God, don't ever let me feel this alone again.

Sunday, 21st March 2019

The girls dragged me out tonight. I didn't want to go. I was planning on staying in with Mark in my house, and just when we were about to settle down, the door went and in came Charlotte.

"Right, you! Off that couch now and get in the shower."

I looked at Mark, who just shrugged. He had a guilty expression on his face. He had clearly been in touch with her.

"I don't want to."

"I'm not asking! I'm telling. Now move!"

Within an hour, I was sitting in a wine bar with Mia, Kelly, Anne, Saskia, Lucy and Charlotte and clutching a glass of fizz. Within two hours, I had been labelled 'The Bravest Girl They Know', 'A Warrior', 'A Machine of Positivity'. I couldn't tell them that I was drinking from the bottle last night like a wino. I couldn't tell them I was throwing up a few hours later because you shouldn't mix Pinot and panic. I couldn't tell them I'd cried puddles. No one wants to hear that. So I said thank you and carried on drinking, telling jokes and saying it would all be fine.

"Have you got private medical?" asked Charlotte.

"I do, but to be honest, I don't think I will get any better treatment than the NHS."

"I'm not so sure about that."

"Don't be such a bloody snob!" barked Anne.

"I'm not a snob!" protested Charlotte. "In this day and age, sometimes you have to pay to get the best."

"And who defines 'best'? It's the same in education. People think if they pay for their kids to go to an independent school, then six years later, they'll have an eleven-year-old who can perform brain surgery, and if they can't, it's the teacher's fault because Mama and Papa kept paying each term. Then there are the people who think grammar school is best, and I was headteacher of one! Grammar schools work for some kids and not for others, so that doesn't make it best. The parents create the snobs of today, not a class system. I've seen kids walk around corridors with their noses in the air and no chin to their name, saying things like, 'One struggles to fold a towel, as one does not have a chin.' The NHS will serve you well, Jo. You mark my words. You don't need to throw money away."

"Well," Charlotte snapped, "all I know is that my friend Melanie's mum had a heart attack and was left in the corridor for days."

"And all I know is that you never hear of all the marvellous work that the doctors, nurses and everyone else who works in the NHS does. You only ever hear stories about stupid people lying in corridors and them making out that no one came near them."

"Well, they didn't!"

"So how did they know she had a heart attack? And was she not fed for the numerous days she was left in the corridor? And what's wrong with your mate Melanie? Can she not tell someone her poor mother has been clutching her chest for days and if that doesn't kill her, malnutrition will? I'm sorry, Charlotte, but it's people like your friend Melanie who say when they gave birth, they were in labour for two months, the only thing that saved them was whale music, and they were stitched back together with a Singer sewing machine."

I laughed, and I couldn't stop. The more I sit with Anne, the more I love her. She takes no shit, prisoners or single measures in her gin. I wondered for a fleeting moment how she would get on with Amara. They would probably end up killing each other, as they're both too alpha and too old to care.

At the end of the night, she asked me to call her during the week to arrange lunch. I've never been to lunch with Anne on my own, but I have to admit, I'm looking forward to it. She may be good for my soul.

Thursday, 21st March 2019

I went to my pre-op today. I had MRSA swabs and what seemed like a pint of blood taken from me for various tests—what they are, I have no idea. I also went for a chest X-ray. I've never had a chest X-ray before and was really disappointed to see it wasn't like the cartoons where you stand in front of it and can instantly see your bones, not to mention that the equipment in the X-ray room was a little antiquated compared to what Carol-Anne was playing with the other week.

I also had to have medical photographs taken of my boobs. There I was, half-naked, standing like Wonder Woman with my hands on my hips, ready to fight for truth, justice and the American way. Apart from school photos, I have never had my picture taken…'professionally', shall we say. And why do photographers need silver umbrellas and sheets of plastic everywhere? I'm sure they will say it's all about the lighting, but I find standing in front of the window gives me some cracking Snapchats. It's just a boob, for God's sake, not *America's Next Top Model.* I'm very disappointed I won't see the photos for approval or have the choice to buy—even as a coaster or a small key ring.

I've told work that I should be back in a couple of months, providing I don't have an adverse reaction to the radiotherapy, which I doubt I will. The way my skin took a battering in Kavos in '94, I think it could have coped with Chernobyl.

I feel a lot more positive about my treatment, and in a few weeks, this will all be over. Mark suggested we go away for a short break before the surgery. So I've decided to finish work at the end of the month and take the week before my op as holidays to get my head in a positive place. I'm feeling a lot more optimistic this week than I was last. It could have been so much worse for me. I could have ended up having a mastectomy and chemo. No boob and no hair, I could not have coped with that. I'm not that strong. I am not that brave. I am not that warrior.

Friday, 22nd March 2019

Mark and I went out with a few of his friends last night. I was dreading it, to be honest, thinking they would all be feeling sorry for me. There were a few hugs that lasted longer than usual, but apart from that, they all carried on like it was a regular night out, which I was grateful for. I'm not sure if Mark had prepped them beforehand. If he did, I was silently appreciative.

For a few hours, I forgot about Tracey. It was just Mark and me, and we had fun. He stayed in mine for the night, saying we had to christen the room since Andy has decorated it. It was either the paint fumes or the eight gin and tonics he'd drunk, but he fell asleep as soon as he climbed into bed, and no christening took place. I couldn't sleep, so I went downstairs to make something to eat.

It was then that I saw her.

She was standing in the dark in the annexe, smoking a cigarette. I knew who she was straight away. The grey leggings, the oversized grubby T-shirt, the greasy bun on top of her head and that horrible, smoke-stained smile.

It was Tracey.

She is everything I imagined, and there she was, grinning at me as she stepped toward the light of the kitchen.

"Don't get too comfy. You won't be around for much longer," I hissed at her.

Then the cheeky bitch laughed at me!

"I'll leave when I am good and ready," she said in a strong cockney accent.

She is the black shadow that I have seen around the house. I only used to see her when I felt her in my breast, but I've been feeling her a lot more lately, and now, maybe because of the drink, I can see her. She's horrible, and I need her out of my house.

"I'm quite comfortable in your annexe," she cackled. "I can't wait for what's-his-name? Handy Andy? Yeah, when he comes around and spruces the place up a bit. He's quite tasty, is our Handy Andy. You been there?"

"Don't be so disgusting!"

She just laughed at this and then had the cheek to ask me to move some of my stuff aside as she needs the space to spread herself out a bit. When she walked back into the annexe, I followed her, but she was out of sight.

I need to tell Andy to hold off on decorating until she is gone. I cannot have her getting comfy! I'll never be shot of her.

Saturday, 23rd March 2019

I got up hoping that meeting Tracey was all a bad dream, but it wasn't. By the time I was halfway down the stairs, I could smell her smoke coming through the kitchen. When I walked in, she was sitting on the worktop, eating a Penguin biscuit.

I tried to ignore her and filled the kettle for coffee while Mark was getting up. She keeps sniffing all the time and rubbing her nose on her arm. I don't know if she has a cold or a coke habit—I'm hoping it's an allergy that will kill her off, but until then I'll just have to wait for 9th April when she will be no more. There is also a smell about her. It's a cross between piss, sweat and old shoes.

Mark walked into the kitchen, completely unaware of the addition to the house, and tutted when he saw the fridge was empty. I could see Tracey eyeing up Mark's arse as he bent over to see if anything was lurking in the salad drawer. The only thing my salad drawer has ever housed is his beer. He should know this by now.

"Why is there never anything to eat in this house?" he moaned.

"There's plenty of Penguins, sweet cheeks," Tracey said.

"Right! Jump in the shower, and I'll take you out for breakfast, and then maybe we could stop at a supermarket on the way back and buy things like fruit, vegetables and meat. I'm surprised you're not carrying eggs on your feet with the number of Penguins you eat."

As I left the kitchen, I saw Tracey licking her lips and leering at Mark. She was making me sick. But then that could've been the crop top she was wearing with the same leggings as she had on yesterday. Her gut was spilling over the top of the leggings, as her cropped T-shirt couldn't contain her porridge-like belly. She looked like a shit Winnie the Pooh.

She followed me back upstairs while I started to get ready and complimented me on my 'nice gaff'. The compliments soon dried out when she sat behind me while I was at the dressing table mirror.

"Not being funny, babe, but you look like crap." She sniggered. "And no offence, but the last time I saw eyes like yours, they were in a fish shop window. All dead and staring at me. Begging for a bit of batter." She started cackling. She clearly loves her own jokes. And I did take offence.

As much as I hate her, she is right, of course. I look dreadful. What will I look like in a month or two? Am I being ravaged already?

"I'll be fine as soon as I put my make-up on. I've just had a rough couple of days, that's all, and you're not helping!"

"All the lippy in the world ain't gonna hide that manky tit, love." Then she left the room and bounced back down the stairs like she was wearing divers' boots.

I didn't even bother with the make-up. I felt I was suffocating in the house and just needed to get out. When we left, she shouted goodbye to Mark—as if he could hear her!

Wednesday, 27th March 2019

Today was my last day in the office, as I'm travelling the next couple of days for meetings about distribution and advertising. Everyone in work has been amazingly supportive. There were some people who started crying, and I had to remind them I'm not dying, I'm having a little surgery and will soon be back in the fold. Lots of presents arrived on my desk, nearly as many as the looks of sympathy but not quite.

It's strange at the moment. I find I'm sitting in the office and staring at people. I can hear them talking of last night's telly or the sales that are on in town or how cheap the Easter eggs are in Tesco, and I want to say, "Hey, by the way, I've got cancer. Can you carry on with your normal life when I'm not in the room, please?" But I don't. I just sit and stare or look at potters' wheels on the internet to distract me. I wonder if Tracey will still be in the annexe when I'm doing my pottery, but why should she be? She'll be gone soon enough, and the only reminder I'll have will be a small scar near my nipple. A small price to pay, I think.

Friday, 29th March 2019

I haven't been home much this week. I've either been down south or staying at Mark's flat. We've booked to go to Spain for a few days, which means I won't have to look at Tracey for a while.

She has now put various ornaments around the annexe including a blown glass fish on my windowsill, various West Ham memorabilia and a picture of a crying clown on the main wall.

"What the fuck is that?" I asked when I spied the picture.

"It's a family heirloom. My mum had it and her mum before her."

"What the hell are you talking about?" I was becoming hysterical. "You're made out of shit and hormones. You haven't got a mum or a nan because no one would allow something like you to stay alive from birth!"

"Untwist your tits and have a Horlicks, Jo. You're starting to get on my nerves."

"Then GET THE FUCK OUT!"

"Newsflash, darlin'. I'm here for as long as you are." And with that, she lit a cigarette and blew the smoke into my face.

When I looked around the room trying to find something to hit her with, I noticed there were numerous overflowing ashtrays all over the floor, and a few cigarette burns have already appeared on my sofa in there. I know it's old, but even still! Only a few more days and she'll be gone forever.

"Fine! Sit here amongst your shit. Enjoy the next eleven days, love. In fact, get some more crap in here. I think a nice dot-to-dot picture would look lovely on that wall. I'm presuming you can count?"

"No need to get personal."

"Or maybe a mosaic from the cigarette butts around the room."

"What's a mosaic?"

"You have eleven days to figure it out."

I walked out, and for the first time, I felt like I could beat her. She is nothing more than a repulsive, odious bully. Maybe my friends are right. Perhaps I am a warrior, after all.

The day turned better. A few of the girls came over with gifts for me, some tokens of hope and love, which I will treasure forever. We all got very drunk, and it was only when people wanted to talk about cancer that Tracey put in an appearance. At one point, she sat bold as brass on the arm of my chair, drinking Blue Nun wine straight from the bottle, laughing at some stories and sneering at others. I wanted to judge her for drinking straight from the bottle, but it wasn't that long ago I was doing the same. Am I Tracey? Is this how people see me?

When they left, she thought it was okay to give me her opinion on each and every one of the girls, and it seems Tracey does not like any of them.

"Saskia is well up herself! If she had tits, I'd tell my mates to move in with her." She tittered.

"You do know that if it didn't hurt me as well, I would quite happily stab you in the face with a fork." I tried to ignore her while I was putting the glasses in the dishwasher but, dear Diary, it's so hard.

"Ah, but you can't. Talking of unfortunate faces, what about that one with the black hair? She well needs a makeover, her. She looks like one of them dolls you practise giving CPR on. And are they all gay?"

"No."

"That Anne seems a bit salty."

"Do you have any friends, Tracey?"

"Aren't we friends?" She laughed.

She was sternly but softly told to fuck off before I climbed the stairs and came to bed.

Thursday, 4th April 2019

Dear Diary, I hadn't planned to bring you to Spain, but here you are, enjoying the sunshine with me. Mark is at the pool, and I've decided to stay on the balcony of our room today. I just wanted a day on my own. I have to admit, I'm very drunk as I write this. Today has not been a good day for me.

I have thought of death today.

I've thought about what difference I've made and how long people will miss me for. I've thought about Mark and what he will do if I am gone. I've thought about what I should wear in the coffin and even what colour the internal silk should be. I've thought about the order of service, the picture that would adorn it, the hymns, the readings and who would say them, the cars and where everyone would go afterwards to talk about what a splendid affair it was. Yes, I have had depressing thoughts, and I don't even drink gin, which is just as well, as no doubt the request for 'Tragedy' by Steps would rear its ugly head again. I've thought about who would carry my coffin and had to dismiss my friend Neil, as he is a lot shorter than the other three pallbearers I've picked. No one wants to see a precarious coffin making its way through the church.

I've also made a list of the songs I want to be played at the wake, which will need revising when I'm sober. I say revising; I mean shortening—the list is long enough for a wake that lasts a fortnight. I'll probably remove 'Another One Bites the Dust' and 'Knock on Wood'.

I know I shouldn't do this to myself, and most of the time, I'm being as positive as I possibly can. But today, it all felt like too much of an effort, and this was a day when I had to go '*there*'. I wrote everything down in the notes in my phone—every last detail of what I wanted—and read it over until I was happy with it. Then I finished my third bottle of wine and deleted the note. No one needs to know it existed. No one needs to know I thought about it except you, dear Diary.

Friday, 5th April 2019

We arrived back in the UK. Am I too mean to pay the extra so I can use my phone abroad? When I took it off airplane mode, a voicemail came through. The hospital wants to see me on Monday. My surgery is on Tuesday! Why would they need to see me the day before? Mark said they probably just want to go over the last few details of my stay. My stay! I pointed out I didn't need to preorder a treatment in the spa or book a table for my evening meal. All I have to do is turn up on surgery day clean as a whistle with a rumbling tummy from a twelve-hour nil-by-mouth stint.

When I called them, they said I have to go in Monday for an MRI scan and to see my consultant. Isn't it a bit late in the day to be asking for an MRI scan? Don't MRI machines need a while to give you a picture? Or are they like Polaroids now? My last MRI experience was with a friend who was so scared they allowed me to accompany her into the room and hold her hand. I removed all of my jewellery and metal belts and so on. However, I completely forgot about the hair grips in my hair. One by one, the machine tugged them loose—when I emerged from the room, I looked like I'd driven up the M1 in a convertible.

We drove home in silence, and when I arrived home, Tracey was waiting for me. She said she missed me, then proceeded to berate me about not having enough food in the house, and could I turn the heating back on, as she was cold? Maybe if she wore something besides cheap leggings, T-shirts or West Ham football tops, she'd keep warm. I noticed the tops of her arms were a dark pink that reminded me of sweaty liver and briefly contemplated vegetarianism. I'm hoping when I go for the MRI, the noise frightens her so much she jumps ship. I doubt it, though.

Monday, 8th April 2019

Mary Callum met me in the breast clinic today. I could tell by her face that something was wrong. It turns out that my disappointing X-ray experience proved disappointing in so many more ways.

"We had a look at some of your scans at the multi-disciplinary meeting, and we think there might be another tumour in there."

"Really?" was all I could say.

"As your breasts are so dense, we've brought in one of the best radiographers in the North West of England to do a further biopsy on you."

Feeling like my breasts could be donated to Pirelli, I was informed it was merely because of my age.

"Could it be a cyst?"

"It could be. That's what we need to find out."

While my first biopsy seemed a necessary step, this one felt very different. This time, *they* were looking for something that even I wasn't aware was there. And after a lot of pushing with the something-and-a-half-p pricing gun, the scanner found the something. Then, as before, the car jack came at me and struggled to dig its way to the centre of my breast, where the radiographer wanted to snip. She poked around in there for over half an hour trying to get to the something. At one point, I thought she was going to put her knee on my chest just to get the probe in further. Eventually, she got there and gave this one a titanium clip too, now known as the *Blue Peter* badge.

Sporting a hospital gown that was thankfully tied at the front, as I had to walk past a number of men on the way, I was navigated to the MRI room, where two nurses helped me onto the bed, as I had to lie on my front. One of the nurses slid a cushion out to reveal two holes to pop my boobs in! As I lay down, the smaller of the nurses got 'under the hood' and pulled each one through a hole.

"It's a bit like milking a cow," she laughed as she tried to coax my B cups to drop a bit more. She was the only one laughing.

After wiring me up to the machine, they scuttled next door to watch the show through the window. I lay there with my arms above my head, face down, and wanted to cry. Only the strict instruction for me not to move a muscle stopped me from sobbing uncontrollably. However, I could feel the tears dropping through the face hole.

"Please let it be a cyst," I whispered.

After forty minutes of pounding, and that was just from the eighties music they selected for me, I was sent back, with two dead arms, to Mary.

"It doesn't look like a cyst, to be honest with you, Jo. So until we get the biopsy results back, we won't be going ahead with the surgery tomorrow."

The tears were bubbling. They wanted to burst and gush, but I kept sniffing.

"Do you want us to get Mark?" He was sitting in the waiting room.

"No, I'll just go, thanks."

Tracey is stuck with me, I kept thinking. I need her out of my life, NOW! I cannot move on until I get rid of this bitch.

Tuesday, 9th April 2019

This would have been my surgery day. I should be on a table somewhere getting Tracey scooped out of me and being grateful for an inappropriately sized plaster and begging for a cardy. But no, I started the day having a shower, and just when I got my head in a positive place, I went downstairs to find Tracey has company.

I say company—what I actually mean is she has moved someone in, and his name is Tyson! Tyson looks mixed-race, although I'm not sure what the mixture is. But if I had to guess I would say part custard because he's thick as, part sloth because he's lazy as, and part *The Sun* newspaper because he's hateful.

I thought Tracey was bad, but he's managed to get right under my skin in a very short space of time. Tracey is clearly all loved up. So much so, they now have a bed in the annexe complete with sheets that have never seen a washing machine and pillows that look like they've been left out in the rain all night.

When I came down, the two of them were sitting up in the bed, smoking and drinking tea. Tracey, with a proud smile, introduced me to the brute.

"Jo, this is my Tyson."

"Is that her?" he asked, and then they laughed.

I closed the door to the annexe, but I can still hear them laughing, and I know it's about me. I had to get out and ended up calling Anne to see if she wanted to go for lunch, which she jumped at. It wasn't long before we were in our local wine bar ordering fish and chips and a bottle of Pinot.

"No offence, Anne, but I didn't expect to be doing this with you today."

"You must be so disappointed. How in the hell did they not find this one? What are we calling this one, by the way?"

"Tyson. Only because they suspect this one is three times bigger than Tracey. They didn't find it because they had no need to look that deep. But apparently, at the multi-disciplinary meetings when they looked at my file, someone suspected there was something else and said an MRI would tell them more."

"So, it's buried deep in your breast, then? You can't even feel it?"

"No."

"Sneaky little shit!"

We ate our fish and chips, mostly in silence. But it was a comfortable silence. Once the waitress took our plates away, we resumed our conversation.

"I take it work have been fine with you?"

"They've been amazing. I did think maybe I should go back to work, but I'm not sure how long it would be for. They could call me back in again for the surgery anytime. I'm not even sure how much I could do in the office—my head is all over the place."

"Have you thought about meditation?" Anne asked.

"I have, but I can't seem to switch off." All I'd ended up doing was making a shopping list and getting a cramp.

"I try and meditate every day. Have been for a long time now. It's helped me a lot through some of my challenging times, shall we say. Why don't you come around to mine in the morning after Kelly has left for school? Don't eat anything, though. Listening to food being digested while trying to empty your mind can be very distracting. And I'm not having you fart all over my Wilton."

I wasn't sure what to say. It was a really kind offer, and I was tempted, but I didn't want to waste Anne's time.

"Look, it's up to you," she said, "but I'm a firm believer in 'a healthy mind aids a healthy body', and while we can't control what Tracey and Tyson are doing to that body of yours, we can certainly reduce your stress levels. Stress feeds cancer, you know, and lots of other ailments including dandruff and verrucas."

"I use Head & Shoulders, and I don't plan on going to the baths," I joked.

"Good! Last time I went in there, I came out a different colour and realised I had a film of fake tan all over me."

After laughing, I realised she had a point.

"Okay, I'll come to yours about half nine, if that's all right."

She promised to have some pastries in, so I'm looking forward to it already. While I may not be able to go into a trance, I would pretend for a pain au chocolat.

I'm not long home now and have come straight to bed. I need to keep myself busy and try and forget about Tracey and Tyson for now. There is still my job, Mark, my family, my friends, my pottery and a fairly hectic social life to keep up with.

Wednesday, 10th April 2019

I went to Anne's this morning. Even though Kelly lives there, you can tell it's Anne's house. There's no denying the fact that she's a lot older than Kelly, and it's evident in their house, which is a large detached with a few antiques scattered around and lots of things screaming DO NOT TOUCH! But it was also very comfortable and looked lived in.

"I've put some cushions on the floor in the back reception room. It's nicer to meditate in there, as you can open the French doors out onto the garden. Unless you want to do it in the garden?"

"Wherever you're comfortable, Anne."

She explained what we would do and how the session would be broken down.

"First, we'll calm our minds and then give thanks for various elements of our lives. We have a lot to be grateful for. Then we'll meditate, listening to our breathing. I'll guide you through that. Then, finally, we'll do some manifestation."

"Manifestation?"

"Asking the universe for what we desire."

"The universe?"

"Well, some people say the universe, some say God. Me, personally, I talk to James Dean."

"Why?"

"Because he had style."

"Who should I talk to?"

"It'll come. Let's just concentrate on technique for now. A word of warning, though. You attract what you ask for. So don't be saying things like 'I don't want chemo'. You'll attract chemo! Be careful how you say things. Use positive words and be specific with your desires."

"It sounds complicated."

"Just ask for a happy, healthy body. You won't go wrong with that."

She guided me through a session that lasted an hour and a half but it only felt like ten minutes. After I finished, I felt calmer, more positive and realised I did have a lot of good things in my life. I also asked for a healthy body, a date for my surgery and a potter's wheel. When I told Anne of my eclectic list, she admitted she asked for health, wealth and a decent coffee stain remover that didn't damage silk.

We ate the pain au chocolat, drank tea and talked no more of cancer. However, when I got home and turned my phone back on, it went berserk. There's been a huge reaction to my postponed surgery with lots of messages coming through. I didn't realise I knew so many people.

Tracey was sitting on my bed when I went upstairs.

"Not so easy to get rid of, am I, treacle?" Me and Tyson were talking last night, and we might have a great big party. I wonder who will turn up, eh? We'll soon find out when we get your MOD results."

"MRI, you thick bitch!"

"MOD. MRI. I don't care just as long as we all have a laugh."

"Tracey, would you mind going back downstairs to your dickhead husband? You'll have to excuse me, as I have to rub my face against some pebbledash."

She wouldn't leave me alone, though. It got to the point where I jumped in the car, with wet hair, and headed straight to Mark's flat. As soon as he opened the door, I started crying. After pouring me a drink, he listened to me. I told him that even though I had a lot of people around me, I felt alone all the time. I told him that my phone annoys me with its constant dinging, and yet I felt guilty as every ding was a message of love. He said he understood why I felt overwhelmed with it all. People are talking about raising money in my honour, for the cancer hospital I attend, and everyone seems enthusiastic about it, but I can't get there yet. But it's the messages I keep getting. I didn't appreciate that I made that much of an impression on anyone, and Mark laughed at this.

"Jo, you are one of the kindest people I know. Whenever anyone is in trouble, you are there. You give them advice, and you tell them straight, which is why people love you. You never ask for anything in return except maybe company when you open a bottle of wine. This is everyone's way of telling you they are here for you now, and you're getting it in one big wave. No wonder you feel overwhelmed with it all. I feel overwhelmed with it, and I'm on the sidelines."

He sorted my head out more with Prosecco and hugs, and for a few hours, I forgot about Tracey and Tyson.

Friday, 12th April 2019

I went to my GP today. I've never been a great sleeper, but now, with the noise from Tracey and Tyson, I'm struggling to drop off. Plus, the added stress they give me with their constant slagging me off has made me break out in various unidentified rashes.

The doctor's surgery had its usual suspects—the old lady with a range of complaints that included a persistent cough and a weak bladder. Judging by the eye-watering smell, I ventured she would be treated for the latter initially. There was also a young mum and dad with their baby, and considering their fretful state, I guessed their precious child was in for its injections. And finally, there was a man at reception arguing with Sour-Faced Lady behind the desk.

The man, in a suit complete with pens in the top pocket, was trying to collect a prescription for his mother, which he'd been told over the phone would be ready. However, Sour-Faced Lady, who could not locate the elusive prescription, felt superior and acted accordingly when Suit Man could not recall the name of the person who had telephoned to say the prescription was ready. As if Sour-Faced Lady had not wound him up enough, she then informed him that his mother would need to contact the surgery herself and put the request in again. By this point, Suit Man felt he only had two options. One: swear at Sour-Faced Lady and haul himself over the desk, *Starsky & Hutch* style, and give the woman a damned good hiding. Or two: stomp off muttering about how the whole system was ridiculous and records should be kept on file. He picked number two, but I was so hoping he would pick number one.

Thankfully, I saw my own GP, Dr. Roberts, today. He has been my doctor for over twenty years, and we are now at the stage where we can talk candidly, with honesty and with humour. He assured me I was in safe hands with Mary Callum. With a bag full of lotions and potions and a sick note to sign me off work for a month, I went home.

Tracey and Tyson were in the annexe, dancing to The Prodigy, and had clearly been drinking a lot, as I spied empty Mad Dog, White Lightning and Carlsberg Special Brew bottles all over the floor. Tracey was shouting for me to join in. I try to ignore her, but it's so hard.

While Tyson doesn't venture much outside of the annexe because he is too lazy, Tracey seems to think it's okay to follow me around the house. She has no concept of personal space—she doesn't even realise she's not welcome. I tried to ignore her while I was in my bedroom, naked and drying my hair. She sat on the end of the bed, asking me about chemotherapy.

"Will you be having chemo?"

"Don't know."

"Will you lose your hair?"

"Don't know."

"But you've always hated your hair. I mean, all that frizz, it's practically pubic. Might be a blessing to lose it all. They say when it grows back, it's grey. You might look good with grey hair, with having an old face and that."

I said nothing.

"You could get it all cut off now and then sell it. Though I'm not sure who's trying to rock the bush look. Maybe people in Yorkshire might want it. They're always wearing flat caps, so maybe they're bald underneath."

"I hope they do give me chemo."

"Why? So you can buy a wig and look half decent for a change?"

"No, because it helps kill you. Now, run along and see to your husband. I think he may have run out of crayons to play with."

When I looked over my shoulder, she had gone. I need to stand up to her more.

Thursday, 18th April 2019

I went back to the clinic today to see Mary and get the results from the MRI. They confirmed that there was a second tumour, which was the same grade as the first, only this one was three times bigger. I knew that already, as it was making itself at home—in *my* home, with Tracey and my biscuit tin! Mary also said the MRI had picked up two smaller tumours in the same breast. As if that wasn't bad enough, she then delivered the news that I had been dreading the most. A lumpectomy was no longer an option, and a mastectomy was the way forward due to the extent of the cancer.

I have to tell you, dear Diary, that I reacted in a way I didn't know I was capable of. Mark, equally stunned but less vocal than I, asked Mary and Abi, the Macmillan nurse, to leave the room. I'm not sure how long they were gone for, but I managed to compose myself by the time they re-entered. I apologised, of course. I even felt embarrassed that I had given such a fine Bette Davis impression with wailing and arm waving of equal proportion. Mary, who had probably seen such reactions before, simply shrugged and smiled and then went on to explain what would happen next.

I only caught snippets. I felt like I was listening to a dodgy radio station when the signal comes and goes. I was hearing most of the essential details but knew I was losing bits here and there. When she finished explaining that I could have reconstruction at the time of the mastectomy and I would certainly be taking hormone therapy for at least five years with maybe chemo and/or radiotherapy, she went on to tell me that she could not carry out my surgery due to absence. As if I'm not panicked enough, I'm now to be passed over to someone who I don't know, who has no idea who I am, and who may have hands like a Sheffield steelworker!

When we left, Mark drove straight to an off-licence and came out clanking bottles like a milkman. We headed to my house, and I sat on the sofa and silently made a start on my first bottle of wine. The annexe was unusually quiet—I think Tracey and Tyson were watching telly. They were undoubtedly in there, as I could smell their smoke even from the lounge.

My first bottle was drunk within fifteen minutes, and I told Mark I wanted to be alone. I didn't want to throw him out, so I took a second bottle of wine up to my bedroom. Before I knew it, I was calling Amara. She listened to me cry again, only this time I made no apology for being drunk. I sniffed, snotted and sobbed down the line for ten minutes.

"I can't believe I'm going to lose my breast. I know it's only small, but it's mine, and it's not even sagging yet. It's still perky and pointing in the right direction, and they're going to cut the thing off me!"

She stayed silent on the phone, listening to me talk about my breast like it had invented the wheel and cured the world of famine. When she could take no more, she finally interrupted me and shouted, "Are you insane?"

"Excuse me?" I was shocked at her lack of sympathy, empathy even.

"That breast is trying to kill you! Why the fuck do you want it? That breast will rob you of your future! Get the fuck rid of it!"

She ranted on for what felt like an age, and when she had finished, I sat on the bed in silence and immediately sobered up. She's right, of course. My breast is not lovely anymore. It's full of shitbags called Tracey and Tyson and pictures of crying clowns. When I put the phone down on her, I realised I quite love Amara and would do for the rest of my life.

19th April 2019 – Good Friday

I woke with a hangover from hell. As I lay in bed and recalled the night before, I could not remember when I had finally given up. Mark was not in bed when I opened my eyes, but his watch was still on the bedside table, suggesting he had just gone downstairs. When I finally made it down, he was in his dressing gown watching *Ben Hur*, completely unaware of the kids screaming in the annexe.

I went to investigate and found Tracey dragging a boy, who looked about seven years of age, off a girl of around the same size. When Tracey saw me, she shouted to the children to look at me.

"Here she is. Jo, I want you to meet my kids. This is Tyler, and this is his twin, Tina. Kids, this is Jo, who will be putting up with my ONE husband and TWO children for the foreseeable. Ain't that right, Jo?"

"I see you've learned to count."

"You were right about her hair!" laughed Tina.

During these formalities, Tyson sat on the bed chewing handfuls of Coco Pops from the box like a stoned camel.

The twins asked me did I have any other biscuits apart from Rich Tea, and when I said no, Tyler took a fit and threw a box of Lego at me. It missed and smashed all over the floor. My head was pounding with the noise, so I quietly walked out of the room, shut the door behind me and went back upstairs to bed.

As soon as I was in bed, though, Tracey appeared and plonked herself at the end, took off her filthy slipper and proceeded to bite her toenails. I asked her where the fuck did the kids come from, and she informed me they had been there a while, but she wanted me to get to know her and Tyson before we met her angels. I told her they were the devil's spawn, and she laughed and took it as a compliment, then spat her chewed nails all over my new bedroom carpet.

I put my headphones in, listened to Marvin Gaye and drowned her out as I fell back asleep.

21st April 2019 – Easter Sunday

Mark dragged me out of bed this morning and told me to pack some stuff in a bag. I don't think he can cope with me being depressed anymore, and quite frankly, neither can I. I put some music on very loud and jumped in the shower to sort my head out. Tracey tried to disturb me while I was dancing naked, but she was told to sod off, and she did for a while.

I went to Mark's flat, and he attempted to cook Sunday lunch. It being Easter kind of threw him in a panic. He's not the best chef in the world, and his repertoire is typical of a man. He's comfortable cooking with mince and feels sophisticated if he has two or more pans on the stove at the same time. His roast lamb and potatoes were not too bad, and he gobbled it up with a grin that lasted from the first mouthful to the last. We then got into our pyjamas and watched Scottish comedies for the rest of the day and night. As we lay on the couch, he slipped his hand over my breast and said he was mentally giving it positive healing vibes. If he ever starts thinking that's a form of reiki, he will no doubt be arrested.

Wednesday, 24th April 2019

I met Amara today for lunch. Most of the lunch was in liquid form, which neither of us minded, and my attitude to her cancer changed today. My journey would be the same as hers, and I needed to know what to expect.

What I didn't expect was for her to have so much humour and to make me laugh so hard with her story. She made me see that what's happening to me is a bump in the road of my life. It is not my life forever more! I just need to deal with it, get better and then move on with the rest of it.

I'm sure all cancer victims go through a stage of 'what will my life be like when this is all over?' I'm not sure I want my old life back, to be honest. Do I want to go back to my job? Maybe this is the time in my life when I say 'fuck it' and start my business selling my ceramics. I don't wish to be rich. As long as I can pay the bills and have enough left over to put by for holidays and Christmas, then I would be happy. I just want to do something in my life that makes me happy, and then, before you know it, I'll appear in *Woman and Home* magazine in a feature about how amazingly independent and inspirational I am. Cancer could be the making of me, or so I told myself briefly.

By the end of our lunch, I had inspected not only the bill but also Amara's reconstruction, which took my breath away. Her breast was so natural-looking and exactly the same as her own breast. The difference this has made to my head is incredible, and as soon as I got her on her train back home, I called Mark to tell him about Amara's fabulous breast.

"You should see it! It looks like her other one. I just wish her surgeon could do mine."

Bless him, he acted animated in all the right places, but I think I called while he was watching *Outlander*. I didn't care that he wasn't as excited as me. He simply listened while I gabbled away like an excited teenager, and at that moment, that was all I wanted.

When I got home, Tracey was clearly annoyed and wanted to know why I was so cheery. I told her it was because she wouldn't be in my life for much longer. She laughed at this.

"We'll see." Then she told the kids to turn up Bob Marley singing 'I Shot the Sheriff'. The irony was not lost on me.

I went to my bedroom and put on some mellow music and meditated. This is the third time I've done it since Anne showed me, and I've realised Tracey doesn't like it when I do. Last time I meditated, it took over an hour, and when I finished, she was waiting outside the bedroom door for me.

"Hey, Jo. Why don't you fire up that internet thing of yours, and we can look for post-surgical bras?" She was laughing hysterically.

"Please fuck off back to your kids."

"Oh, they're fine. Come on, let's see if we can find anything half decent. Isn't it funny to think you have drawers and drawers full of pretty bras that you can't wear again?"

"I might be able to."

"You'll be lucky to hide your hideous new tit in a vest. Will Mark want you then?"

"What did I do to deserve you?"

I cried for at least two hours after that. I know Mark loves me, but you hear about men leaving their wives after mastectomies. And he's not even married to me.

Thursday, 25th April 2019

Andy called me while I was at Mark's flat. He was due to start some prep work on the annexe but called to say he thinks I should have a structural surveyor to look at it. I had noticed some cracking on the walls, but Andy seems to think the problems could be a cause for concern. When I put the phone down, I told Mark.

"I told you to get a proper survey done on that house!"

I just had a homebuyer's survey, as I figured the house had been standing since 1930, and if it were going to fall down, well, surely it would have done it by now. However, the annexe was only around eight years old.

"Look, I know someone who might be able to have a look at it. Let me make a couple of calls."

After about half an hour, Mark had arranged for a man called Jerry to look at the annexe next week. This is all I need on top of everything else.

Friday, 26th April 2019

Mark and I went back to the breast clinic today to meet my new consultant. I don't know why, but I was expecting a burly man from 'up north' with a dismissive and unsympathetic attitude, complete with uncaring hands, seeing as I'd been pawned off onto him. I couldn't have been more wrong when I clapped eyes on Navid Makkar, who had a way so gentle I swear he wafted into the room.

Looking like a Bollywood film star, he settled into a chair in front of me. I can't say 'sat' as that implies a degree of force, and there was no force; he simply settled onto the chair like a feather. I liked him immediately and noticed he had hands like a child pianist, which made me smile even more. He took me behind the curtain, and as soon as my bra was off, I launched into the YMCA routine with the enthusiasm of a *Britain's Got Talent* finalist. He smiled approvingly all the way through and only let the smile slip when he began pinching my nipple and twisting it like he was trying to find Radio 4. He would stand back to look at it periodically, then flick it some more. I wanted to tell the thing to do what it should, but I wasn't sure what it was supposed to do and if indeed it would even listen to me in the first place. It seems my body likes to do its own thing now, so I left Navid to it.

He insists I call him Navid. I felt privileged doing so but then remembered that the year is 2019, not 1819, and if I dropped a hanky on the floor in front of him, it was very likely I would have to pick it up myself. His voice was gentle as he told me that the reconstruction was still possible, and they also had to remove the sentinel node while I was being operated on. This is the node that is feeding Tracey with estrogen—and Hobnobs, the last time I saw her. A radioactive injection, the day before the surgery, will be able to tell them which node is keeping Tracey, Tyson and her offspring in the style to which they have become accustomed.

"A radioactive injection? Does that mean I'll look like the Incredible Hulk by Christmas?" He said nothing.

He explained that once all the surgery was completed, the team would look at maybe offering chemotherapy.

"Chemotherapy? Does that mean I will look like Phil Mitchell by Christmas?" Again, nothing.

Not realising I was trying to have a joke with him, he went on to say I will definitely be on hormone therapy for at least five years.

"Does that mean I will look like Magnum, PI by Christmas?" I think Navid now understands I have a slight obsession with Christmas, and not knowing whether to answer me, he simply offered a lip twitch.

We then went over the options on how to reconstruct. I never realised I would have a choice. So, option one is an implant with a supportive mesh, which is essentially made from pigskin. Or option two is to take flesh from my abdomen and create a whole new boob from that. Option one has a quicker healing time and can be done by Navid. But the downside is if I have to have more surgery at a later date, there is a chance I could lose the implant. Option two is more natural, as it's made from me; I'll also have a tummy tuck to boot but will end up with a vast abdominal scar and will have to go to a different hospital under a different doctor. I have already made my mind up, but Navid has given me until 9th May to think about it and pencilled me in, just in case, for 15th May for the mastectomy with an implant. If I decide I want option two at any point up to 9th May, then I am to call Abi, the Macmillan nurse, and she will make the arrangements for me to transfer.

After showing me some before and after photographs of his work, Navid glided out of the room and left me with Abi. I admitted to her how relieved and impressed I was by Navid, and she said she could physically see me relax the minute he walked in. I told her I would definitely be heading for the implant option, and she agreed that in my case, it was probably best, and we would have to take the risk that no more surgery would be required. I was laughing to myself at the speed I had decided. I deliberated longer leaving O2 to go to Vodafone.

She then produced a box of implants, which Mark and I found amusing, and a body drain, which I found less so as this will be hanging out of me when I come around from the surgery and will be swinging from my body for about a fortnight. The drain, the size of a sports water bottle, will be attached to a long pipe, which will be buried somewhere in my new boob. Mark switched off from this bit and carried on playing with the implants. He looked disappointed when he had to pop them back into Abi's playbox and left with only me and my handful of leaflets, as usual.

Monday, 29th April 2019

I met the girls for tea this evening, and it was nice to talk about other people's lives apart from my own. The only time I felt a little different was when Saskia turned up with a bouquet of flowers. She insisted they were made for a customer who didn't collect them, and she thought I might like them. I knew it was a lie, but a sweet lie.

Mia moaned for most of the early evening about Rob and how lazy he was and how he still doesn't ask her anything about her day-to-day life. She then turned to Lucy.

"Have you not got a fella, then?"

I felt so sorry for Lucy. Her face went purple, and I could see Charlotte was trying to think of something witty to say.

"No. I had. But it ended. Quite recently, in fact."

Lucy didn't speak much after that. She hardly touched her meal, and as soon as the desserts arrived, she made her excuses and left.

I walked out with her to the taxi rank outside of the pub. "I'm not going to ask if you're okay because it's quite clear you're not. Do you want to come around to mine this week and talk?"

"No. I'm okay."

"Lucy, this is the first time I've seen you refuse tiramisu. Your head is clearly mashed."

"You have enough on your plate."

"Don't you fucking dare!! I might have cancer, but I'm still your mate! Please do not let this thing affect you and me. You used to tell me everything, and all of a sudden because I'm having an operation, I've been demoted to an acquaintance. Don't you fucking dare do this to me, Lucy! I couldn't bear it!" I was crying. It came from nowhere. The thought of my friendships being affected by this disease was too much for me to bear.

"Can I come around this week?" She was sobbing.

We hugged and made arrangements for Wednesday, and after putting her in a taxi and taking a few deep breaths, I walked back into the pub smiling and telling everyone that Lucy was fine and had simply come on her period. I think most of them bought it.

Wednesday, 1st May 2019

I woke to find Tracey trying on my clothes while Tina was clip-clopping around the bathroom in my high heels. She asked if she could sit on my knee while I went for a wee, and when I said no, she screamed at her mum to tell me to let her. Tracey ignored her or didn't hear her, as she was singing 'Isn't She Lovely?' at the top of her voice while she tried to squeeze into my Ramones T-shirt.

"Do you have anything in a larger size?"

"No, because this isn't bastard Debenhams! And get that top off before you stretch it!"

"You're right. Don't want to make it bigger when you'll have less to fill it out with in future."

"I'm getting an implant. I'll be filling it out just fine."

"You think? You might have one pointing south and the other north-west. You might find a jumper is your best friend in future."

"You know what, Tracey? You're right. I'll buy myself some jumpers, and I'll get you one as well to cover that monumental gut of yours!"

She shook her rolls in front of me like a belly dancer.

"My Tyson loves a bit of meat." She giggled.

"Then why not go downstairs and let pumpkin-head eat off the veritable buffet called YOU! Let's see how many Cheesy Wotsits you can stuff into that cavernous navel of yours."

"Do you think it's big?"

"Tracey, it has an echo!"

She whipped off the T-shirt and put her own back on. I swear she looked like she was sulking. I seized the moment and put on my meditation music, and she told Tina they had to go.

"She won't let us hang around when she starts chanting like a flaming Buddha. She'll be wearing orange sheets next and listening to George bleeding Harrison."

I ignored her, and an hour later, when I opened my eyes, they had both gone. After showering, I went out and did some shopping for food for Lucy and me and then came home to tidy up. For the rest of the afternoon, I forgot I had additional guests in the annexe.

By the time Lucy turned up after work, I was halfway through a bottle of wine and a George Michael album, and most of the dinner was cooked.

We didn't mention Dave for a while. She spoke of everything else including a loose gutter that was causing damp in her flat before she talked about him, and I think it only became a subject because I forced it.

"So, Dave? Before, during or after tiramisu?" I stood there, clutching her favourite pudding.

"During."

I plopped two large portions into the bowls, handed her one, and she began.

"I gave him an ultimatum."

"I didn't think you would ever do that."

"He said about her wanting to buy something. To me, if he did buy it, he was showing a long-term commitment."

"What was it? Like an eternity ring?"

"No, a timeshare in Benalmadena."

I wanted to laugh, but I'm her mate.

"Benalmadena, eh? The hotspot of southern Spain. I can see the long-term commitment there."

"Don't take the piss!"

"Sorry. But I thought you were going to say they were having a baby or something."

"It doesn't matter that it's some shit timeshare in Spain. It's the fact he's talking to me about it two hours after me getting a bikini wax because he likes it bare down there. So, I asked him if he had any intention of leaving her."

"And?"

"He said he wasn't sure."

"Fuck."

"I know! In the end, I said I'm not there to be his little tube of glitter in his boring life until I'm out-glittered by a shitty flat in Benal-fucking-madena."

"Then?"

"Then he said that IF they did split up, the timeshare would be part of the divorce settlement, and I would benefit from it!"

"Is this guy for real?"

"I just stood there, Jo. I stood there with a chuff like a peach thinking 'You weren't worth the wax!'"

"What did you see in him in the first place?"

"I don't know."

"Seriously. You need to know. If only to get over him."

"He liked me."

And there it was. Lucy, with her self-esteem dragging on the floor and her ego not far behind, screaming for a massage.

"The man in Bargain Booze likes you, and you have never given him a second glance. What was it about him?"

She sat for a moment to contemplate, and when she did eventually speak, her voice was no higher than a whisper.

"He made me laugh. He made me laugh like I've never laughed before. He liked my music. He didn't mind that I had lumps and bumps. He said I smelled good, and he kissed amazingly. And he had this look that was so intense you felt you were on fire sometimes. But then I wanted to know more about his wife, and it was obvious things weren't right and he was sad about it. At first, I didn't mind being his Band-Aid—it was fun, you know. But the more I realised I needed him, the more I saw the man and not the lover. And he was a mixed-up man that I got mixed up with, and I shouldn't have done."

Her eyes were full of sorrow. I want to say tears, but they weren't. Was it a good thing that she wasn't crying? Or is she bottling things up, which some people say is worse? We opened another bottle of wine and started to make plans for a night out when she could go out on the sniff. We knew without asking that Charlotte would want to join us.

"And if Rob doesn't find out soon if Mia takes one sugar or two in her Ovaltine, then I think she will be joining us as well."

Friday, 3rd May 2019

Jerry, the structural surveyor, came to the house today. I was pleased to see that Tracey and her brood were out. I'm not sure where they went, but they left Jerry and me in peace. It was Jerry's head-shaking that made me nervous, so I left him to it while I made him a cup of tea. Mark said he was friends with Jerry's brother more than Jerry himself but knew enough to know he was good, wouldn't mess me about and had a brilliant sense of humour, which, judging by his face, had been left in his Vauxhall Meriva parked on my drive.

He sat to drink his tea at the small table in the kitchen and started with a tone not dissimilar to Mark's about getting a proper survey done before I bought the house. Once he was satisfied that I was suitably chastised, he went on, using a lot of building terms and structural references, to tell me that the annexe was falling down. I asked him a rough cost to fix it, to which he said the whole thing was practically rotten and it would be cheaper to knock it down and build an entirely new extension. He also said it would need doing sooner rather than later, as the main house was at risk.

After another cup of tea, he warmed up a bit and gave me some names of builders he trusted and who would give me a fair price. When he guessed how much it would be, I knew I would have to speak to the bank about a loan. Would a bank give me a loan with my current health? I doubt it. Where the hell am I going to find the money? Should I just knock down the annexe and not rebuild? But the whole reason I bought the house was to have the space to do my pottery, and the main house isn't big enough.

Jerry departed through the annexe, leaving me standing in a room full of Tracey's crap that was threatening the rest of my now beautiful home. Thanks to Andy and Farrow & Ball, of course.

Sunday, 5th May 2019

I am dying as I write this, dear Diary. What a Saturday night that was. Mark and I decided to have a few friends at the house, our 'couple friends'. We thought only ten or so would turn up but went into panic mode when the number settled at twenty-four.

Rob and Mark kept the local shopkeeper happy with their constant trips to get more drinks. When we all realised it was nearly ten o'clock and fear set in about supplies lasting, Rob retrieved my wheelbarrow from the shed, which was returned twenty minutes later with seventy-two cans of lager, two bottles of gin and a lot of wine—I don't know how many bottles of the latter.

The night became very hazy. I remember being in the bathroom and arguing with Tracey.

"I won't tell you again. Tell Tyson to put the fucking Pringles back!"

I also remember being in the kitchen asking her why she dressed like a piss-stained tramp, which she said was my fault!

"I don't have to take this abuse, Jo. If it carries on, I'll just tell Tyson to give you a hiding."

"Tyson couldn't hit water even if he fell out of a boat!"

It was at that point, when I was laughing and crying at the same time, Mark announced—to everyone—he was putting me to bed.

I decided today that my destructive drinking has to come to an end. I think as far as odds go, I would put a fiver to win on my liver killing me before the cancer does. I briefly toyed with the idea of calling the bank manager tomorrow about the loan but then decided to speak to Mark to see if he thought I had a better chance of getting a loan after my surgery.

Monday, 6th May 2019

I ordered a head scarf off Amazon, and it arrived today. I felt sick as I pulled it from the packaging. I ordered a brown one, so it was a similar colour to my hair. I sat in front of the dressing table mirror for ages looking at myself, wondering what I would look like with no eyebrows and no eyelashes. Gollum sprang to mind. Eventually, I tied the scarf to my head, trying to tuck every single hair to give the illusion I was bald underneath. The reflection in the mirror reminded me of my gran, only her scarf had rollers underneath. Chemotherapy is going to throw me back to the 1970s.

I then started to play with my make-up. I put more eyeliner on, trying to imagine my eyes with no eyelashes, and coloured my eyebrows in to make them look more 'synthetic'. When I finished, Tracey was standing behind me, looking over my shoulder at my reflection in the mirror.

"So, this new job of yours on the *Black Pearl*—you get a parrot with that?"

She was right. I looked like a freak. I whipped off the scarf and sobbed, but I still heard Tracey say, "Just stay in, mate. No one wants to look at that."

I'll have to stay in for the rest of my life unless it's Halloween or I get invited to a Pirates and Princesses party.

Thursday, 9th May 2019

I was back at the clinic today, and Navid was just as nice as I remembered him. Even Mark commented on his manner and said it might have been a good thing that Mary wasn't my consultant anymore. I had to agree, especially when he asked me where I wanted my scar and said he would try and save some of my areola.

We went through the risks of surgery, which ranged from a dicky tummy to death. He asked me to sign a form saying I was prepared for either and anything else in between. It felt like the surgery was going to happen this time. I was finally going to be rid of Tracey, and all of this would soon come to an end, starting 15th May.

When I left the hospital, Andy called to see how I had got on with Jerry.

"I'm just waiting on his report, but I've decided that the annexe is coming down," I said.

"I think that's for the best and was hoping you'd say that. What I thought was we could make a start while you're in hospital. That way, you won't have to put up with all the noise and the mess. We'll get it sorted for you by the time the builders turn up."

"That would be amazing, Andy. I'm staying at Mark's flat after the surgery for a couple of weeks."

"Oh, he'll look after you. Good idea, that."

"Let me know how much this is going to cost."

"Don't be daft, Jo. I'm not charging you for this! The only things you need to pay for are the skips."

"No, Andy!"

"I mean it, Jo. I know the builders are setting you back a pretty penny. I just wish I could do more, to be honest. You were amazing when Mum died—me and Saskia always say we wouldn't have coped if it wasn't for you."

Saskia's and Andy's mum, Norma, had died last year. It was a sudden heart attack, and it had understandably floored them both. It was apparent after a couple of days they didn't know where to start with arranging a funeral, and neither one of them had the mental strength to do it. I had help, but I managed to organise most of the day by myself. I didn't mind; I was glad I could do it.

"You've got enough on your plate. Let me do this, or our Saskia will chop me balls off."

I started to cry. Cancer is making me so freaking emotional. I haven't cried this much since I watched the film *Beaches* about ten years ago. I was a mess for a fortnight and still well up now when anyone mentions Bette Midler.

Friday, 10th May 2019

Mark and I went out tonight. It was our last night out before everything changes. We had a good talk, and Mark was insistent that nothing is going to change and it was all in my head. But it's not, and from next week the evidence will be over half of my body. He challenged my feelings, asking how I would feel if the tables were turned. I know it would make no difference to me if anything were to change with him physically, but breasts are a big deal to men. Men reinforce the sexuality of them, which is then absorbed by the rest of the woman.

My sexuality is important to me—to all women—but it was something I took for granted. I thought the only things that would threaten me being sexy would be weight gain or old age. No one ever thinks that it could be challenged by a scalpel, do they? And if Mark can never bring himself to make love to me anymore, a man who has been with me for years, a man who loves me on a level I am not sure I could find with anyone else, then how would another man find me attractive? Especially if I'm resorted to wearing ugly bras for the rest of my life. What is the better option for me? To have sex with the ugly bra on to hide my mutilated body or to show the mutilated body because then at least he can have access to the natural one? Whichever way I look at it, one thing is for sure: this is going to affect my sex life one way or another.

And what about how I dress? Will I have to wear polo-neck tops for the rest of my life, like Steve Jobs?! Will cardigans define the new me? I'll need to start shopping in shops like...I don't even know where they sell cardigans, for God's sake! Do they make them anymore? There's a lady in work who has had the same cardy hanging off the back of her chair since I started there. Does she have it because she can't find a replacement? Or does she simply not give a hoot what she looks like? Will Mark still love me if I start wearing cardigans?

He told me he's informed work that he will be on holiday for a few weeks while he looks after me. His work has been very supportive to both of us and sent a beautiful bouquet to my house. Mark put a post on social media saying that from next week, I would be staying in his, and if anyone wanted his address to direct-message him. I noticed his phone was beeping more than usual as the night wore on. At one point, he sighed, saying I was a popular little bunny as he looked at his phone. I hated being responsible for the disturbances, but he made me feel a little better when he looked up and gave me his million-dollar smile. Never mind the sex, dear Diary, I'm not sure I could live without his smile. It makes everything just right in my world.

Saturday, 11th May 2019

After a day of shopping for new hospital pyjamas, Mark and I picked up a takeaway. I was just about to tuck into my chicken chaat and start an episode of something on Netflix when he began.

"How would you feel about us living together?"

"What? Permanently?"

"Yeah."

"But I've only just moved in. I'm still figuring out which key opens which window, and I'm not sure the house alarm sets when I leave the house."

"No, I mean I could sell this flat and move in with you." He looked nervous when he suggested it. "I've been thinking about it for a while, and I thought you might have asked me when you were buying the house."

"But I never thought you wanted us to live together."

"Jo, I want to marry you!" He seemed more surprised when he said this than I was hearing it. I looked at him, and at that moment, I realised Mark and I have been hiding a lot from each other for the past couple of years. I think deep down I have always wanted to marry him; I just never dared hope. After what happened with Stu, I never wanted to feel that vulnerable again. The funny thing is, it was a conscious decision years ago, and for some reason, I guess, my subconscious took over and kept telling me that it was best to live on my own and keep Mark at arm's length, in an emotional sense. How long had he wanted to marry me? How long had I wanted to marry him? Why had I wasted all this time?

"Well?"

I didn't need to think about it. "Of course I'll marry you." He wants to marry me, even with a dodgy boob! "But can we wait?" I made the excuse of waiting for everything to settle down before we thought about it properly, and he agreed.

"But I'm moving in as soon as you're well enough after the surgery."

The truth, dear Diary, is I want to see if his feelings change when he sees me after the surgery. He said he's calling some estate agents tomorrow to get the flat on the market as soon as possible, and that's making me nervous. He'll be giving up his life to start one that he may not like in the future. My illness has changed so much about me already, so God knows what I'll be like after the surgery. Will I even want him? What if I can't cope and I reject him because it will be easier to be on my own? With all of this silently swimming in my head, I suggested he rent his flat out and keep it as an investment. He's toying with the idea and said he'll get some advice when the agents come and give a valuation.

So, officially, we are unofficially engaged or the other way around. Providing Mark proves to be the man of my dreams and doesn't run a mile or find a girl called Zoe, then I'm going to be happy for the rest of my life.

Monday, 13th May 2019

Spent most of the day in my house trying to sort things out before I go into hospital. While I packed my overnight bag, Tracey sat on the bed and took the piss out of my Primark pyjamas.

"Why aren't you wearing your posh Ted Baker ones?"

"Because when I am dealing with a tramp like you, why in the hell would I be wearing my Sunday best?"

But between you and me, dear Diary, my Ted Baker pyjamas are a little slim, and I'm worried about them being able to accommodate the drains. Yes, I have to have two drains, apparently. One goes at the front of the breast and one further back or one at the top and one at the bottom. I'm not entirely sure. When Abi was explaining, I just kept thinking that the contents were going to look like Campbell's tomato soup which, lucky for me, I never liked anyway.

"So, Mark proposed, eh? I'm surprised, seeing as you will only have one boob and all."

"Not everyone is as horrible as you."

"Oh, no, there are some that are worse."

She was right, in a way. I knew what I was dealing with, and I knew I could get rid of Tracey and her ugly brood. There were a lot of people not as fortunate as me.

She just sat on the bed and watched me as I tried to sort out some of my drawers. She seems a little off her game today. I think she knows something is coming her way. I wish I could see her face when the digger comes and tears down the annexe. Where will she go? I don't care as long as she takes her husband, who I swear is imbecilic, and her two children, who I'm sure if they were allowed to grow up would fancy each other and be fairly proficient with the banjo.

Tuesday, 14th May 2019

I went for my radiation injection today. This is so when I'm in theatre they can locate the node that has been delivering takeout hormones to my tumours. When I asked the nurse what sophisticated equipment they use these days to detect the 'hot node' as they call it, she pointed to a large metal box on her desk, next to her banana and Müller yoghurt. Said box had a couple of windows which housed the gauges. The last time I saw anything like this was in the film *E.T.* when the scientists were trying to find the little alien. I was quite shocked at the crudeness of it all. I naively expected, in this day and age, to be on the table and they would plug my boob into a USB port, which would give them a PowerPoint presentation and a Google map to locate the offending node. But no, they will wave a metal rod near me and wait for the 'crackle'. It all felt very...well... Russian, if that's not offensive.

Mark drove home while I clutched my boob the whole way, as it felt a little strange. He's staying at my house tonight, which will soon be our house, I suppose. Now the decision has been made, I'm so happy, which seems bizarre at a time like this. But I have to find the positives; otherwise, I will go insane.

My phone has been busy today with people sending their love and positive vibes, all of which I have appreciated to the point of periodically crying. All this love has kept me positive for tomorrow. The day when I can say I am cancer-free. The day when I get a new boob that isn't trying to kill me. And hopefully, the day when I start to feel a little less scared. But the past few weeks have given me so much more than fear. I have learned that strength does not come from within, it comes from love, and I've felt an awful lot of it lately.

It's true what they say—that in dark times, 'you find out who your friends are', and I used to think that was a negative statement. Yes, I had people who said they would be there and weren't, but not many, and I get that. But I've discovered I'd interpreted that statement wrongly; I have more friends than I realised. Some days that has knocked me for six, but in a good way, and that is where I found my strength. From that strength, I've found it easier to be positive: I still try and dance in my knickers each day, still try and meditate a little so I can ignore Tracey and her ever-increasing brood, still look in the mirror and tell myself it's all going to be okay. And it will be! I have a lot of people in my corner, including a team that will soon be evicting the bitch called Tracey.

Wednesday, 15th May 2019

I didn't sleep much last night. Either my head was keeping me awake or my tummy grumbling was. I have been nil-by-mouth for a whole twelve hours. As most of them were in bed, I can't understand why I'm starving, as I normally wouldn't eat anyway! But for some reason, I wanted a fry-up around half two this morning!

I kept clutching my boob in the dark. I'm not sure how I feel about it now, to be honest. When I looked at it last night, I wanted to tell it off. I feel like it's betrayed me and let the rest of my body down. And then I looked at it again, and it seemed so innocent, as if it wanted to say it was sorry. Clearly, starvation has made me delirious.

I went downstairs while Mark was in the shower. Tracey and Tyson were still asleep, and I crept into the annexe and sat beside her. Her face was all red and blotchy—I can only presume radiation does not agree with her. She woke up and stared at me for what seemed like a very long time. I gently grabbed her jaw with one hand and then squeezed it hard.

"Get to fuck," I whispered.

She just smiled at me and didn't say a word as I walked out.

Mark was very quiet the whole way to the hospital, and I kept catching him sighing—a clear sign of nerves with him.

When we arrived on the ward, we were greeted by a gregarious nurse called Pam, who within fifteen minutes of me arriving had me in a gown, paper knickers and surgical stockings. Mark asked if he could take a picture, and even though I refused, it was nice to see him giggle at the sight.

Navid soon arrived on the ward, clutching a new Sharpie pen, which quickly went to work over half of my body. Slashes, dots, arrows and long wavy lines were soon hidden again by my medical gown, complete with arse hanging out of the back.

Mark's serious face returned when the jolly porter turned up to wheel me to theatre. It was at this point I realised I hadn't been scared before; I'd just thought I had. Pure terror was racing around my body as I said goodbye to Mark and was wheeled to Theatre 1. I wanted to be sick but there was nothing in my stomach. I wanted to shout to the jolly porter to stop. But what could he stop? He could stop wheeling the trolley, but I would still be sitting on it riddled with disease and fear. The only way I could eliminate either or both of those was for the jolly porter to keep pushing me further into the bowels of the hospital.

After passing through numerous double doors and along lots of green corridors, I was wheeled into a small room and introduced to four people who all seemed to know what they were doing, thank God. Before I could catch my breath, one was sticking monitor pads to me, one was inserting a cannula into the back of my hand, one was filling a needle (I think), while another held my hand and occasionally stroked my face, telling me it would be all over soon.

I let them busy themselves with my body and glanced over to the stool in the corner of the room, where Tracey sat. She wasn't smiling now. It seemed she was only interested in what the medical team were doing and hardly noticed me at all.

Then a man, who reminded me of Jim Robinson from *Neighbours* for some reason, came over, took my hand and asked me what I liked to drink. I think I said Prosecco, but I can't be sure.

The next thing I remember is waking up with Navid pushing down on my chest and asking a nurse to change a drain. I looked at the blood-filled sports bottle in my surgeon's hand, then looked at the clock expecting it to be midday—the time I was supposed to be in the recovery room. I was right about the location, but the clock said half three! Navid, as if he was telling me a bedtime story, explained that there had been some complications in theatre regarding me bleeding and a hematoma. All I kept thinking about was Mark and my family and friends and how they would be panicking at the length of time I had been gone. When I mentioned the time and asked if I was okay, Navid assured me I was and instructed a nurse to pass a message to the ward to inform Mark.

By five p.m., I was back on the ward, and Mark came with some of the girls. They didn't stay long, which I was kind of pleased about. I was tired, and I wanted to think about what had happened to me. I was also aware that I could feel a huge 'thing' beneath my gown and panicked for a moment, thinking they had put the wrong size implant in. What if they put a 'DD' in by mistake? You hear of these things, don't you? I'm not sure where, but it's not that hard to make a mistake like that, surely? I looked down at the hidden mounds and was relieved to see they looked the same size. These doctors know what they're doing, I suppose.

Knowing I'm fussy with my food, Mark and the girls had brought enough to feed a small family for a week, and I'm only in for one night! I asked Mark to take it all home and maybe give some of it to the builders for their break tomorrow. While he'd been worrying why my operation was taking so long, he'd distracted himself by playing project manager, overseeing the demolition of the annexe. He said it has all gone, and Andy and his builder mates have cleared most of the debris away in readiness for the next lot of workmen to start rebuilding.

Mark is funding the new extension, which will be more conservatory in style. Mark likes to call it an orangery because the roof on this is more substantial than a conservatory. He jokingly threatened not to pay the bill after I said how pretentious he was. I'm glad he had that to take his mind off things today. Like I have said, dear Diary, he's a fretter, and he probably would have been wound up to the point of huffing and puffing himself into a dizzy spell.

Thursday, 16th May 2019

I spent the night on the ward with two other women. I thought the ward would only be for breast patients, but it seems I'm the only one.

The lady opposite me has had a varicose vein removed from the back of her knee, while the woman next to me has had her haemorrhoids dealt with. Both were painful, I'm sure, but I felt a little lonelier when they turned off the lights, as I'd hoped I'd be with ladies all mourning the loss of one breast or, unthinkably, both.

The haemorrhoid lady should have also been operated on for her restless legs—she couldn't keep them from swishing all night like she was doing the Riverdance against the rubber-covered mattress, whilst varicose-vein lady was a snorer. Her open mouth made me want to screw up bits of paper and flick them in her direction.

The night nurse seemed surprised at dawn that I still hadn't slept. Judging by the mascara rings below her eyes, she'd clearly managed a sneaky hour or two. I asked the healthcare assistant for some brown toast, which when it arrived looked more like Weetabix, and two rounds of white bread. The bread had been for a swift dip in the toaster at some point that morning, judging by its jaundiced hue, but I ate it anyway, as I was hungry, and thought of the builders eating the now-longed-for chicken salad Mark had put back in the fridge last night.

It was at that point, even though I was in more pain than I ever thought possible, that I decided to go to the bathroom and try and make myself look a little more 'well' so I'd be discharged sooner rather than later. With the aid of Elizabeth Arden and Chanel, Pam the nurse declared me fit and waved me off by noon with a large bag of tablets and a kiss, and I headed back to Mark's flat, swinging my blood-filling drains.

On the drive home, I told Mark that Navid had removed the dressing, and he and Pam had helped me put on my post-surgical bra, which is the colour of weak tea.

"How does it look?" he asked.

"I didn't look at it. I'll maybe look later today."

I knew that wasn't true as soon as I said it. I didn't want to look at it. I didn't want to look at my body ever again, to be truthful. If Mark wants to look at it, then that's up to him, but I don't have to, and I don't need to either.

Friday, 17th May 2019

I've managed to avoid mirrors for a whole day, which if I were in my house would be a lot harder. Mark has one full-length mirror by his front door, a large one in the bathroom and a small one in his bedroom, and that's it. I try not even to look down at my body. I know from the hospital that they are the same size, but I just cannot bring my gaze to anywhere except straight ahead or the ceiling.

When I'm not avoiding mirrors, I'm obsessing over the contents of my drains. One is filling up rapidly with what looks like Ribena, while the other is nearly empty with only a splash of what looks like Lucozade. Apparently, from a medical point of view, Lucozade is good. Having to drag them everywhere is starting to piss me off, though. Even when I'm lying down, I have to make sure they don't roll off the bed and end up tugging at my body.

Mark seems to have been in a constant state of panic since I came home. I can't tell him how much pain I'm in, as this might send him over the edge. But the pain! It's the kind of pain that's so bad you can't cry. The sort of pain that makes you obsess over what time it is (waiting for my next tablet fix). The sort of pain that robs you of much-wanted sleep. The sort of pain that keeps reminding me that my breast is in an incinerator bin—presumably. The sort of pain that tells me I'm a cancer victim.

I have never felt like a victim, until today.

Saturday, 18th May 2019

My life the last couple of days has been a repeated four-hourly cycle of food, drink, tablets and sleep. I now have an app on my phone that gives a gentle but distinctive reminder when my tablets are due and which ones I should take. Upon the first few chimes, Mark is on his feet burrowing through what can only be described as a sack full of various tablets. He watches me swallow what he has found in the sack, fixes my drains and pops me back under a blanket. He will then stare at me until the phone jingles again for my next lot, and they're not always the same offerings as the previous round.

To be fair, he is starting to relax a little, evident by him not jumping to his feet every time I simply shift in the chair. Today was the first time we properly laughed since I left the hospital. Today was the day he had to help me have a shower.

So, the instruction from Navid was that the area from below the neck to the hips was not to get wet under any circumstances. A challenge, yes, but we rose to it and laughed at our ingenuity. Fortunately, Mark has a two-man shower in his flat, this space being previously tested in a far more amorous way, shall we say. With Mark in the shower with the back legs of a plastic kitchen chair in with him, I took a seat, naked except for a Disney World cagoule zipped up to my chin. Mark, in his holiday shorts, asked me to lean back while he washed my hair, leaving the front of my body outside of the cubicle.

We laughed all the way through the exercise with his hairdressing patter, while I sat there holding my two blood-filled drains aloft like the Statue of Liberty, in my coat. Once he towelled up my hair, the chair was removed, and I joined him in the cubicle, where he washed my legs and essential bits and bobs. As he washed my arse, he said I looked like I was carrying two pints back from the bar. The rest of my body was given a gentle wipe with a facecloth, and he dressed me in new pyjamas. Completely helpless as I was, Mark dried my hair, popped it into a wonky ponytail and finished with a look of love that I will remember for the rest of my life. He hasn't taken the vow, 'in sickness and in health', but when he does say it, I know it's a promise he will keep.

Monday, 20th May 2019

I'm still fairly helpless, so Mark has been helping me put on my bra. I stand with my back to him so he can't see anything—I have yet to look myself. I'm not sure when I will do that again. The thought still terrifies me.

I was back in the clinic today, and I have a new nurse called Eliza. She checks I am healing properly and thankfully has warm hands and a lovely, friendly nature. I like Eliza. She continually compliments me on how I take care of myself and do as I'm told, and this is all evident in how I am healing, which is perfectly, apparently. When she removed my dressing, I looked at the ceiling. I didn't think she'd noticed, but clearly, she had.

"Your reconstruction is great. Navid has done a really lovely job. He's such a perfectionist."

Of course, she would say that. She's not going to remove the dressing and shake her head like a builder giving an estimate, is she—tutting and sighing at the same time?

Powered by panache, Navid glided into the room and inspected the Lucozade-like contents of my drain. "This can come out, Eliza."

Eliza caught my face of panic.

"It won't hurt. I promise I'm really gentle."

Within five minutes, she had disconnected one of the Campbell's soup containers and began to tug at the tube buried in my body. I'll admit it didn't hurt, but she failed to say that it would feel like someone sucking spaghetti through me. After she'd applied a dressing to the open wound and given me a leaflet on exercising the area, I left feeling a little lighter. However, as we went back to the car, I started to rant to Mark about them giving me their opinion on how it looks.

"They aren't going to say, 'Oh, he's made a right pig's ear out of that. Never mind, eh!' As if!"

Mark stayed quiet. I don't need his opinion. Well, not just yet anyway. I'm not bothered about the reconstruction at this point. I need to know if all the cancer is gone. I need to know what the next step is going to be. I need to know if I have to have chemotherapy. How will I cope? How will Mark cope? I have found a decent wigmaker about twenty miles away and places where I can get eyelashes. But will I be able to cope with all of that? I can't go to the Co-op without make-up and the clack of a stiletto heel. And the sickness? And the steroids which balloon you? I'm not exactly a stick to start off with. Can I refuse steroids? What the hell does a steroid do? I need to find out. Even though I have shied away from the internet the last few weeks, I think I may have to research a little more in case I need to challenge some decisions made on behalf of me and my body.

Mark checked on the house today and said they'd started work on the new foundations for the extension. He said Andy's been keeping an eye on things too and told the builders that he was family, so they feel he has a bit of authority. I laughed at this but was also extremely appreciative of Andy's white lie. Why is everyone being so kind? I can be such a cow sometimes, and they all know it.

Tuesday, 21st May 2019

Today was a big day. Mark looked at the reconstruction this morning before putting my bra on for me. I asked him if he wanted to look at it, and without hesitation, he said he did.

I kept my gaze squarely on his face as I removed the second ugliest bra I own—the weak-tea-coloured one being the first. As soon as it dropped, he began to smile. Not broadly, but enough to show a hint of relief and even raise an eyebrow in amazement. I still didn't look at it; I just kept watching his face.

"It looks amazing, darling." His voice was shaky.

He kept smiling at me and didn't insist on me looking at it when he helped me put on a clean bra. He simply hooked up the back, kissed me on my shoulder and helped me into a shirt. He went into the kitchen to put the kettle on, and I sat on the bedroom floor and cried. I cried for a while. I wasn't sure why—was it relief at his acceptance of it or my cowardice? Where is the woman people turn to when they're in trouble? Where is the woman of opinion and conviction? Where is the woman who drinks cocktails and tells creepy men to 'move along'? Where is the woman who dances in the rain and doesn't care if people are watching?

Where the hell have I gone?

Friday, 24th May 2019

I've had a week of visitors and have now formed a schedule of three slots: early shift at ten a.m., leaving around twelve p.m.; next lot at one p.m., leaving around three p.m. when I take my favourite tablet, Tramadol. These yellow and green beauties knock me into a stupor for a couple of hours, after which I wake in time for my six p.m. visitors. The weekends are reserved for family and anyone who can't fit in with the midweek table due to any 'unforeseen circumstances'.

Mark also has a routine of mopping and hoovering each morning before all the visitors of the day and popping out while I'm having a nap to replenish stocks of Cadbury Mini Rolls (always a hit), Tunnock's Caramel biscuits and Hobnobs.

Get well cards now cover every surface, and Mark declared that if I get any more flowers, he'll have to start taking Piriton. We're at the point where when any flowers arrive, we pray they're already arranged in a bag, as Mark has not only run out of vases but has also used all his pint pots.

The pain is subsiding a little each day except for a periodic contraction from the replaced muscle stitched back to my chest wall. With each tightening, I break out into a small sweat, swear like a sailor and wish I was drunk. Navid said these tightenings are perfectly normal, so I don't worry; I let Mark do that. I do wonder if he worries about the results of the breast tissue they removed as much as me. He's never spoken of results still to come. He only talks of tablets, the content of my remaining drain and would I like some soup? He's bought gallons of the stuff. He clearly thought that when I lost my breast, I would wake up craving *Carrot & Coriander*, *Cream of Chicken* or *Cock-a-Leekie*. Does he not realise that looking at my drain each day has probably scarred me from ever liking soup, Lucozade, Ribena or Vimto ever again?

Monday, 27th May 2019

I have finally had my second drain removed! I can now go to the toilet and pull down both sides of my knickers at the same time. And I can have a shower without the cagoule. I still have some plasters, but those are all strapped under a waterproof dressing.

Raising my arm is still not allowed, so washing my hair is a challenge and can only be achieved if I stand with my head to one side like I'm trying to get water out of one ear. I've discovered there is a small mirror in the shower cubicle, which I avoid looking into. Mark came in while I was showering and didn't bat an eyelid at my new mound. I tried to hide it as I stepped from the shower—I'm not sure if he noticed. He handed me a towel just like he always used to when I got out of the shower.

We went over to my house today. As we pulled up to the drive, I felt a little sad. The house doesn't look the same, and when I went in, it didn't feel the same either. Yes, most of it hasn't changed, but that air of familiarity about it has gone. Maybe it was seeing strange men in my kitchen using the kettle, or maybe it was heading to the door from the kitchen, which now overlooked a building site.

The annexe was not only gone, but the blown glass fish, the West Ham memorabilia and the crying clown picture were gone as well.

And for a fleeting moment, I felt lost. I wanted them back.

I was slightly disgusted I felt that way. Surely, I'm not wishing for Tracey! Mark caught the look on my face and said it would be different when the orangery was up. I do hope he's right, as I'm not sure I will ever love my home again. Will it ever feel like it belongs to me?

Friday, 31st May 2019

I had a good day today, mentally wise, I mean. I meditated, which I am really enjoying now, and then spent an hour dancing. Mark was in work, as he had to attend a meeting, so I took advantage of the empty flat. I didn't plan it, but a good tune came on as soon as I stepped from the shower, and before I knew it, I was dancing around the flat in nothing more than my underwear. It made me feel alive, properly alive, like the blood was rushing from my fingers to my toes. I caught myself laughing as I shook my hair and after an hour was only defeated when the pain reached a level I could no longer ignore. But it was worth it. It felt like a day when a little bit of me reminded the rest of me that I was still here.

When Mark came home, I was still bouncing around like a child and asked him if he could get me a bottle of Prosecco. This will be my first drink since the surgery, and I will be drinking for the right reasons. Not because I need it to help me cope or to blot out what I'm going through but for the reason that I want to sit with Mark and watch some nonsense on TV and feel good. He didn't hesitate and came back with booze and an Indian takeaway, while I found a comedy for us to watch. I lasted until about ten p.m., which is late for me these days, and then said I was ready for my bed. Mark always insists he take me to bed. He likes to stay up late and will go back to watch something manly once I'm planted under the covers. He helped me, as usual, to put on my pyjamas.

And then in my fizzy fuzziness, I decided.

"I want to look at my reconstruction."

There was no conversation about it. He just smiled and nodded. "Okay."

Taking me by the hand, he pulled me into the bathroom until we were in front of the mirror. I felt sick with nerves, stood there with my bra on, and as Mark reached for the clasp, I wanted to scream for him to stop. But I could hear another voice inside me, a very quiet voice; it was telling me it was time. It was telling me that it would be okay. It was telling me that Mark would help me. It was telling me that I had to accept. I stood stiff as Mark undid the clasp.

"Are you ready?"

I silently nodded.

He gently slid the straps down from my shoulders, revealing my old familiar breast and its new friend. I'm not sure how long I looked at it before I spoke. I looked down at my new cleavage and then back at my reflection. I turned to the left a little and then to the right. The most obvious thing is there is no protruding nipple anymore, but Navid has managed to save most, if not all, of my areola. A thin, jaggedy scar, about three inches in length, runs vertically from the centre of my areola to underneath the breast. My cleavage is a little 'off', and from the side, it looks smaller than its natural mate, but before the tears came, I managed a "Wow."

I thought the reconstruction would look like an old balloon. Like the ones you find behind the couch two months after the party, all lumpy and wrinkly. But this was not that. This was not only a reconstruction; this was good enough to call a breast. I caught Mark's face in the mirror, and he was smiling at me as if to say 'I told you'. I stood naked for a while, and Mark and I talked about it and looked at it, a lot.

It's still too sore to touch, but we gave it a proper inspection, including the scar and how neat it was. He helped me back into my bra, and we marvelled at how you couldn't tell that anything had changed while I was wearing one. Even the 'off' cleavage was corrected, and when I peered down, it looked familiar.

I kept thinking of Navid and how I had not said just how amazing he was and how lucky I was to have been in his hands. I will when I next see him.

Saturday, 1st June 2019

Kelly and Anne had the girls over tonight. I was in two minds about whether to go, but as the day wore on, I realised I was ready to go somewhere else that was familiar but gave me the feeling of getting out. I'm starting to get cabin fever, and I'm also missing my mates.

Anne had made an enormous pan of curry, and Saskia brought one of her homemade lemon drizzle cakes, no doubt made because it's my favourite. Strange to say, but there was a sense of relief just being with them. It could have been relief to know that my old life still existed or because being with the girls gave me an audience to moan and vent.

"You got all your painkillers?" asked Kelly.

"I do. I'm a proper little smackhead looking for my next fix."

"How is the pain?" asked Mia.

"Horrendous."

"Have you looked at it now?" asked Saskia.

"I have. Would you lot like to see?" There were a lot of nodding heads.

As I stood, they all came closer, except for Anne.

"Hang on, I need me glasses!"

"My tits aren't that small, Anne!"

Once they were all standing in front of me, I felt I should give them a warning.

"Now, this is not a breast anymore, and there is no nipple. He's given me a shape, so be warned, and if anyone pulls a face, it'll be the last one you pull in front of me!"

I had on a white shirt, which I unbuttoned, and then I apologised for the ugly bra. I didn't unclip it; I simply slid the soft cups towards my collar bone and took a deep breath.

"Fucking hell!" Charlotte squealed. "That's fabulous. It looks nearly like the other one."

"What do you think, girls?"

"Charlotte's right. That's incredible. Your surgeon must be an artist," said Anne. "Do you think he could do anything with these?" And with that, she pulled up her top and bra at the same time to reveal two voluminous breasts.

"Jesus Christ, Anne!"

"I'd love for these to be lifted. Look! They're practically covering my navel! I mean, to reconstruct one of these, the doctor would have to skin a pig!"

"I think there's enough skin on there for a surgeon to play with," said Mia.

They all sat for half an hour eating curry and discussing what surgery they would like to enhance their bodies. For a moment, I wanted to remind them that I hadn't had cosmetic surgery. I hadn't had a boob job. I hadn't walked out of hospital feeling like a new woman. But what was the point? They knew what I had been through, and it would have only made the poppadums harder to swallow.

By the end of the evening, I was drunker than I realised, but that could have been aided by the Tramadol, and the night ended with Mark tucking me into bed.

Tuesday, 4th June 2019

I'm in panic mode now. Tomorrow I'm back in the clinic to find out all the results of the surgery and the histology report. I can't stop thinking about chemo and how this will devastate me. The brown headscarf is still hidden in the drawer, and I keep wondering if I should have worn it more around the house, simply to get used to the look of it.

Mark suggested we go to my house and see the orangery, as it's more or less up. It just needs all the finishing touches, but essentially the structure is there. What if I don't like it? I can't move now! Not when so many people have worked on it and paid for it.

I hate change, and everything about my life lately has changed. I don't feel like me anymore, and nothing in my day is familiar. My routine has gone, my house has changed, my body has changed, and I can't stop thinking about Tracey. When will I get her out of my head? I told Mark to postpone the visit to the house until tomorrow after clinic.

Wednesday, 5th June 2019

Navid and Abi walked into the usual consultation room today. I'd managed to convince myself that I'd been overreacting to things lately, and all would be well. As Navid walked in, I noticed my file was a little thicker than the last time I'd seen it. A few weeks ago, it had housed a few sheets of paper, mainly stickers bearing my name and NHS number. But now it was the thickness of a Freeman's catalogue, and nowhere in there was a page of Slimma Slacks. My pages were full of medical terms, diagrams, lots of ineligible notes and empty sticker sheets. Lots of them.

He opened the file and gave me a sympathetic smile. I knew that smile. It wasn't a happy smile. It's the smile that says, "Brace yourself, kid. I'm about to mash your head again."

"So, we have the histology report, and unfortunately, we found more cancer."

"Shit."

He passed me a box of tissues.

"A tumour around four millimetres was in your sentinel node."

"Fuck."

"We have no choice, Jo. You need more surgery so we can remove all of your lymph nodes and check there is no more cancer in them. We said this could be a risk doing the reconstruction straight away."

Every nerve in my body was pulsing, and each pulse was hurting me all over.

"Will I lose my implant?"

"We will try every precaution to ensure that doesn't happen and keep infection risk to a minimum."

I sat there numbly for a long time. I couldn't believe they had found more cancer, and because of this, I now have to have more surgery to remove the rest of my lymph nodes—an axillary clearance, they call it. I took a gamble, and now I have my implant in the middle of the table as the stake in my poker game with cancer. If this surgery throws in an infection, then I can say goodbye to my new boob and be left with one side of my chest completely flat for at least twelve months.

Navid went on to explain the short-term risks—losing the implant, high chance of chemotherapy—but the one that slapped me in the face was the increased risk of lymphoedema. This horrible condition of permanent swelling of a limb or even all of them made me want to shout ENOUGH! But I didn't. I just sat there stunned and watched Navid flick through his diary looking for a date for the surgery.

"When?"

"My next available surgery is the nineteenth of June." He looked at me with sorrow and sympathy.

"If my lymph nodes have cancer in them, then that's bad. That means I could have cancerous cells somewhere else in my body?"

He nodded.

"But if they're clear, then that's good? That means the sentinel node caught the cells, and the rest of my body is fine?"

He nodded.

"How in this day and age is there not a scanner that can see if there are any tumours in there without having to cut me open again?"

He shook his head in agreement, saying it was a shame that this was the only way to check them, especially after I had been healing so well from my first surgery. If there's cancer in any of these nodes, then it could be anywhere in my body. I could be riddled. I feel like Tracey literally took a shit in my body, and instead of flushing the chain, she had a dirty protest because she was being evicted. She probably told Tyson and the kids to do the same. All of them, shitting in my sentinel node and leaving it there to fester.

Again, Mark and I walked out of the clinic trying to digest the news of more cancer being found and maybe more still lurking in my nodes and God knows where else. I sent a text to some of the family and some friends and told them the news. They all echoed the same message about keeping positive, but I'm not sure I have the strength anymore to keep shrugging, to keep smiling.

All I feel I can do is keep breathing.

Thursday, 6th June 2019

I spent most of last night awake. Mark snored gently next to me, and I was glad he was sleeping. I know he's been struggling lately. I'm on a lot of painkillers, so it could have been that, but I'm sure I heard Tracey laughing outside Mark's bedroom door. I sat up and strained to hear her, but then Mark stirred, and the laughing stopped. I didn't hear it again, so it must have been my imagination. I'm digesting more tablets than the Rolling Stones did in the sixties, so that's got to have some hallucinogenic effect.

We went over to the house today. Again, it all felt unfamiliar, and the whole time I was there, I was incredibly angry. I wanted to shout at everyone to leave my fucking house alone. I wanted to say we were happy when it was just me and the house and the Farrow & Ball. Why were all these people messing with it and changing it and thinking they knew best? These strangers seemed more familiar with my home than I was. Some of them had probably seen bits that even I had never seen. But I didn't say anything.

The orangery is a little smaller than the original annexe, and I wondered why, but I didn't ask. It's all shiny and new. Very unlike the original building that seemed to fit with the rest of the house. This new addition was simply that—a new addition, which would probably serve as well as its predecessor, so maybe I was being a little harsh.

To be fair, it seems a lot lighter and brighter, and the builders have done a good job trying to line up the walls to where the annexe joined the gable wall of the main building. Mark likes it, but he could see my reluctance to offer an opinion. I suppose with time it will grow on me. At the end of the day, he's paid for it now, and I have no choice but to simply accept it.

Saturday, 8th June 2019

I went to the dentist today to get my teeth cleaned. My dental hygienist, Billy, is a friend and follows me on social media. He had a huge hug for me and asked me how I was. I gave him the usual upbeat "Fine." He went on to tell me about how he and the rest of the surgery were going to handle my oral hygiene in future. His whole plan is geared around me having chemotherapy—worst case, he said. There are several things both he and I can do to keep my mouth comfortable if this happens to me. Sore mouth, ulcers and painful gums are all part and parcel of chemotherapy.

When he was done rattling out his plan, he finished me off with a hug.

"We'll look after you."

I started to cry, then told him off for making me cry.

"This will cheer you up." He produced a mock-up of his Save the Date cards and wedding invitations. Very blingy, very Billy and totally gorgeous. The wedding is next February, and it will be my first gay wedding. I hope I find a decent wig in time—and it's not too windy on the day!

Monday, 10th June 2019

I was back in the clinic today with Eliza. Again, she was saying how brilliant my reconstruction is and that I'm healing well. I wanted to say that Navid's work may be getting flushed down the toilet soon if the axillary clearance surgery goes pear-shaped. But I didn't. I wanted to say I was actually starting to like the reconstruction and it could be getting whipped away from me. But I didn't. I just smiled and said I was glad she was happy with it.

She took my photographs again—more 'before' pictures to adorn Navid's photo album. I wondered if he ever printed them off and put them behind cellophane pages of an album that had a blurry vintage picture of snowy mountains on the front. I wondered if he ever ranked them. Where would my boob be in the ranking? Right now, I didn't care if it came last as long as the implant stayed in my body. What's the point of these photographs anyway if I'm to lose the implant? Will they take photographs of me afterwards if I lose it, draped on a chaise longue looking into the distance? Will they need a picture of just a scar? I doubt it. Who would want to see that? What would be the point? Would all my previous images just end up in the recycle bin in the clinic's hard drive? My chest would just become another statistic.

Would it be better to lose the breast straight away or have reconstruction and then lose it? Is the reconstruction like a halfway house, letting you come to terms with the surgery and the cancer and everything else, and then, just when you're strong enough, they take the implant away? Or is it just better to wake up, no mound there at all and simply start to heal straight away? The latter seems so much more straightforward and yet the most terrifying. At the end of the day, it is not my choice. It is the choice of my surgeon and my body, and all I can do is watch and accept.

People say that you're brave when you have cancer. I'm not brave; I just have to get on with it. I don't have a fucking choice!

Tuesday, 18th June 2019

I must be deafening God with all the praying. I am literally walking around the house, muttering to myself like a dissatisfied husband. *Please let this operation go okay tomorrow. Please make sure I don't get an infection. Please make sure that what they take is all cancer-free. And I promise I won't be bitchy anymore. I promise to be a better person. I promise to be the most amazing wife to Mark, and I promise to look after my body in future.*

Wednesday, 19th June 2019

At the hospital, I was relieved to be greeted by Pam, the gregarious nurse from my last visit. She remembered me and gave me a huge hug and kiss. I was also in the same bed as last time, for which I was glad. It seems silly, but a little familiarity made me relax slightly. I was given my gown, surgical stockings and a pair of paper knickers that were only fit to poach eggs in.

"I'm not being funny, Pam, but do you have anything bigger than these? My arse is the size of Reading—I'm sure each Tramadol contains five hundred calories."

She agreed that the knickers would be pushed to fit a twelve-year-old and soon came back with a far more voluminous pair, which made me wonder whether I was as big as she seemed to think I was. That or she thought I had a penchant for poaching eggs by the dozen.

Mark begged for a picture. Again I refused, and before he could argue, Navid was standing behind him like D'Artagnan, smiling and brandishing his new Sharpie pen. This time, he drew pretty pictures all over my left arm, armpit and a little towards my implant. I wanted him to write 'BE CAREFUL IN THIS AREA' around the implant, but he just did a sweeping arrow instead. Maybe that means the same thing in doctor language. I hope so.

Once Navid had left, the same jolly porter, who also remembered me, slapped me onto the trolley and wheeled me to Theatre 2 this time. I was disappointed to see it was exactly the same as Theatre 1. Why they'd be different, I do not know. Again, four people who all knew what they were doing were milling around and plugging me into various things.

I wasn't as scared as last time, and Tracey wasn't sitting in the corner watching us. The anaesthetist asked me again what I liked to drink, and while I was wondering what else I could say apart from Prosecco, I was being woken up by a nurse called Natalie. By the time she had finished her introduction, I was aware of the most excruciating pain across my chest and down my left arm. When I told her the pain I was in, she gave me a shot of morphine. I waited and waited, and the pain became worse. I was aware that my legs were swishing all over the bed, and after what seemed like hours, another nurse instructed Natalie to give me a wee bit more morphine as I was clearly in a lot of pain.

My gratitude only lasted twenty minutes, by which point it was evident this was having no effect on me.

"Is it actually going into my body?"

Another nurse, whose name I can't recall, shone a torch in my eyes and said my pupils were like pinheads.

"It's definitely going in there, Jo."

A consultant came into the room and asked what the problem was, and when the nurses explained, he instructed them to change the painkiller. They were now injecting Tramadol and paracetamol intravenously and telling me to try and relax.

Within fifteen minutes, I was wondering who had performed the miracle, as I was asking for water, rearranging my newly acquired drain and apologising for the fuss I made.

"Don't apologise," said Natalie. "We just need to find the right painkillers sometimes. Morphine doesn't agree with everyone."

An hour later, I was back on the ward and asking for a cup of tea, after which I had a long sleep before Mark and some of the girls came in to visit me. They didn't bring food this time, which I was sad about. This escalated to devastation when I was given a plate of something that was supposed to be cottage pie. I'm not sure if they called it that because it had been made in a rural dwelling in Dorset or if they had used the recipe for cottage pie as more of a guideline in the hospital kitchen. There was white stuff on top and brown stuff underneath, and that was the only resemblance I could find to a cottage pie. After declining to take part in a hospital version of a Bush Tucker Trial, the plate was returned in the same state as it was presented half an hour earlier, and Mark went off to scour the corridors for a vending machine. He returned with a packet of Hula Hoops, a KitKat and a sorrowful look.

There were two other women on the ward with me. One had had a lumpectomy, while the other had had a mastectomy with no reconstruction. This was to be offered to her at a later date. I felt less isolated than last time. It shouldn't really matter why the other patients were in, but it did to me, and I was glad I was with 'boob' women this time.

We were all pretty synched when it came to sleep and wanting tablets. And when we were awake, I would go as far as to say it was fun. At one in the morning, we talked of lousy food in hospitals, grumpy nurses (we had one on the night shift) and ugly bras. I began my one-man routine on how unattractive a woman feels after surgery and the lingerie industry compounding our vulnerability by making flesh-coloured post-surgery bras.

The thing is I've never seen flesh that colour in my life, pre- or post-surgery. Do they make them that colour thinking they'll blend in? Do they think the wearer won't notice they've had a breast removed? Who are these women who walk around in total ignorance until it comes time to remove the bra and see the devastation underneath? And that's only if they can find the clasp in the first place. Remember—it's flesh-coloured.

Our laughter was disturbing the other ward, according to the grumpy night nurse. I barked at her that laughter was the best medicine, but she clearly thought Tramadol was, and at certain points in the night I had to agree. A couple of hours later, we were awake again, like three crack whores looking for our next fix of painkillers.

By then, my hunger pangs were also keeping the other ward awake, and I asked for tea and toast.

My ward mates joined me, and we continued our bonding session over anaemic toast and a conversation about B&Q.

Thursday, 20th June 2019

Pam had a student in tow today, a lovely girl who was eager to learn. She stood by my bedside while Pam regaled her with my history, about which Pam was an expert—well, the last two months anyway. The child kept throwing me a concerned look and then would smile when she could see I was taking it all in my stride. Plus, I was high as a kite.

When Pam finished, I asked the student nurse had she ever seen a reconstruction before.

"No."

"Would you like to?"

"If you don't mind." She was really enthusiastic.

"Well, you are here to learn, so you might as well learn properly."

While they swished the curtain around my bed, I took off my pyjama top, and Pam helped me remove my bra, as I still had the drain hanging from underneath my armpit. I was soon standing in front of the student while she oohed and aahed at it. Pam pointed out that my surgery was pretty good, and they didn't all look like mine, but it was an excellent example of mastectomy followed by an immediate implant.

"Come and feel it then," I said. She groped it gently. "Can you feel the difference between them?" I asked.

She continued to feel and study its shape. Between Pam and me, she soon learned that the breasts are not the same. They don't look the same. They don't feel the same. They don't act the same. Christ, they're not even the same temperature. By the time the curtain was pulled back, Pam and I felt we had done a good deed for the day, and I was offered a cup of tea for my efforts. It even came in a cup and saucer; clearly, I'd made Tit Teacher of the Year.

While I drank my tea, Pam asked if I would be happy to do that again in future for other women who struggle to decide if they want reconstruction. I said I would, and she suggested I speak to Abi, the Macmillan nurse. I was really flattered she asked me. Could I be a decent role model for women at this most vulnerable time? I'm not sure. I might have the rack to show them, but did I have the right rapport for them to walk away feeling better? I'd hate to make them feel worse! This will need some careful thought.

It was then that Navid walked in with a smile, and I immediately felt 'safe'.

"We removed all of the lymph nodes, and the operation went well. They were quite high in the body, which is good, so hopefully, we won't have disturbed the previous surgery too much."

He checked the drain and told Pam to remove it immediately even though it was filling with something that resembled Rioja.

"But it's still collecting fluid!" I protested.

"The longer we leave that drain in, the more chance you have of an infection."

I would have ripped it out of my body there and then if I could. Call me paranoid, but I asked if I could wash my hands and use the sanitiser before we started, knowing they'd ask me to press a dressing against the hole left behind. Pam soon snipped at a couple of stitches and the drain was pulled through my body, leaving me jelly-legged.

Mark came to collect me, but this time I insisted he take me to my house. I haven't been home for over a month, and the builders are all done. It just needs a good clean and making pretty, which Andy said he would help me with, once I've decided on the colour. I'm not bothered what colour it is, to be honest. I told Mark he could pick, but this threw him in a spin like he'd just come off the waltzers. Why do men find it so hard to pick a colour? And if you put any kind of pressure on them, they choose the most inappropriate colour on the chart and then need a lie-down.

It still felt strange when I walked into the house—not as much as previous visits, though. Mark headed straight for the extension while I went to get changed and sort out my meds. He came bounding up the stairs like a puppy, excited about how brilliant the new annexe was, and said I needed to come down and take a look. I said I would—later. At the moment, I just want to rest.

Friday, 21st June 2019

I went to bed too early last night and woke around three. The pain was raging in my arm, and I needed to go downstairs to get some tablets. I walked into the kitchen, aware of the new addition just off it. Should I look? What if I didn't like it? I figured I could always practise the face that says 'It's wonderful, Darling!' when I came to look at it again and let Mark think it was the first time I'd seen it.

As I swallowed my tablets, I heard her again. That laugh! I told myself it was just my imagination, but I was sure I heard her. I eventually took a breath, turned on the light and went into the orangery, as Mark still insists on calling it. I have asked him if we can now call it a studio, and he seems to quite like that suggestion. He clearly wants to sit in the pub and talk about leaving something 'in the studio' like he's Nile Rodgers or, more accurately, Tony Blackburn. People who have orangeries and call them orangeries watch Carol Smillie and wear cords. We do neither.

The builders have done an outstanding job, and Andy has already started work on a sturdy shelving system where I can dry out my work. As I turned to leave, I spotted something on the bottom shelf. It was tucked at the back, and I only noticed because the shelves are slatted. I reached in and brought it into the light…and felt every nerve in my body jolt. There in my hand was the blown glass fish that had belonged to Tracey.

For a moment, I wondered who had put it there. But that was a stupid question, and there was no one to ask. I couldn't see Tracey; I'm not even sure she's in the house anymore, but I admit, dear Diary, I did look over my shoulder. I put the fish back on the shelf for now. Hopefully, it will disappear eventually, just like its owner.

I went back to bed but couldn't sleep. The pain from this surgery feels worse than the first one, even though it was a smaller operation. So I watched TV—I say watched; I was entranced by the sign language lady in the corner translating a soap opera. I sat there, trying to catch the signs for the swear words. I haven't watched anything that intently since I last saw *The Generation Game* conveyor belt. The programme finished, and I was still none the wiser if Jackie had indeed cheated on Carl or Craig—I can't remember the names. If the tablets continue to give me broken sleep, I may find out tomorrow night if Jackie did cheat or at least learn who is who.

Monday, 24th June 2019

I went to Anne's this morning to do some meditation with her. That's what I tell her, but I'd be lying if I said the Danish pastries she gets in for afterwards aren't a bit of a draw.

We talked a lot about looking for positives in the most challenging times, and every scenario I gave her she could find the silver lining. She is a wholesome person to be around at the moment. Funny—when I think of all the girls in the gang, I'm finding she's the one I need the most. I need them all for different reasons, but there's something comforting about her. My mum is long gone, and I rarely think of her, but maybe, subconsciously, I need someone to nurture me a little.

"You losing weight?" she asked.

"I'm trying to cut out a lot of crap in my diet. The only time I treat myself is when I come here," I admitted.

"Well, don't be losing too much. Your body needs calories to get itself better, so I'll keep getting the Danishes in. But I might go somewhere different. That baker up the road has started doing everything gluten-free. They'll be throwing pumpkin seeds in the crusty cobs soon and calling themselves artisan and charging four pound for a French stick."

"That's not a positive attitude."

"It is. I can say quite positively I will be heading to Waitrose for my pastries in future."

"Oh, yeah, Waitrose. They're known for their fine selection of cheap Eccles cakes and iced buns."

"I don't mind paying through the nose at Waitrose, but I'm not getting ripped off by someone who thinks draping a gingham tea towel over his sliced white will distract me from his filthy apron."

I tucked into a cinnamon swirl and drank peppermint tea while Anne rummaged in the sideboard in her front lounge. She soon returned to the dining table with what looked like old photo albums and delicate paper bags that seemed to be holding very little. I watched her silently as she sorted them into a pile that only made sense to her. She picked up a small, flat, white paper bag and pulled a photograph from within. I could only see its white back, but Anne's face told me the other side was pleasing to her. Her smile slipped a little as she passed it over to me. The picture was of Anne in her twenties, with another woman who appeared slightly older. Judging by the hairstyles, it was taken in the mid-eighties, and they were all dolled up for a night out. She walked towards me and stood behind me, looking at the photograph over my shoulder.

"That's me and my sister, Rosalind. But we called her Roz." I noted she said 'called'. "We were off to a new club in town that night. Nineteen eighty-four, that was. I was twenty-three, and she was twenty-five. Look at our hair! Stiff as plywood, it was."

"Where is she now?"

"With the Lord, I suppose."

"What happened?"

Anne moved back to the head of the table and sat down. She absent-mindedly opened a photograph album but didn't invite me to look.

"Like yourself, she found a lump. But the silly cow ignored it. She said she only ignored it for a few months, but we all suspected longer. It was in her breast—the same as yours—but by the time she went to get it sorted... well, it was too late."

She heard me gasp.

"Oh, love, don't think what happened to her is going to happen to you! She was a silly girl. A fearless girl. And that's what we couldn't understand. She was too frightened to go to the doctor's. Said she was embarrassed about a doctor looking at her boobs. How ridiculous is that? She actually went in the end because she had backache and wanted some strong painkillers, and that's when they started testing her."

"Was it in her spine?"

"Jo, it was everywhere," she whispered. "So much has improved since then, I do wonder if she had it now, would they be able to help her? Then again, you can cure some cancers but not stupidity." I detected Anne was still a little angry over her sister's death.

"Tell me about her."

She looked up and smiled and then started to pass photographs my way, explaining who was in them and where they were going. It seemed Anne and her sister had been inseparable.

"When she died, she was the only one who knew for sure about my sexuality. She kept going on about me coming out because the charts were full of Bronski Beat and Erasure. She saw life too simply sometimes. Well, I thought she did. But looking back, she had the right idea. She shunned anything convoluted or complicated.

"I find as I'm getting older, I care very little about people who care very little about me. There was a time I wanted to know why they didn't like me, then I realised one day that I don't like certain people for silly reasons, and I probably give certain people silly reasons not to like me too. Am I bothered? No. But years ago, I would have been.

"You'll probably find when you come to the end of all this cancer nonsense that you put up with even less crap in your life."

I thought about what Anne was saying and concluded she was right. There have been times when I've felt some things were not worth the effort—specific people or arguing my opinion. I hadn't realised, but having cancer has made me question everything in my life, and most of the questions end with 'will it make a difference?' I see that as a positive.

"She was dead before she was thirty," Anne said.

"Did she marry?"

"No, but Lenny wanted to before she got really sick. She said no. She told me Lenny didn't suit being a widower, and it was easier to get over your girlfriend dying than your wife."

"Where is he now?"

"Last I heard, he got married and went to live in Canada. His job took him there. All his family are gone now. He could be dead for all I know. I hope he's had a happy life. I liked Lenny."

She carried on passing photographs and talking of her childhood Christmases with her mum and dad and Roz and various pets across the years. There was no writing on half of the prints, and she guessed the years according to the fashions worn. She laughed at a picture of Roz in a shiny puffball dress.

"Someone should have told that girl no one could pull off taffeta after Lady Di's wedding. She was going to a new nightclub called the Blue Bazooka, I think. She went with some fella who had an Austin Allegro and the best highlights I've seen outside of a Duran Duran video. She cried when he dumped her for his hairdresser. I don't know what she saw in him. His hair might have been nice, but he had shocking breath. It was so bad, his teeth had all fled by the time he was thirty."

"Ew."

"She had some strange men in her past. She was with one fella, his name escapes me, but he could start a fight in an empty room. She'd get herself all dolled up, and then he'd knock on the door for her, and within thirty seconds, the doorstep was like the final scene of *The Karate Kid*!"

I had to laugh and so did she.

"She sounds brilliant," I said.

"She was. You'd have liked her. She was me, but more. She was more funny, more pretty, more…I know this sounds funny…but…well…more alive."

"And where is the positive in all of this?" I asked, even though the answer was obvious.

"She was MY sister. She taught me how to ride a bike. She taught me how to drink. She taught me to stand up to people. But more importantly, she taught me that lesbians shouldn't be seen dead in legwarmers." She stood up and started to scoop the loose photographs back into their little bags. "Go and put the kettle on, while I clear up this lot."

I went into the kitchen and thought about Roz. If only she'd been born twenty years later. Not only has medicine improved but so have people's attitudes to being sick. Her odds today would no doubt have been much better. I'm lucky to have found my cancer in an age when so much can be done. I'm lucky that I have options. I'm lucky that I will survive this. It will be a long time before someone pulls a picture of me from a little paper bag.

Thursday, 27th June 2019

I was back in the clinic today with Eliza. She noticed I was struggling to raise my arm and called Navid in to have a look. After a brief examination of my armpit, which I so wish I'd shaved as it was looking like Diana Ross was camping out in there, he declared I have axillary web syndrome. It is a condition that affects a small number of people after having an axillary clearance. It's also known as cording and no wonder. These rope-like cords feel like they're spreading from my armpit to past my elbow.

"Raise your arm a little more," Navid instructed, then without warning administered the most barbaric tickle I have ever felt. With all his fingers and his might, he dug hard into my armpit to snap the cords. Before I could punch him, he stopped and smiled at me like he'd just given me the best orgasm ever.

"What the hell was that?!"

His smile disappeared for a moment, but then I realised I could now raise my arm above and behind my head—which I hadn't been able to do for a few days—and his smile returned. Clearly, he'd been in this scenario a number of times, and his smug grin was honed to perfection.

"Make sure you keep that arm moving. I hope you're exercising every day."

"She's like a bloody windmill," Mark piped up from behind the curtain.

I decided to tell Navid and Eliza about my morning routine, whether they were interested or not.

"I start with grateful meditation to keep me positive. They say healthy mind, healthy body. Then I do regular meditation to calm my mind. My mate Anne showed me how to do it. Do either of you do it?"

They both shook their heads and carried on washing their hands and putting instruments away.

"Then I finish off with a half-hour session of physiyoga—a mix of your exercises, Navid, and some of my old yoga routine. I also do a little weightlifting for my weak arm. I say weights—it's actually a large bottle of body cream. It was either that or an old tin of hot dogs. I may have to invest in some proper equipment if I want to keep lymphoedema at bay and make sure my arm is more useful than simply filling a sleeve."

"Lymphoedema is quite rare, you know," Eliza said, trying to reassure me.

"I know. But I'm terrified!"

"You're doing all the right things, Jo. We're really pleased with you."

I felt a little happier hearing this, but it was short-lived. When I got back to the house, I felt like another dark mood was descending on me. I've been struggling for a couple of days, trying to coax positive Jo from the shadows. There are times I want to curl up and stay in bed all day, but I know I would feel worse at the end of it. The visitors are still streaming in with a plethora of gifts, which sometimes makes me feel guilty for putting people out and making them spend money on me they could be spending on themselves.

Don't get me wrong, dear Diary, I *am* grateful, but I feel they're visiting someone who is much nicer in their heads, and when they arrive, they're disappointed to find it's only me and I'm not that much fun after all. I suspect half of them only come to look at the new studio. Yes, Mark agreed we could call it that and wants to put a sign on the door from the kitchen in case anyone needs to know where it is. IKEA and their floor stickers have a lot to answer for.

Friday, 28th June 2019

We had friends over today. The sun was out, so we sat in the garden. Mark and company began to get tipsy while I spent most of the day in the bathroom inspecting my armpit, which seems a bit bigger than the other. I told Mark, and he said it was probably just a bit of swelling from my last surgery—perhaps I'd been overdoing the exercises. I've now upgraded the body cream to a large tub of fairly dense body butter. Who said I can't take on a challenge?

Our visitors were gone by six p.m., when Andy popped round for his next lot of instructions. He brought some flowers and a box of fudge from Cornwall. Andy hasn't been to Cornwall as far as I know, and judging by the best-before date, the holidaymaker that actually bought it went a while ago. Even still, it was nice that he thought of me, and a well-practised, "Oooh, my favourite!" followed after he presented it to me like one of the Three Wise Men.

Saturday, 29th June 2019

I woke up this morning in a lot of pain. When I went to the bathroom to inspect the swelling, I immediately shouted to Mark. I am half human, half bagpipe. The scar from my last surgery looks like it's going to split open any moment, spilling tyres, fish and a number plate from New Jersey (why is it always New Jersey?).

As it's Saturday, I can't call Eliza or any of the staff from my usual clinic. I have to call the local general hospital, which has a reputation on par with Hitler's SS. Could I last until Monday when my breast clinic was open? Could I bear the pulse that was throbbing in the lump? It reminded me of the opening bars of 'Does Your Mother Know' by Abba. Did I actually have any clothes that could accommodate this ever-growing lump? Maybe I could knit it a small hat and pretend I was carrying a baby.

I made it to lunchtime, and when my Tramadol gave up trying to kill the pain, I called the hospital. I then spent forty minutes on the phone to someone so inept I was tempted to ask, "Is your mummy there?" After battling my way through various help desks (I do wonder if there are more receptionists in the NHS than medical staff), a range of various grade nurses and I think a cleaner at one point, I was eventually put through to a ward sister, who ordered me to go to the assessment unit.

Mark and I had planned a day of fun of some sort and maybe a meal later. His day of fun was now cancelled, but with a bit of luck, we might still make the meal.

I found the assessment unit and several harassed-looking staff within—I wasn't sure why, as there were hardly any patients to assess. It wasn't long before I was called by a nurse, who was impressed when I rolled up my sleeve without being prompted. Blood pressure taken from my right arm—which is the only arm they can ever do it on now—and bloods extracted, I was told the results could take up to two hours and sent to the waiting room. Why did they need blood in the first place? I just wanted someone to look at my third boob in my armpit, which was now a 36G. Mark just shrugged when I told him about the wait. He's now a natural and declared he was off for a newspaper. He came back ten minutes later with a bottle of water and a look of disgust.

"What's up? No newspapers?"

"Can you believe the newsagent's only had *The Sun*?"

"That's because only decent papers are bought."

"I'm disgusted the shop was selling it in the first place."

He knew people in Hillsborough—those who don't know someone who went undoubtedly know someone who was affected by it. Buying *The Sun* in this area is a clear sign of disrespect. Reading it in public labels you a troublemaker or a southerner, the latter being the best option for the reader and his teeth. So no newspaper. Instead, we amused ourselves with the racing on the telly, taking empty bets on which horse would win and keeping tally of our imaginary winnings.

After two and a half hours, a small man finally called my name. With a stethoscope hanging over his designer clothes and an expensive watch, he looked important, and once I sat down, he apologised profusely for my wait. He'd been notified that I was on my way and had instructed the ward to tell them the minute I arrived, but he never received the message and was only aware of my presence when the blood results landed on his desk. He asked me to remove my rather voluminous batwing top, the only thing to accommodate my ever-growing child's head. Being unable to shave the area for a while, my baby had a good head of hair, but even without the aid of a machete, he quickly concluded I had a seroma.

"What's that?"

"It's when fluid builds up around the surgery site."

"Will you drain it?"

"Your blood test results indicate no infection, so I'm not going to touch it."

He suggested I see Eliza on Monday, and maybe she could drain it. He clearly didn't have the stomach to pierce this one and watch all the contents spill out like a tsunami.

I couldn't blame him; I didn't want to see that devastation either, especially all over his Jasper Conran shirt.

By the time we left, Mark and I were too exhausted to go for a meal. We ended the night with a bucket of chicken, two bottles of wine, tablets and a pissed dance to 'My Sharona', the words changed accordingly.

Monday, 1st July 2019

I called Eliza first thing, and she beckoned me to the hospital I know and love to see if she could help Sarah the Seroma. I feel that anything on my body that has a better hairstyle than me deserves a name.

Eliza took one look, and her lips went into a thin line. Reluctant to touch it, even though she wasn't wearing a Jasper Conran shirt, she went to fetch Navid. He arrived like Glinda the Good Witch of the North and smirked when he saw it.

"It's not that big."

"Are you kidding me?"

"There are some women who literally walk around with their hands on their hips, they're that big."

"Will you drain it?"

"No. We could risk an infection and compromise the implant."

"But it has a rhythmic throb that keeps making me sing 'I Need You Tonight' by INXS."

This did not affect his decision to refrain from the drain, and off he went in his bubble smelling of lemon with a hint of coconut, leaving me with Sarah the Seroma, who looked even more pissed off than me.

"Come back on Friday," said Eliza. "We'll make sure it looks okay before the weekend starts."

Disappointed, I left the hospital with my armpit baby but no 'It's a Girl' balloon or even a kiss from the nurse to wish me all the best with my new addition. Do these people not realise that this thing keeps me up all night as well?

Wednesday, 3rd July 2019

I had another bad night sleeping last night even though Sarah the Seroma is starting to settle down and is shrinking. I do hope the nurse doesn't chastise me for her being underweight. I know I'm not sleeping because of the results that are due on the 9th. This wait feels more sinister than the last one. What if the cancer is in my lymph nodes? Then could it be in my lungs? Liver? Brain?! Strangely, part of me doesn't want to know. I heard that Paul McCartney didn't tell Linda she was terminal, and she was horseriding the day before she died, completely unaware. I want to be like that, even though I can't ride a horse.

I joined a social media group full of breast cancer sufferers, but now I'm not sure if it was such a good idea. I feel the only people who are posting are the ones who are at death's door. It's killing my efforts to remain positive, especially when the feed is peppered with posts with details of so-and-so's funeral and thanking everyone for their kind words. I am affected when I read these posts, don't get me wrong, but I'm not entirely sure *how* it's affecting me. How do I feel sorry for someone I don't know? But then

I wonder if my family would take comfort from something like that. I doubt it very much.

I got up early and went downstairs. For some reason, I went straight to the studio to inspect the shelving cabinet. The glass fish is where I left it. Why is this fish haunting me? If I was going to be haunted by an object, could it not have been a Fabergé egg? A Tiffany lamp, maybe? No, I get a skanky blown-glass fish from the era when people thought Wrangler's were cool and racism on TV was classed as comedy.

I sat in the corner of the studio for a while, remembering the family that was in this space before, and I started to cry. Had I rid myself of them all or were they hiding in my wardrobe ready to pop out when Mark and I were about to make love one night?! I didn't know whether to laugh or carry on crying when I had a vision of Tracey shouting, *"Atta girl!"* while Mark and I bounced around the bed.

I carried on crying, truth be told. Fear is feeding my tear ducts at the moment. I'm doing well to keep it together in front of people, even the visitors who come and cry all over me. Why are they crying? I'm the one in pain. I'm the one with this teasing death sentence. I'm the one who's lost her breast. I'm the one who can't feel half of her arm. I'm the one who can't shit for days due to all the tablets. I'm the one with a beachball in her left armpit. I'm the one who can't lie on her front. I'm the one who can't take anything off a shelf higher than her knee. I'm the one with hair like a maniac because I can't style it properly. I'm the one who feels like she's doing a battle with Death every day! So why are these people crying more than me?!

When I finished crying, I sat in the studio until the sun came up. I prayed to whomever might be listening and said sorry for being so mean and having bad thoughts about people who love me and get upset.

As well as a new boob that clenches as soon as it feels a breeze, I now have guilt.

Friday, 5th July 2019

I went back to see Eliza today, who was pleased to see that Sarah the Seroma had upped sticks and moved out. So much so, she could now see three visible cords running through my armpit, courtesy of my new syndrome. Far gentler than Navid, Eliza asked me to take a deep breath as she snapped each of them between her thumbs. At least she gave me a warning, and when she finished, I was capable of bringing in a 747—I was grateful. Sweaty, but grateful.

I'm going out with the girls tonight. This will be my first proper night out since all my surgery. There was a dress that I wanted for the night, and when I went to buy it, the shop didn't have my size. For once, I played the cancer card, asking was there anything they could do. Without hesitation, they took a larger dress to a seamstress, took it in for me and then sent it to me by courier so I would have it for the night. See? There are good people in the world.

The dress has a very low neckline with Bardot sleeves, and it wasn't until I came to try it on that I realised I didn't have a strapless bra I could fit into. Also, lack of bowel movements for nearly two months has taken its toll, and I look like I'm due in December. While I was panicking, a voice told me to dig out a swimming costume—a strapless number that was a little on the tight side might do the trick. When I tried it on altogether, it looked okay.

The thing is, dear Diary, I'm not sure I want to go now. I'm terrified of getting drunk and falling over and hurting myself, or someone bumping into me, or someone simply looking at my chest and pointing. I'm meeting everyone at eight o'clock, but with the way my hair is behaving at the moment, I should have started getting ready four days ago. I've got more chance of making Paul O'Grady straight. But I want to look pretty tonight, as this may be my last night out for a very long time—dependent on chemo or horseriding lessons.

Saturday, 6th July 2019

What a brilliant night that was! Yes, I was the first to leave, but it was still gone midnight, and I walked in a straight line after I said goodbye to them all. I drank cocktails all night and felt like Jo was back in the room. I was only reminded that I was sick by well-meaning friends who kept asking me if I was okay. And I was. I was fine.

"How can someone who has been so sick look this good?" said Charlotte.

It was that comment that made me relax. It was the audible gasp when I walked in that made me feel like a woman. It was the empty chair waiting for me in the middle of the whole group that told me they would look after me. And they did.

Mark was pleased to see me when I arrived home. I'm not sure if it was relief that I could still walk tipsy in high heels or the fact that I'd had a lovely time. The night ended with Mark and me fooling around, and I forgot that Tracey might be in the wardrobe.

My head today is fine, but I'm exhausted, more than usual. I can go from feeling like I could run a marathon to feeling like I've just completed one in the space of ten minutes. This constant undulating makes me question every activity that is suggested, including walking around the supermarket or being able to hold out for a whole episode of *Killing Eve*. So, because I was so tired, I stayed in my pyjamas most of the day, while Mark showed people around his flat. He thinks someone is going to put an offer in. I hope it's sooner rather than later. I'm too used to having him beside me each night now, and him still having his own place means he hasn't quite moved in.

Monday, 8th July 2019

My stress levels are now through the roof. My skin is flaky, my arsehole doesn't know whether it's coming or going, and I'm exhausted but not sleepy. I'm hardly talking to Mark in case he brings up the subject of results and wants to *chat about it*. There's nothing to chat about until I find out if the lymph nodes are clear.

I had a quick peek on the cancer support group, and every post I find is frightening me. I'm praying so much my knees are flat, and I'm constantly chanting to myself that 'I have a healthy body', as per the advice in the book *The Secret*, and thanking the universe every morning that I'm still here. What with praying, manifesting, meditating, reiki, dedicated masses, having enough healing crystals to build an igloo and the good old NHS, surely I'm in with a fighting chance.

When I think of tomorrow, I imagine Navid telling me that Tracey is dead. He produces my manila-coloured file, and instead of medical notes, it's full of black-and-white photographs of Tracey's dead body. Her eyes are open, her yellow tongue lolling out of one side of her mouth, and she's wearing a Christmas jumper with I'M ON

THE NAUGHTY LIST across the front. He asks me to identify the body, and I give an enthusiastic nod. When I ask how she died, Navid confirms she died from being hit on the head with the shovel of a small JCB or a Massey Ferguson—the make is yet to be confirmed. He then produces more photographs of Tyler and the kids, who look like they were in the middle of a game of Twister when they met their demise. I also notice there is a dog in the picture. I'm not sure what breed it is, but I do know it's the ugliest dog I've ever seen. When I question Navid about the dog, he tells me his name is Sentinel, and he choked to death on a Twister spinner.

But it won't be like that. It'll be medical terms and lots of words that end in -therapy or more surgery that takes place a week on whatever day.

Tuesday, 9th July 2019

The journey to the hospital was quiet, horribly quiet. I don't think we even noticed that the radio wasn't on. We sat in the waiting room and tutted that the telly was on ITV. We were missing *Homes Under the Hammer*—a staple ingredient of all hospital visits, it seems.

When my name was called, I wanted to ignore the nurse. I wanted to sit and watch Eamonn Holmes give his opinion on this summer's florals. I wanted that more than anything else when she called my name. I could hear Mark silently saying *let's do this* when he stood up.

The nurse ushered us into the familiar room of table, chairs, an examination bed and hand sanitiser, and Mark and I sat. We sat for what seemed an age. We sat very still, terrified to move. Soon, Abi and Navid walked in with enthusiastic smiles, which they always did anyway. They could be about to tell you that they found cancer in your head, but not to worry as they would be chopping it off and reconstructing another from a melon, quick-cook spaghetti and fuzzy felt. The smile was always the same when they walked in, followed by the dreaded thud of my now-weighty manila file that probably registered on the Richter scale.

Navid didn't dance around it.

"All of your nodes are clear. You had thirteen in your body, and we took them all, and the report says that there was no cancer evident in any of them."

His smile broadened, and I looked at Abi, who gave an enthusiastic nod. I went to speak; I remember that. But I couldn't get any words out initially. The huge lump in my throat was bobbing between my forehead and my knees.

"Really?" I eventually squeaked.

I remember being on my feet and kissing Abi. Then Navid put his hand out for a handshake, and I told him to behave and threw myself against him. Then I remember Mark was crying and smiling at the same time. The relief was so palpable; he looked like a different man.

"So I'm cancer-free?"

"Yes."

"Like, proper cancer-free?"

"Yes."

No more surgery. No more drains. No more slots in Navid's busy diary.

After telling me about what to expect at my oncology appointment, he asked me to jump on the bed so he could check my webbing. Again, without any warning, he dug his fingers into my armpit and started snapping the cords like an angry harpist. Through gritted teeth, I swore and apologised at the same time for calling him a twat.

"Please ignore me. I'm so sorry." Navid and Abi found this amusing and said they'd heard worse. Maybe some people forget to apologise.

It was at this point I had to ask him. I couldn't help myself.

"Navid, can you please say 'Tracey is dead'?"

He looked confused, and Abi smiled.

"Is that what you called your cancer?" she asked. I nodded, silently hoping they wouldn't laugh at me.

Navid smiled at me. "Yes, Tracey is dead."

I didn't have the black-and-white photographs like I'd had in my dream, but this was better. This was real. She was gone.

Wednesday, 10th July 2019

My phone has gone into meltdown. The news has spread that Tracey and her trampy family are dead. I'm half-relieved at yesterday's news, but I still have a whole new medical department to get to know in the hospital.

My oncologist is a Dr. Menon, and I met him today to discuss my therapy going forward. However, we were not called by Dr. Menon, we were called by another doctor. He mumbled his name, and it sounded like Dr. Showaddywaddy to me, so I just shook his hand and gave a polite hello. He brought Mark and me into a room not too dissimilar from Navid's, and the doctor perched on the end of the examination bed like he was sitting on the bonnet of the latest model Ford Capri. He then produced a laptop with a graph that he didn't initially refer to and decided to go straight in with the course of action.

"So we'll start you on three weeks of radiotherapy. Then we'll give you a course of chemotherapy. Then we'll give you a tablet each day. Then we'll give you a monthly injection to suppress your ovaries. Then we can look at getting them removed. Then we can also look at an injection that you take every six months to help the onset of osteoporosis."

When he finished, I sat there, shell-shocked, like I had been put through a clothes mangle, while Mark collated all the leaflets that were being passed to him by a very pale nurse in the corner. I thought I was coming in for a chat! I thought a discussion was to be had! Navid had always said that radiotherapy was not a good option, as it compromised the implant. Now Dr. Do-wah-diddy was saying I needed it every day for three weeks?! Did this guy know who I was? Had he read my file?

"What are my odds of cancer coming back if I don't have the radiotherapy?"

"Fifty per cent," he said flatly.

I looked at Mark in a state of shock

"Fifty per cent, Mark. It's a no-brainer. I have to take the radiotherapy with odds like that."

There goes my implant, I thought.

But Mark just looked at the smug doctor, still perched on the end of the bed, and I could see from Mark's face he was angry.

"Can I ask, Dr…er…I'm not even sure who you are, quite frankly, but have you attended any of the multidisciplinary meetings the team have each Thursday?"

These meetings were to discuss the treatment of all the patients, and the team included surgeons, nurses, therapists, etc.

Dr. Who-did-a-doody's smile slipped, as did his steadying leg. "I've attended a couple," he admitted.

A couple?! What the hell is going on?

"Also, you have come in with your shiny laptop but failed to explain any of the data that is included in these pretty graphs." Mark was at his 'I Don't Give a Shit' level, customarily reserved for cold callers and Nigel Farage.

Shifting a little on the bed, the doctor proceeded to read numbers but not explain them, which confused me and wound Mark up even more.

"Where's Dr. Menon?" snapped Mark.

"He'll be here…erm…soon," he stuttered.

My head felt like it was going to burst. All I kept thinking about was losing the implant because of the radiotherapy, losing my hair because of chemotherapy, losing my ovaries because of my cancer type, and to top it all off, he added that there was a 90% chance of me developing lymphoedema! I've been exercising my stiff arms so much I have biceps like Rambo to keep this condition at bay, and now he was saying with a shrug that it was all a waste of time.

Mark's nostrils were flared, and I wanted to run out of the room and find Navid. I wanted him to tell me it was all okay, and I could go back to his care. It was at this point Dr. Menon walked into the room. He didn't glide or come in a bubble or float in on a cloud of Creed. No, he came in, gave a well-practised smile and then sat on the edge of the bed that Dr. Diddy-dum-diddy-doo had just vacated.

"My name is Dr. Menon. I'm your oncologist. I presume that Dr. Didgeridoo has explained everything to you. Do you understand everything so far?"

He looked like he was about to move on, but then I finally found my voice.

"Actually, I'm surprised how this conversation has gone today."

"Why?" he challenged.

"Well, for a start, I was told that radiotherapy was not on the cards as it would compromise the implant. In fact, Navid didn't even discuss it with me, as it was not an option."

It was at this point, when I saw the look he gave his colleague, that I knew I never wanted to get on the wrong side of my oncologist.

"Why are you talking to them about radiotherapy?" he snarled.

Dr. Menon apologised and asked the ever-shrinking nurse to take all the leaflets relating to radiotherapy out of Mark's hand. Without wanting the cretin to get away with what he had just put me through, I interjected.

"No, hang on a minute! What about my fifty per cent odds of this cancer coming back?"

"Excuse me?" asked Dr. Menon, clearly confused.

"Isn't that what you said?" I threw an accusatory finger at Dr. Should-a-had-a-slappa.

"That's everything thrown in," he whispered.

What the fuck was the man talking about? What was *everything*? Was he even qualified? Was this some kind of work experience thing?!

Dr. Menon explained that radiotherapy was not an option—for all the reasons Navid had said—and that we would look at other treatments. He said he'd also explain my statistics to me properly. I'd like to tell you, dear Diary, that Dr. Cock-a-doodle-doo looked sheepish, but he didn't.

Dr. Menon continued and explained chemotherapy would only slightly improve my chances of cancer not recurring, and it was entirely up to me if I wanted it. I said that after all the research and advice from a friend who is a cancer specialist in another county, I felt that pumping my body full of poison could be more damaging. He smiled and said he agreed in my case and instructed the nurse to take back yet more of Mark's leaflets.

The whole time, Dr. Zip-a-dee-doo-dah leant against the wall, his feet crossed like he was waiting for an interview with *Top Gear*. I wanted to punch him. If it was up to him, I'd have been walking out of the clinic with no boob, no hair and no ovaries. I only went in for a fucking prescription! Did he not realise what he had just put me through? Did he not realise just how close he was to getting a beating from Mark? And I wouldn't have stopped him. I would have chanted *Easy! Easy! Easy!* through the whole assault.

I told Dr. Menon I wanted hormone therapy, which he agreed was the best place to start and snapped at his inept assistant to get me a prescription, which was soon produced and handed over with a brief talk about menopausal symptoms.

"You may experience headaches, hot flushes, night sweats, abnormal vaginal bleeding or discharge, pain in the pelvis, leg swelling, chest pain, shortness of breath, numbness in your face, difficulty speaking, vision problems, nausea, fatigue, mood swings, depression, hair thinning, constipation and dry skin."

"I experienced all of them one weekend a couple of months back after a hefty bender," I said. "As long as it doesn't give me cancer, I don't care."

I was then instructed to take my first one as soon as I could today. Dr. Menon ordered the insipid nurse to make an appointment for me the following week to see him and get my blood taken.

Once dismissed, Mark and I practically ran away from the hospital. We went straight to the pharmacy, and while we were waiting for the hormone tablets, I told Mark I didn't want to talk about what had happened. My head was that smashed, I couldn't process what I'd just been through. His lip-biting indicated to me that he did need to talk about it, and soon, everyone in the pharmacy was aware of Mark's feelings towards Dr. Menon's assistant.

I let him vent; otherwise, it would never go away. He needed to get it off his chest, and I needed the pharmacist to bag my pills quickly, as there were a growing number of concerned faces in the shop. Mark didn't hold back, and his language was as colourful as a Pride parade.

"It's still a good day though, babe," I reminded him. "I've got the treatment that I wanted, I'm keeping my hair, and I'm keeping my implant."

"I'm sorry, darling. You're right. Why don't we go somewhere and have a nice lunch?"

"That's a good idea. Best find somewhere quick, though. I've just taken my first tablet, and my menopause is due to start in the next half hour."

Thursday, 11th July 2019

I sat up most of last night while Mark slept next to me. I was on the iPad, looking at all the various treatments that were still on offer to me. They want me to have a monthly injection, which will suppress my ovaries and stop them from producing estrogen. Side effects of this are not just menopausal symptoms. No, this treatment actually puts your body in a menopausal state. But if it decreases the chances of me getting cancer again, then I'll take it. However, I've been thinking… why not just take the ovaries out? It's not like I want any children, and neither does Mark. So, instead of pumping my body with more medication each month, why not just take them out? The bed is probably still warm from my last surgery. Plus, perversely, I want to see if Theatre 3—the only one I've not been in—is the same as Theatres 1 and 2.

It seems Dr. What-a-divvy is keen for me to have an additional injection every six months, which helps prevent osteoporosis. However, the side effects of this injection are far more alarming, including necrosis of the jaw! As soon as I saw that, I decided, right there in the dark, not to take that one. Surely there are things I can do with my diet and some exercises that will help prevent osteoporosis. I wanted to keep looking, but after taking a strong painkiller so I could type, the side effect of drowsiness kicked in, and I soon fell asleep.

Friday, 12th July 2019

I called into work today and gave them an update on what was happening with me. I'm at the point now that whenever I recall what has happened to me, I feel like I'm talking about someone else. Is it a good thing to detach myself from it all? Is this a subconscious coping thing? Amara wasn't in, so I spoke to a girl in HR who I didn't know. She took all the details and made a note that a further sick note would be on its way. Amara already knew. This just made it more formal.

Andy was in the studio today, finishing off the painting. I plumped for a cheery shade called Sudbury Yellow—by Farrow & Ball, of course. I figured the sunny colour would lift my spirits whenever I walked in. Andy was clearly taken by it.

"If there's any of this left, Jo, can I take it home?"

"Of course."

"I reckon half a tin would be enough to do my mum's breast wall in the lounge. She saw the colour on my hands yesterday and said how lovely it was."

I looked around the room and started to imagine it as a potter's room. It was easier to see it all now it was more or less a blank canvas.

"I'm going to be off work for a couple of more months, so I have plenty of time to sort this space out."

"It's loads better than it was," said Andy.

"You reckon?" *she* said.

I heard her!

But when I looked, she wasn't there.

Wednesday, 17th July 2019

Mark and I went to the oncologist's today to discuss my next lot of treatment. Dr. Menon was pleased to hear that I had not experienced any side effects with my daily dose of Tamoxifen but looked slightly disappointed when I said I would not be taking the zoledronic acid to help my bones.

"I'm sorry, the risk of necrosis is too high."

He respected my decision and said that we would have to monitor my bone density if that was the case, as my risk of osteoporosis was high if I was taking ovarian suppression drugs.

"Will you be taking the monthly injection?" he asked.

"Oh, yes, I want that. In fact, can we just take out my ovaries? That has to be better than pumping my body with drugs each month."

"Let's see how we get on with the injections first. Shutting down a woman's ovaries can be quite traumatic. If you don't react well with the injection, at least we still have options. Whipping them out is not always the best way forward initially."

I could see his point, and Mark also agreed that Dr. Menon was talking sense.

"I want to take some more blood from you and test your vitamin D levels. Vitamin D is vital for healthy bones. You look like you have a healthy diet, so I doubt there's anything to worry about."

I had read up on vitamin D and knew I had to eat more eggs and oily fish as well as getting outside in the sun more. It was then that Dr. Menon produced a diary quite similar to Navid's to book me in for my first ovarian suppression injection. It's all set for 7th August. The day when I start the last of my cancer therapy. My first monthly injection for at least the next five years, maybe ten. Who cares? As long as it stops the buffet that fed Tracey and the likes.

Friday, 19th July 2019

Mark has sold the flat and got the full asking price. It's good to finally have some good news that isn't cancer related. He's made a decent profit on the flat and suggested we keep fifteen thousand back for the wedding. I don't want to spend that much on a wedding. I just want to have a quick wedding and go home with a curry. When I suggested this, he was aghast.

"Seriously?!"

"Yes, I just fancy a registry office and a quick pub lunch."

"No, Jo! I'm sorry." He looked hurt. "Do you know how many times I've smiled over this wedding? Knowing that you will be my wife one day? Do you know how many times I've sat in my car thinking I was going to lose you? How many times I thought of life without you? Too many! And now I've been given the chance to look after you for the rest of my life, and I want to celebrate that. I want to show everyone that I am marrying the most amazing person in the whole world."

"Steady on," I sniffed.

"Look, it doesn't have to be a flash church thing with vintage cars and flowery bridesmaids. But I do want a day that reflects us. I want a day where all the people who've supported not only you but me as well can help us celebrate being alive together!"

I knew he'd worried about me a bit, but I'd naively imagined he was only concerned about the day he was living in. I never imagined he was worrying about the future—my future, his future. I never thought about him imagining life without me. I cried more as I thought of him in his car, all alone.

"Okay, babe. Whatever you want," I said. "But nothing formal. I want music and dancing and people eating bacon butties."

"Done."

And then he kissed me, and I felt truly loved.

Tuesday, 23rd July 2019

I went shopping with Charlotte today and spent most of the day in the local department store's lingerie section. I had a basket full of bras to try on but was stopped by a stout lady with a tape measure around her neck before I went in the changing room.

"You can only take six items."

"I'll be buying more than six items!"

"Policy, I'm afraid."

Charlotte leaned over the small counter, which the lady stood behind.

"Listen, love. She has fourteen bras in that basket, and she's trying them all on in one go. She's just had a mastectomy, so if you think we're running in and out of your changing room swinging half a dozen bras at a time because it's policy then you can think again."

She looked shocked, and her gaze instantly went to my chest.

"We have a fine selection of post-surgical bras," she whispered.

"I'm done with beige!" And I scooped the basket from the counter and walked into a changing room without waiting for her to argue. Charlotte and I giggled in the changing room and began trying the bras on. By the time I finished, and realising it was ridiculous to buy them all, I opted for six that I thought Mark might like too. Included was a peach satin bra that I knew he would love. When I tried it on, I was pleased with my shape in it.

"Do you feel pretty?" asked Charlotte.

I silently nodded. I wanted to cry. I never thought I could look like a woman again, never mind pretty.

"Let me buy that one for you?"

I protested, but I could see it was something she really wanted to do.

"Everyone was buying you presents, Jo, and I had no idea what to buy. I mean, I wouldn't know where to buy a healing crystal, and I'm not the type to write soppy words in a card. But underwear—that I do know. Now promise me it'll see some action?"

"It will, but you do realise, the whole time I'll be thinking of you now!"

"Whatever rocks your boat, kid."

Wednesday, 24th July 2019

I spent the morning having a long bath and decided to de-fuzz my whole body so I could try on my new underwear at home. I wanted to feel pretty again. After digging out my best body cream and slowly rubbing it all over, I pulled out the peach set first. I was still surprised at how well it fitted, and while I looked at my reflection in the mirror, I saw her. I didn't turn to look at her. She was leaning against my bedroom wall and watching me.

"Very nice," she sniffed.

"Why are you here, Tracey?"

"You really need to ask?"

When I turned to challenge her, she was gone.

Friday, 26th July 2019

Andy has finally finished all his jobs in the studio. At last, it's ready for me to use. I've not ordered a wheel yet, as I want Johnny from class to help me pick one, and I've not been there for a few months. He's kept in touch by text—I only have to call him and he will be round to help me.

Before Andy left, he went to his van and came back with a bottle of champagne. "This is from Saskia and me. Sis said you should toast to your new dreams."

"Of course I will." I gave him an appreciative peck on the cheek.

I walked him to his van and thanked him for all his work over the last few months. "And not just the work, Andy. You've been amazing, looking after me."

"We all care about you, Jo. So don't scare us like that again."

"You'll still come and see me, won't you?"

"Yeah, 'course." I doubted it, though. Andy was shy, and unless you needed him to paint something, he struggled to interact with you. It's a shame, as I really like him and not because he's Saskia's brother; it's because he's a decent bloke.

After I waved him off, I went back into the house and straight to the kitchen, where the champagne was on the kitchen counter. I lifted it to put it in the fridge, but before I knew it, I was tearing at the foil, thinking, *fuck it*.

Before I knew it, I was two-thirds in. I had the music blaring from my small portable speaker and was dancing around the studio to 'Big Yellow Taxi'. I spied the glass fish, and it was then that I shouted at her.

"Tracey! Oh, Tracey! Come on. I know you're there. Lurking in the shadows, no doubt sweating like meth with a headache because you haven't had your daily fix of Um Bongo!"

"I like Sunny Delight, actually."

I spun and there she was, sitting on the floor, trying to cross her legs like they belonged to someone else and they wouldn't do what she wanted.

"Had a few, Jo?"

"I'm celebrating, actually."

"Really?"

"Yes, really!" I snapped. "I have this beautiful studio. Mark has practically moved in—you know, Mark? The fella you said would run like Usain Bolt as soon as you'd finished munching on me. Yes, well, he's sold his flat, and get this—we're getting married."

"Married? You? At your age? And surely you ain't got the cheek to wear white. What with your track record before you met Mark?"

"Oh, I'll be so white you'll struggle to see me in a snowstorm." I stooped down and moved my face close to hers. "I'll be white from head to toe and all the underneath bits as well. Including lacy knickers and a lacy bra." She looked at me with disgust. "Where's Tyson and the kids? I believe you had a dog hidden from me as well."

"Well, some people are funny about pets, ain't they?"

"Is that what it was to you? A pet?"

"Think of it as a guard dog."

"Why aren't you with them?"

"You know why."

"Tracey, I'm going to drink the rest of this champagne. Then I'm going to dance to Whitney Houston with my eyes closed. When I open them, I want you gone. Do you understand?"

"Whatever you say, Jo."

I warbled through 'I Wanna Dance with Somebody', and when I opened my eyes, she was indeed gone.

Tuesday, 30th July 2019

Dr. Menon called today. Apparently, my blood results indicate that I'm deficient in vitamin D. He's asked me to come in and chat about it. When I asked him if this will delay my Zoladex injection, he said we'll chat about it on Friday, when he wants to see me.

How long have I been deficient in vitamin D? I'm starting to suspect a while, as my knees could call dolphins when I walk up the stairs. Have my bones been crumbling for years and are now on the verge of turning into talc? Does this mean I can't have my ovaries out? Does this mean I can't even have the monthly Zoladex injection? If I can't have that, then my risk of cancer coming back goes through the roof.

Why can't they just tell you over the phone?!

Thursday, 1st August 2019

I met the girls tonight for tea at the wine bar. It was supposed to be one of those nights when you have a bite to eat and maybe a little Pinot. It turned into a full-on session, and no one wanted to go home. Once we were at a certain point of giggling but sober enough to be serious, Charlotte began questioning Mia about her and Rob.

"Has he improved at all at home?"

"No. I think I've married the dullest man in the world. I go home and cook tea and then watch him scratch his balls all night while he watches football. I'm as bored as an undescended testicle."

"Have you tried some sexy underwear? Maybe do a little dance. I went shopping with Jo the other day for lingerie. Maybe I could help you too."

Mia blushed. "Maybe."

Lucy was at the bar getting some more wine, and Kelly noticed she was talking to a man.

"Who's that?" We all shrugged and noticed he was playfully hitting her on the arm. She giggled and hit him back.

"Play fighting?" I remarked.

Anne tutted. "That's how it usually starts."

Lucy came back carrying two buckets and with a broad grin on her face.

"And who was that?" I asked.

"Kieran." We all stayed silent and continued to stare at her. "I used to go to school with him. I had a little crush on him, and it turns out he had one on me too." She was giggling. I wasn't sure if it was sweet or sickly. "Anyway, he asked me out, and we're going for a drink on Friday."

"Blimey, she must have beaten your record, Charlotte," said Anne. "What's the quickest time you've been asked out on a date?"

"An hour and ten. But to be fair, that was a stranger, so can we really compare?"

"Oh, come on!" Lucy protested. "The last time I saw him, he had his school tie tied around his head and thought he was sexy dancing to Madonna."

"Another scenario of how it usually starts," muttered Anne.

"So what's the score with him?" I asked.

"He's single and has been for two years. Was with Belinda Meadows for ten years, but she left him for an accountant down south. Apparently, he found them in a car—you know…at it. He said he was on antidepressants for a year after that."

"You know we're supposed to be having a laugh, right?" said Saskia. Lucy ignored her.

"But he's okay now, and he's off the tablets."

"And you found all this out while having a play fight and ordering two bottles of Prosecco on ice?" I said.

"She's efficient. I'll give her that," said Anne. "And I also give her the crown of Fastest Puller, so you need to up your game, Charlotte."

Anne was only winding Charlotte up, but it was hard to tell whether Charlotte thought it was funny or not. She remained silent, so I'm plumping for the latter. She's quite precious about her 'copping off' crown.

"How's all the new underwear?" she asked, trying to change the subject.

I shrugged noncommittally. Most of it was still in the drawer, complete with price tags. I felt different once I had it all home. It was exciting when I was trying it on in the shop, but when I got home, I realised it was simply hiding what was underneath. It wasn't going to change anything. With or without Tracey's visit, I think I would have felt exactly the same. Disappointed and slightly depressed.

"Do your boobs look fabulous in them?" asked Saskia.

"I don't have boobs. I have a mound and a tit."

"My dad drank in the Mound & Tit for years," said Anne. "It was a miners' pub, and a good time was had by all who went there. So don't knock it." She winked, and we all laughed. "No one knows what's under there except us, Mark and the doctors. You're still beautiful, and the main thing is you're still here."

Anne was right, and I knew she was thinking about her sister. How could I moan about anything? She pulls my mood back into the light when it wants to lurk in the shadows. I wondered for a moment if she would consider being by live-in life coach.

After at least a half dozen bottles of Prosecco, we decided to call it a night. Some of the girls were taking the following day off, some were working from home, but poor Kelly had to go in.

"What are you doing tomorrow?" I asked Charlotte, trying to keep her upright as the taxi pulled up.

"Judging by the way my legs won't cooperate, I'm thinking I'll be starting the day with a bottle of Gaviscon. You?"

"Nothing much." It wasn't the time to mention the emergency oncologist appointment about my vitamin D levels and the fact that my skeleton could resemble dust.

Saskia and Mia joined Charlotte in the back of the taxi and blew kisses as it pulled away. Across the road, Mark was waiting for me with a smile, as always.

Friday, 2nd August 2019

I went to see Dr. Menon with only a slight hangover for company today. He had a genuine smile when he greeted me, which threw me a little.

"Your test results have come back, and your vitamin D levels are very low. We expect them to be low, but yours were very low indeed."

"Yes."

"So, we need to start you on a fifteen-day course of supplements, and then you'll need to take one tablet every month."

"For how long?"

"We'll be monitoring your bone density every few months, so we'll just see."

"How do you monitor my bones?"

"A simple scan."

"Is this going to push my hormone therapy back?"

"No, not at all."

Why couldn't he have just said all of this on the phone?!

"How can I help increase the levels? Why are they so low?"

"Practically everyone who lives in the UK has low vitamin D. However, with you being mixed race, that makes it worse."

"Eh?"

"Your body needs more exposure to absorb the sun."

I sat there and could hear Yoda saying I had much to learn about the *dark side.* Then I thought of poor Mark. Any temperatures above eighteen degrees require a baseball cap and a dig-out for last year's Ambre Solaire. While I, on the other hand, need it to be at least twenty-five degrees before I feel I can remove my coat.

"You tend to find Asian people or people with darker skin have low levels. The tablets will elevate them. Please don't change your diet, eating more yoghurts and drinking more milk and such like. Let the medication do the work. Otherwise, you'll end up with stones." He vaguely pointed to his side and pulled a face that was enough for me to cross Activia off the shopping list.

I walked out of the clinic relieved but also slightly annoyed. I had imagined so much worse, and all it meant was I was to take more tablets for a couple of weeks. By the time I got home, I realised I was kind of glad that my vitamin D levels were low, as it meant they would monitor my bones more closely, and surely that is a good thing? My GP will send me a letter to attend the scan, so hopefully, I shouldn't have to wait too long.

I admit, dear Diary, I went to bed as soon as I came back from the hospital. Mark's convinced I'm doing too much, but we all know it's a hangover.

Wednesday, 7th August 2019

Today was injection day. I went to a different clinic—the one where they administer chemotherapy. There were lots of side wards off the corridor, each having half a dozen comfy chairs ready for patients to receive their cancer-killing medication. My room is known as the Rapid Room, probably because of the speed they can give an injection compared to chemotherapy. I now have a mental map of the hospital and feel I could direct most people to anywhere on site, including car park payment machines and the best attended toilet facilities.

A lovely nurse named Katrina called Mark and me into a bright room that smelled of lemons. I don't know why, it just did. The walls had pictures of the local area in years gone by, and they distracted me while Katrina prepared the injection.

"This will be injected into your tummy." She waved a box in front of me, and I hoped it was the contents that would be injected, not the actual box. "You may get some bruising, and it may be tender for a few days. You understand all of the side effects?"

"Basically, this will start my menopause."

"It will—" she looked at Mark "—sorry—" and they both giggled. "Some people find a little cough helps when I inject it."

"I'd rather have a little anaesthetic."

I stayed seated and lifted my top as she knelt on the floor in front of me.

"And cough."

It sounded like a staple gun had gone off and felt like someone had snapped an elastic band against me. I was pleasantly surprised. Katrina was either good at injecting or I was as hard as nails. I was absolutely fine.

"It can take around three weeks before you feel anything—if you feel anything at all. Some women sail through the treatment while others are very sensitive to side effects.

"She'll be the sensitive one," said Mark. "She once fell asleep on a roller coaster after taking a motion-sickness tablet."

While he convinced Katrina that it was true and embellished the story further, I sat there wondering if I felt different. I didn't.

"So we'll see you in four weeks, Jo. Here's your appointment card, and remember next time you come we will inject the other side of your tummy."

I said I hoped she would be administering my next one as she was so gentle, to which she informed me the whole team was lovely. I will no doubt meet them all over the next five years.

Monday, 12th August 2019

I met Amara today. I've been looking forward to catching up with her for a long time. There's a new restaurant that has opened in the city, and when we said we both wanted to go, we booked it immediately.

The restaurant didn't disappoint in interior design or food, and after a few wines, we stopped talking about work and cancer and just talked about girly stuff, which was lovely. Then, before the dessert came, we trotted off to the toilets together so Amara could check out my reconstruction.

"Oh, Jo, that's sensational. How clever are these surgeons? That scar will disappear in no time. And the one under your arm will look like an armpit crease soon. It looks amazing. No wonder you're pleased. And with your bra on, you can't even tell."

I was pleased she liked it. Strange, I know, but as she has a reconstruction herself, I felt she was informed and experienced enough to give me an honest appraisal. A cleaner tried not to look in our direction as I popped my bra back on while Amara and I suppressed our laughter.

"What must she have thought? Me groping your boobs in the toilet like that." She was laughing and spooning rhubarb mousse into her mouth at the same time.

"I feel like everyone's had a look at my tits recently, so one more won't hurt."

We finished the day off in a wine bar of her choice and drank cocktails until I felt I was at my limit to negotiate public transport. We promised to catch up soon, and I said I'd come into the office to talk of my return, which she shushed me over.

When I got home and went upstairs, Tracey was waiting for me on the bed. She had the glass fish in her hand and was polishing it with spit and her sleeve.

"Nice time?"

"Lovely, thank you." I was shouting to her while I peed in the en suite.

"She seemed impressed with your boob."

"She thought it was fabulous. No thanks to you."

I walked into the bedroom and sat in front of my dressing table, ready to take off my make-up. As I smeared my whole face with cleanser, Tracey decided to sit behind me on the bed and watch. I took my time and kept looking at her, and she would occasionally smile but didn't say anything.

"You're very quiet, Tracey." I spun to look at her.

"I know," she moaned. "Don't have much to do these days."

"Then just go," I suggested.

"I would if I could, but I can't."

When I stopped crying, she was gone.

Thursday, 15th August 2019

I went to physiotherapy today to see if they could snap some of the cords from this axillary web syndrome. I can now feel them in my torso, around my back in my shoulder muscles and as far down as my wrist. Esmé, the physiotherapist, had a good rummage around and concluded that the cords were too deep to be snapped but could be stretched, which would help with mobility.

I wished I'd taken a strong painkiller before I went, as by 'stretching' she meant digging her thumb into my armpit as far as she could and then dragging it down the length of my arm, pulling the cords along the way. I admit, dear Diary, my eyes did water, and I mentally called her a name that I'd be ashamed to confess to a priest.

Esmé was also very hands-on and gave my new breast a grope that made the other breast remember something similar happening to it outside a youth club some decades back.

"It's all moving nicely in there," she said.

What was 'all'? All that was in there was a muscle and an implant in some pigskin. There must be plenty of room in there for the three of them to move about.

Once she was happy and had used half a bottle of massage oil, she wiped me down like I'd just emerged from a car wash and sent me off with an appointment card with written details to see her the following month.

I drove home, sticking to my top, stinking of jojoba but a lot more nimble at roundabouts. 'Look for the positives', as Anne would say.

Wednesday, 21st August 2019

I think this injection is finally kicking in. I spent at least an hour in the shower crying. I don't even know why I was crying. I haven't done that since I was a teenager, and even then, it was usually instigated by something, such as Charlene and Scott getting married on *Neighbours*, and I had a fairly heavy session of the blues when Duran Duran decided not to tour in my area.

I need to get a grip of myself. I can't be like this when I go back to work, having hour-long showers, and I'll have to go back—if only to pay the water bill!

Friday, 23rd August 2019

Apart from the emotional incontinence, I've had a quiet week. No appointments with anyone. I've been completely lazy watching box sets, eating Jaffa Cakes and looking at wedding dresses. We've not set a date yet. We've just said we would know when the time was right to have that conversation, and when we did, we would try and get married as quickly as we could.

I had the girls over tonight. Mark was out with some of his climbing friends and said he would crash at his flat, as he expected to be very drunk. What will happen when we're married, we are yet to discover. Will he stop getting so drunk? Or will I have to put up with his lecherous advances, repetitive repertoire ('are you okay?' is a firm favourite) and his morning breath that could quickly tarnish brass? He'll likely have to sleep in the spare room, subject to a bed being purchased—from IKEA no doubt.

It was a funny night with the girls. Typically, they are either serious or funny. Tonight was both. The humorous element came from Lucy and her disastrous date with Kieran.

"He spent the whole night talking about Belinda, and when he wasn't talking about her, he talked about the tablets he was on and which were the best and why. I got a review of every antidepressant known to man—I felt like I needed a prescription for some myself by the end of it!"

"Well, at least you'll know which ones to ask for when you get your prescription," said Anne.

"Plus, he's a vegan."

"Oh, fuck that!" shouted Saskia. "I don't mind people who restrict their diets to whatever. But what is it about vegans where they feel the need to tell everyone about it? Hi, I'm Stefan, and I'm a vegan! Who cares, Stefan? And then they become known as Stefan the Vegan. We don't say Mel the Vegetarian or Harry with the Milk Intolerance or Sandy with a Gluten Allergy. Did you eat on your date?"

"No," replied Lucy.

"Proves my point! You didn't even go and eat, and you still know he's a vegan. They bore me to death inspecting labels in the supermarket like the food is full of Anthrax. He probably doesn't realise his depression is his subconscious telling him to eat a bleeding kebab."

"All right. Calm down." Kelly was laughing.

"Well, I won't be seeing him again," said Lucy. "I told him at the end of the night that I didn't think I could fancy him that way."

"Good! Vegans usually have appalling breath anyway." Saskia had to have the last word.

"*Did* he have appalling breath?" I whispered to Lucy.

"It was a little musky," she whispered back. I was glad Mark wasn't vegan or depressed. Though I'm not sure which is the lesser of the two evils, to be honest.

"Jo, is it okay if our Andy pops in for a second? Mum left her notebook in mine the other day, and she needs it, so Andy said he would pick it up tonight."

Within half an hour, Andy was standing in the lounge, looking a little scared by the sight of six half-cut women. I asked him about his mum's breast wall and was she happy with the colour. He seemed to relax when we were in territory he was familiar with. Before Saskia handed over the notebook, she gave a quick introduction to everyone. He nodded at everyone but smiled at Lucy, who smiled back. I clocked the look and stifled a giggle. He soon left, and I turned to Lucy.

"What's going on with you?"

"What?"

"As soon as you're within five feet of a single bloke, they go all googly-eyed."

"*Is* he single?" Lucy asked.

Saskia looked surprised. "He is."

Lucy nodded approvingly.

"Come off it! You don't fancy our Andy, do you?"

"I thought he was fit."

"I've always thought he was nice-looking, to be fair," I said.

There was an awkward silence. This was new terrain for us. Is it okay to fancy your mate's brother?

Anne broke the uneasiness rising in the room with, "The important question here is, is he a vegan?"

While Saskia was going on about how no one in her family would be able to give up meat, her phone pinged.

"Well, Lucy, that's some powerful allure you have there. Andy's asking about you."

After some to-ing and fro-ing, it was concluded that Saskia had no problem with passing Lucy's number on to Andy. I thought about if Mark and I split up, would I have allure like Lucy? Would a man walk into a room full of women and only notice me? Would I want to be noticed? It was then I saw Tracey sitting at the back of the room. She didn't speak; she didn't even smile. She just sat there and stared at me.

"I'm thinking of leaving Rob," Mia blurted out. When I looked over at Tracey to see if she had reacted to this, she had vanished.

"What?!" I said.

"I think I may have made a mistake. He's so boring, and he isn't interested in me at all."

"You're just settling into each other, that's all," I tried to reassure her.

"We have nothing to talk about," she protested.

"Mia," Charlotte started, "you've probably spent the last two years talking about your wedding. Am I right?" Mia nodded. "There was a reason you said yes to him when he proposed. But what you need to ask yourself is if you said yes simply because you wanted a wedding. If the answer's yes, then yes, you've made a mistake. But I figure you're not that stupid or shallow or vain."

"I wasn't bothered about a big wedding."

"So you said yes to him and not a wedding?"

"Of course!"

"Then remember why you said yes because all those reasons are still there. You no doubt wanted to look after him, he no doubt makes you feel safe, and he does love you. Otherwise, he would never have said 'I do'. Good men are hard to find, and you have a good one. You just need to talk to him."

"I have!"

"No, you haven't. You've moaned at him. Talk to him and tell him exactly how you feel. Show him how upset you are because, let's face it, you don't want to leave him really, do you?"

"No." Mia started to cry, and Charlotte scooped her up into her arms. Who would have thought it? Man-hungry

Charlotte would be the one to give Mia marital advice. But then I realised—that's all Charlotte actually wants. She wants a man to look after her and to be able to look after them. The funny thing is, I'm not even sure Charlotte realises that herself.

"I just thought that once we were married…well…"

"You'd have your happy-ever-after? You thought Rob was going to plant true love's kiss on your wedding day and you'd spend every night making him falafel with bluebirds on your shoulder? Life ain't like that. Men will never kiss you the same as the first one. Men will piss you off some days and make you laugh on others. And most men don't know what falafel is. You don't have a boyfriend anymore, Mia. You have a husband, and that's a whole new ball game. The rules are different now. You can't just run back to your mum's anymore. Sort it out because at the end of the day, you have a good man there."

Everyone nodded in agreement while Mia looked around the room, still clutched to Charlotte's chest. Mia apologised for bringing the vibe down on the evening, but once we turned the music up, we soon forgot about men, and I didn't see Tracey for the rest of the night.

Wednesday, 4th September 2019

Mark and I went for my second hormone therapy injection today. I'd like to say it was as painless as the first, but that would make me the biggest liar in the world! I was greeted by a nurse called Minnie, and there was nothing mouse-like about her at all. She had a voice like Sylvester Stallone, the build of an Olympic shot-putter and hands like inflated marigold gloves.

"Did you know this is the biggest injection we give to anyone?" she began.

"I don't want to know!" I tried to be light.

"It's massive!" I ignored her while she rummaged with her equipment. "Would you like to see the needle?"

"I'm sorry, Minnie, but please stop talking to me." I was willing my body to relax and trying to concentrate on my breathing. She knelt in front of me, just like the other nurse had, but there the similarities end. There was no warning, no request to cough or even an indication that instead of injecting me, she would proceed to dig it into my stomach like she was bedding plants.

"You bled a little there," she said when she pulled away.

I looked down and was reminded of John Hurt in the film *Alien*. I wanted to say so much at that point but realised I was sitting in my bra on an open ward.

She began to mop up the blood. "Do you normally bleed like that?"

"No. Never. The last time, I didn't even bruise. I wonder why that is, Minnie?"

My veiled accusation was lost on her. She twanged her gloves off her disproportionate hands and brightly informed me that it was likely I would bruise this time. I wanted to say 'or bleed to death', but by then, she had stuck a wad of something to my tummy and told me to get dressed.

"Go to the desk, and they'll make your next appointment. See you next month."

As Mark and I walked through to the clinic reception, he said I should tell them I didn't want Minnie in future.

"I can't do that! They're a team here. I say something like that, and they'll all have it in for me. For the next five years! No, I just have to hope I don't get her too often. It's not like she did it on purpose."

"You're in agony!"

"I'm not. I'm being a baby. I've had a boob cut off, remember? This is nothing."

"You're nails, you." He kissed the top of my head. I wasn't hard as nails, though. I just wanted to get home and eat a bowl of paracetamol, lie down and call Minnie fit to burn for the rest of the day.

It was a good thing Mark had come with me and was driving. When we got into the car, I discovered I couldn't fasten my seat belt over my injection site. I held the belt over me, and as I watched in the side mirror for any passing police, I noticed Tracey in the back seat, although she wasn't paying any attention to me. She seemed quite content looking out of the window. I watched her until we pulled up to the house, and I think she was gone when Mark was helping me out of the car.

Once inside, I went and lay on the couch while Mark ran around making me tea and getting me painkillers. He had a meeting to attend and was running late. I told him he didn't need to come with me to every injection, but he said he wanted to go to as many as he could. To be honest, dear Diary, I was glad he was there today. I don't know how I would have driven home.

I curse you, Minnie, and your mutant hands.

Thursday, 5th September 2019

Anne has had a mini-stroke! I called on her this morning to do some meditation, and as soon as she answered the door, I knew something was wrong. God forgive me, but for a moment I thought she was drunk. It was when she told me Kelly was out and asked if I wanted to call back later—even though the pastries were on a plate as per usual—that I knew something was seriously wrong with her. From my first-aid training in work, I suspected it could be a stroke.

The ambulance didn't take long, and Kelly arrived soon after. Within twenty minutes of them all arriving, they were off to the hospital, leaving me to lock up the house.

When I eventually got home, I sent a group text to the rest of the gang to let them know and nominated myself to find stuff out and pass it on instead of us all texting Kelly every five minutes.

It was hours later when Kelly did text. Anne was diagnosed with having a mini-stroke and, according to Kelly, was more or less back to normal, except for having no memory of the morning, me or the cinnamon swirls.

I updated the girls and told them I would get some flowers and have them in Anne's living room before she was home tomorrow. By the time they'd all transferred money into my account, I had enough to fill her bedroom as well.

Friday, 6th September 2019

I went to Kelly and Anne's house early this morning. Kelly had already gone to school to hand over to another teacher and had left the key behind a loose brick for me to get in.

I stripped the bed for them and put a wash on. I remember when I came home from the hospital and Mark had washed the bedding in my house and in his apartment. Just getting into a clean bed made me feel so much better, and I had no doubt Anne would feel the same.

I had over a hundred pounds in my account from the girls for flowers, which seemed an obscene amount to spend on something that would be dead in a week. Instead, I spent fifty pounds on two large arrangements and bought a voucher for Kelly and Anne's favourite restaurant in the village for when Anne was up to it.

It was while I was remaking the bed that it happened. I wasn't sure if it was because I was unfit and my left arm was useless, but I was suddenly aware I was warm, really warm. Then I felt a trickle of sweat meandering its way between tit and mound.

My first hot flush! It's official! I'm menopausal!

I could see my ovaries wilting like a wet Wicked Witch of the West screaming, "Curse your cancer! My youth is dying! Dying, I say, along with all my estrogen-filled eggs. Oh, my beautiful world!" then being snuffed out with a final *poof* of Zoladex.

It soon passed, and I sat on the bed, wondering what to do next. Should I text someone and tell them? Mark? No, I couldn't text him. He'd left late for work after a lazy morning of lovemaking. I didn't want him coming home to find me all shrivelled in the bed telling him my libido had been collected with the recycling bin while he was checking spreadsheets. I thought maybe I should note the time and see how often the hot flushes came. But then it dawned on me that I wasn't in labour. No one else would actually give a shit if I were having a flush—maybe I should take the same approach.

I smiled to myself, thinking about how close I was to buying a cardy.

Sunday, 8th September 2019

Me and the girls went over to see Anne today, and she looked perfectly fine. So much so, she was keen to use the restaurant voucher that night.

"But you've only just come out of hospital!" Kelly protested.

"Oh, behave! I was only in there five minutes! I've spent more time looking for my car in the multistorey car park. I'm fine."

Kelly won the argument after we all took her corner, and Anne went into a sulk, but Kelly promised her they could go later in the week.

"Well, I'm not going on Tuesday. They have two-for-one on a Tuesday, and the grey brigade come out that night. All sat there, slurping soup, and even after dessert they still dig out a Fry's Chocolate Cream that's been in their handbag for at least six weeks to give it that authentic flavour."

I laughed. "My nan used to love them."

"Well, I hope she shared it with you. You can see them all in the restaurant, rummaging in their pockets and trying to open the wrappers without anyone noticing in case they have to pass a bit to their mates. I swear some of them could peel an orange with a boxing glove on!"

I followed Kelly to the kitchen to help her make the tea and cut up the red velvet cake Saskia had brought. It was Anne's favourite.

"Don't think I didn't notice all the housework you did around the house," Kelly remarked as we made the tea. "Including the bed."

"It's nice to come home to a clean bed when you've been in a strange one."

"You're not supposed to be doing stuff like that. You're still recovering yourself."

"I had my first flush while I was making your bed."

"How was it?" She looked a little shocked.

"Hot! It didn't last long, but I will admit to finishing your bed in only my underwear."

"Is there anything you can take?"

"Nothing. I can't even take herbal stuff, as there's some evidence it can stimulate estrogen in your body."

"Shit! From a plant?"

"Yep. So, I am now your sweaty friend for the foreseeable."

She hugged me. "I love you, my one-titted, sweaty friend, and thank you again for everything. I'm so glad you and Anne are friends. Out of everyone, you're the one I wanted her to like the most."

"Why?"

"Because I love you the most. But don't tell the others." She sniggered and grabbed the tray; I followed her into the lounge.

We stayed for another hour and then all left at the same time. When I got home, I kept thinking about Anne—what if she'd had a big stroke instead of a mini one? I couldn't help but compare her illness to mine. At least I had a warning that my sickness was coming. At least I had time to come to terms with it and consider my options. But to have a stroke while you're arranging pastries one morning—it scares the shit out of me.

For the first time in my life, I felt lucky to only have had cancer.

Wednesday, 11th September 2019

I've had another day spent crying like an old black-and-white movie star. Every time I walked past my bed, I threw myself on it and burst into tears. I hate these injections and what they're doing to me. I pride myself in being positive. I try and find the fun in everything and anything. But Zoladex is the vampire of any happy emotion I'm clinging to.

I thought doing some yoga might help—until I noticed that the mound is puckering when I clench, which sent my mood spiralling to the depths. And who met me at the bottom? Tracey. She was sitting on the bed when I finished my latest bout of wailing into the pillow. I looked at her and sniffed.

"I hate you."

"I know."

"When will you go?"

"That's out of my control. And I suspect it's out of yours as well, sweetheart."

"Don't you sweetheart me," I hissed.

"Look, don't get aggy with me. You got what you wanted. You got your reconstruction. You kept your hair. You even got a proposal, so why you bitching and crying all the time?"

"Because I have to take tablets every day. Because I have to have an injection every month to stop you from moving back into my life."

"And here I am."

"I'm never going to be able to get rid of you, am I? What the fuck?!"

"At least you have someone. You've got all your mates and this house. Who have I got? Tyson and the kids are gone. I haven't even got the dog to keep me company."

"You don't deserve anything! You're a parasite!"

"I did you a favour."

"You did no such thing! You made me sick, and I will be constantly reminded of that every day."

"What? When you take your stupid pill?"

"No! When I look in the fucking mirror and see what you did to my body, you bitch!"

"Is that it?"

"What?"

"You think you're so special. Well, you're not! Get off your high horse cos you need to realise you're riding a fucking donkey. I didn't pick you cos I think you're great cos you can make a bed when someone's had a stroke or sort people's love lives out or make shit plates out of clay. I picked you cos I could, cos you were there, and cos I couldn't be arsed to go to anyone else."

I didn't know what to say to her. She was right, though. I was nothing special. Why did I ever think it would happen to someone else? For all the times I had given to charity, I never thought that one day those donations could help me. How could I have been so naïve? How could I have been so blasé about my life, my health, my vulnerability?

I walked to the bathroom and washed my face, which made me feel a bit better. I went downstairs to watch TV, and Tracey sat beside me for a while, but once the programme got interesting, she went to wherever it is she disappears to.

Saturday, 14th September 2019

Mark's officially moved in. The sale completed today, and in four trips, with Andy's transit van, we finally got all his stuff in.

Over the last few weeks, we've been selecting what to keep from my house or his. It was a reasonably painless exercise. We soon realised that my soft furnishings were the best, while he had all the top-of-the-range electrical stuff. I've sold my washing machine, fridge, microwave and TV while Mark's sold his sofa and bed. The new owners of the flat have inherited a lot of free stuff including plates, a vomit-inducing rug and half of IKEA.

There's still too much stuff, but we don't care. We said we'll see what gets neglected and makes the grade over the next few weeks. Those poor items that don't make it through to the next round will be going to the tip.

I can't believe he's moved in. I still feel like this is just my house. How long will it take before I can say it's ours? Perhaps because he paid for it, it feels like 'ours' when we're in the studio, which is strange in a way, as that will be the only room in the house that is all mine, my space.

All of our friends are pleased that we've finally taken this step. We should have done it ages ago. Cancer has made us both realise that there isn't time to waste. It's not like we're on a ticking clock. Well, actually, we are. I think before I was ill, I knew I was going to die one day, but I figured I would be old and grey in a nursing home, dribbling oxtail soup down my chin. Cancer makes you hear that clock. All of a sudden, you become aware of the ticking. Sometimes it's quiet, but even when it's hard to hear, you're aware of it. It's always there. Sometimes it's loud, and the only way you can drown it out is to do something, plan something, see someone, tell someone.

The best way to ignore it is to live.

Monday, 16th September 2019

I went to the doctor's today for my latest sick note. I have been getting sick notes for two months at a time, but this time, I asked for six weeks instead. While I'm still having lots of symptoms such as the pains in my muscles and the uncontrollable crying, nothing is stopping me from returning to work sooner rather than later. My appointments have taken on a pattern now, which means I can revolve my work life around them, as I know when they're going to pop up.

I called our HR department and told them I'd like to return to work on 28th October. They sounded pleased I was coming back and said they'd arrange a meeting for me to see someone in Occupational Health and organise a phased return.

I'm not going to lie, dear Diary, I'm scared about going back to work. I feel my brain has gone to mush and I've forgotten how to do my job. I'm also worried about having a hot flush and a crying fit right in the middle of a meeting.

The doctor was very understanding and said if I didn't feel I could return then to come back for another note.

He went as far to say he wasn't sure I had dealt with my illness emotionally. I could not be any more emotional if I tried, and I have no choice but to deal with it when all of that emotion is running down my face. I told him I was fine, and he silently nodded as he passed me the note.

When I left the surgery, I felt I was missing a trick. Is there a standard way of dealing with cancer? Had I gone rogue with my own unique mode of survival? I didn't feel I had neglected myself emotionally. I know exactly what I've been through and still continue to go through. Is this not why I meditate, do yoga and drink far too much Prosecco? I've been watching comedies for months to keep positive. I haven't allowed anyone to say negative things in front of me and have completely avoided negative people. I try and find ways to help people, so I'm passing good vibes on. I stopped feeling guilty for having cancer, as guilt is a negative emotion. But most of all, I've danced every day—in the shower, in my underwear, while I dry my hair—I even wiggle my arse when I brush my teeth. I would twerk to a hymn if I knew it would make me feel good.

So I'm sorry, Doctor, I don't agree. I think I've been dealing with my emotions just fine. Yes, they might overwhelm me a little lately, but that's just because I've only done two rounds of Zoladex. Wait until I know all its moves and then we'll see who has the upper hand.

Friday, 20th September 2019

I went out with the girls tonight. We all went to the wine bar except for Kelly and Anne, who were at the restaurant using the voucher we bought. They met with us later, and Anne looked really well.

They'd been there for an hour when I noticed Anne giving Kelly a nod, which she reciprocated.

"Anne and I have an announcement to make."

We all stopped and stared.

"Are you two getting married?" Charlotte asked.

"No. We're going travelling. We've been talking a lot this week, and I've decided to take a career break for a year."

"And I've decided to rent out my house," added Anne. We all sat for a moment, slightly stunned. The silence became apparent as we tried to process what had just been said. I felt the need to pierce it.

"Where are you going to go? What about your health, Anne? Aren't you frightened you'll have another stroke?"

"I'd rather have a stroke trying to see something than sitting in my armchair being frightened of life."

"Me too," agreed Mia.

"I'll follow all the doctor's orders and give myself the best chance not to have another one, but that's it."

"What's all this about?" asked Charlotte. "Is this like a Make A Wish thing? Are you dying?"

That was when I knew that Kelly and Anne could also hear the ticking clock. To leave their lives behind for a whole year, it must be deafening.

"No, on the contrary, Charlotte." Anne smiled.

"We've contacted an agency online, and they sort it all for us. They help with transport, accommodation and trips."

"Where does it start?" I asked.

"We fly to Paris on the first of January," said Kelly.

"January?!" I squealed. "That's only a few months away!"

Around the table, the mood dropped like a stone.

"We thought you'd be happy," whispered Kelly.

"We're just going to miss you, that's all. It's a wonderful idea, isn't it, girls?"

Saskia raised a glass and made a toast. "To living."

After the toast, I went to the toilet for a cry, as usual. I had grown fond of Anne and would miss her terribly, probably more than Kelly, not that I would tell anyone that. When I came out of the cubicle, Anne was there waiting for me.

"I'm going to miss you too, kid." She opened her arms, and I let her scoop me up. We said no more in the toilet. In silence, she waited as I fixed my make-up and took a deep breath. Then she moved to the door, indicated for me to smile and opened it.

When we re-joined the girls at our table, I was relieved to hear the subject had changed. Lucy was being pushed to reveal the details of her date with Andy.

"Oh, you've had a date then?" I asked.

"A date? She's seen him every night this week," revealed Saskia. "I'm surprised she's here tonight, to be honest."

"Every night?" Charlotte sniggered. "Blimey, he must be good!"

"Not like that!" Lucy protested. "He's been charming. Probably the sweetest man I've met."

"Our Andy?!" Saskia looked aghast.

"To be fair, Saskia, your Andy is quite sweet," I said. "I've always liked him."

"You like him because he gives you mates' rates when he does your painting."

"It's not just that!"

Lucy went on to regale us with details of her week and all the dates she'd been on with Andy. She looked really happy and blushed at certain points in her stories. I'm made up for her.

Even though it was a good night, I still felt sad when I got home. I felt sad that Kelly and Anne would soon be leaving and at the thought of Lucy and Andy, which is ridiculous. Everyone is moving on, getting on with their lives, while I'm still in the cancer arena. Even though I don't have it anymore, I still feel like a cancer patient. Will this feeling ever go away?

Wednesday, 25th September 2019

I had a stand-up row today with the pharmacist. Every time I put in a prescription, they don't have the drugs I need. They always have to phone someone to see if they can get my medication, and whoever it is they're calling refuses to answer the phone.

The row came about when they tried to fob me off with an inferior brand. The hospital says you should not mix your brands of tablets, as some of them can give you more side effects than others. When I said I couldn't accept the tablets offered, the pharmacist said they needed to make a call. Fifteen minutes later, I was told they'd continue to try and call whoever and could I come back in an hour? Which I did.

An hour later, still no tablets. They'd forgotten to make another call, and once again, I was told to come back another hour later. Which I did.

By lunchtime, I was still without tablets. I asked the pharmacist for my prescription back so I could go to another chemist, but they couldn't find the prescription and advised me to go to the doctor's to get another one. I blew my stack!

By the time I'd finished screaming about cancer, mastectomies and incompetent pharmacists, he was back on the phone, at my suggestion, to another pharmacy, which had them in stock. I was *yet again* told to come back an hour later, to which I said I would be back four hours later as I was tired of doing the fucking Hokey Cokey and next time I came I wanted it to be the last.

When I returned at four, my tablets were there.

"We've even got an extra supply for when you come back," said the pharmacist.

"Did you grow up next to a nuclear reactor?! Do you honestly think I would come back here?!"

I came home and meditated just to try and calm myself down. It didn't work, so I drank Prosecco instead. That did the trick.

Thursday, 26th September 2019

I saw the physiotherapist today. My arm has been feeling strange, and I'm worried I'm developing lymphoedema. I measure the arm every two hours, which I know is excessive, but I'm worried sick.

As soon as I arrived at Esmé's office, I told her about my latest obsession and asked if there was anything she could say to me to wean me off my tape measure addiction.

While she greased her hands, I stripped off from the waist up and climbed onto the table. She went straight to the area I said was strange and pummelled my mound like she was playing air hockey.

"It's just webbing, Jo. It's all really stiff, and it's spread down the arm and across the chest to the reconstruction. That's why it feels strange."

"Are you sure?"

"I'm almost positive. Has the measurement changed at all?"

"No."

"Then I'm sure it's not lymphoedema. Let's do some exercises and see if we can loosen it all up and stretch some of the internal scarring."

After a massage, which was agony and pleasurable at the same time, we did some yoga together. She could tell I'd been doing the exercises she'd advised on the previous visit, and with some kind of compass, she could see my mobility range had improved by fifteen degrees. Apparently, this is amazing. While I exercise every day, I'm no Jane Fonda, but Esmé went on to tell me about all the women who say they're exercising and clearly aren't, then bitch about moving like C3PO.

"Let me see you next week, and if you still feel that there's an issue, we can refer you to the lymphoedema clinic."

My heart sank. I wished I hadn't said anything. I started to feel that just talking about it was going to make it happen, as if I was attracting the inevitable, and if I'd kept my trap shut, then it would all go away.

Back home, I immediately had a shower to wash the grease off. My mound feels a little looser and softer, to be fair. I realise I need to massage it more, even though it knocks me bandy. I'm okay looking at it, but to touch a part of your body and only feel it in your hand confuses your brain. So, because of that, I've avoided the area, except for washing. Even Mark isn't allowed there anymore. What's the point if I can't feel anything?

As I was massaging Bio-Oil into my scars, Tracey appeared. She perched on the edge of the bath, still wearing filthy leggings and a T-shirt that had a Care Bear on the front.

"How much will they fade, you reckon?" she asked, watching me apply the oil.

"Don't know. We'll see."

"You measured that arm since you been home?"

"No."

"Are you gonna?"

"No."

"I'll give you 'til teatime, and then you'll be pulling that measuring tape around your arm like a smackhead."

"It's fine. I'm just being paranoid."

She watched me the whole time I was massaging my scars, which I found slightly creepy. I went into the bedroom and put the music on through my phone, dancing as I got dressed. Tracey stayed in the bathroom. She usually follows me from room to room, but she just stayed on the edge of the bath, and every time I walked in there, she silently watched me.

When I went downstairs, I kept the music on and started Mark's tea. As far as I could tell, Tracey stayed in the bathroom. It's been strange with her lately. She seems a lot quieter and at times a little lonely. She doesn't seem as aggressive as she once was, and when I see her, I feel less angry.

I'm not sure if that's because I'm recovering, meditating or drinking a lot of Prosecco. Whatever helps, I suppose.

Friday, 27th September 2019

I went for my first bone scan today. It seems pushing me into the menopause could have a detrimental effect on my bones, so they need a baseline result. I then have to go every now and again to see if there have been any changes.

The waiting room was like the casting couch for the film *Cocoon*. I was the youngest in there, by far. I guess osteoporosis usually only hits you when you're older. But then again, menopause should not have hit me until I was older.

When I was called, I was taken to a large room and was asked to lie straight down on the bed. No gappy gowns! No injections! I could even keep my trainers on.

"Do you have any underwires in your bra?"

"I do. I can take it off." I was wearing the peach silk bra, which had become my favourite. I had no qualms about whipping it off and casually draping it on a chair for her to admire.

"No, we'll work around it." Then without warning, she groped through my jumper, found the wires and gave them a firm shove over my chest. I wanted to admonish her for treating my delicate underwear with such dismissiveness, but while I was thinking of something to say without sounding like a tool, she strapped my feet to a large block at the foot of the bed.

"Stay still." And then she disappeared.

The machine began to whir, and a large arm swept over my body. The sound reminded me of the photocopier in work. Five minutes later, I was unstrapped, and I was able to pop my boobs back where they belonged.

"Can I just say, you smell lovely!" She gave a large sniff. I felt if she had seen my bra, it would have been the highlight of her day. "What is it you wear?"

"Jo Malone. Myrrh and Tonka Bean."

"Never heard of it. Is it expensive?"

"About eighty pounds, I think."

"I can't afford that!"

I wanted to say I wasn't selling it to her.

"Maybe get your fella to buy you some for Christmas," I suggested and scooped up my bag, reading from her body language that she was about to tell me the tale of her fella or the fact she didn't have one. I reached for the door and gave a squeaky goodbye over my shoulder.

I should have the results in a week. Fingers crossed I have bones as dense as my breasts. Or breast, now.

Wednesday, 2nd October 2019

I went for my monthly injection today and prayed the whole journey there that I wouldn't encounter Minnie again. Someone must've been listening, as I met a new nurse whom I liked immediately. She gave me the injection without fuss or feeling the need to provide me with commentary throughout, and within twenty minutes of check-in, I was back on the road.

I decided to call in at Anne's on the way home. I haven't seen her since her and Kelly's announcement. When I arrived at the house, there were two men loading what I recognised to be one of Anne's sideboards into the back of a van. She saw my confusion as I walked up the path.

"You moving out already?"

"No, I'm just selling some bits and bobs. The antique shop in Avon Road took a few pieces off me. That's them finishing now."

When I went into her lounge, it looked sparse. Two of the sideboards had gone, as well as a large display cabinet and a writing bureau.

"I look like I'm in witness protection." Anne chuckled. "But to be honest, I should have gotten rid years ago. I'm sure the wood from that bureau was from the *Marie Celeste*. Most of this belonged to my mum and dad. I kept it all for sentimental reasons, which is daft. Why should I feel any closer to my mother simply because I have her smelly old sideboard? And Kelly never said a thing. She must've felt she was living in a bloody time warp."

"Are you selling everything?"

"That's the idea."

"But what about when you come back?"

"We'll have a huge shopping trip." She laughed. "There's a couple of things I want to keep in storage, though. Pictures mostly and some of the china, but apart from that, it can all go. Then I'm going to get Andy in, and he can paint it all, ready for rental."

"You won't have problems renting this. Everyone loves this road."

"I would have had problems if I'd left it like *Acorn Antiques*. I need it to look modern, minimal, European, as you lot do now."

"You should get my Mark over. He'd have this place looking more Swedish than the chef from *The Muppet Show*."

"Anyway, to what do we owe this impromptu visit?"

"I've just had my injection and thought you could give me sympathy while making me a cup of tea. But you must be tired after all the shifting of furniture."

"I shifted nothing! I just pointed at stuff and they loaded the truck. They didn't even accept a cuppa."

"Well. There you go then. You've not wasted the boiled kettle, so crack on," I joked.

I was only going to visit for an hour. It turned out to be four. We talked of her and Kelly's up-and-coming adventures and how much she would be able to cross off her bucket list. It got me thinking about my bucket list and all the things I had yet to do. It scared me slightly when I realised how little I've achieved in my life. What if my diagnosis had been terminal? It would have been too late to do all the things I wanted to do. For the first time, I felt very mortal. It's not like I ever thought I was immortal, but like I say, now I can hear the ticking clock of my life.

I'm not even sure what's on my bucket list. Sure, I want to travel. I want to do the usual things—drive across America in a Ford Mustang, be pulled by huskies through marshmallowy, snow-laden trees—you know, all that crap. But there are other things, strange things, that I've often thought I would love to do. Such as:

1. Walk in a huge, flamboyant costume in the New Orleans Mardi Gras.

2. Look into the mouth of a volcano.

3. Swing my legs off the Great Wall of China.

4. Spit off the top of the Eiffel Tower.

5. Wash an elephant (not in a zoo!).

6. Dance to the Argentinian Tango.

7. Camp in a desert and look at the stars.

8. Wash my hair in a waterfall.

9. Host a fabulous party on a yacht (with a select group).

10. Learn the piano.

A strange list, I know. But these are some of the things that have crossed my mind and made me smile. I've swum with sharks and dolphins and various other aquatic creatures. I've been in the jungle and found it sweaty. I've climbed trees in the blue mountains of Jamaica and picked coconuts, but I haven't done the things that I actually want to do. Can I do any of these before I die? Some of them are easier than others. When should I start crossing them off? If I start now, I may feel like I'm terminal already. But if I leave it, when will be the right time? At what point in your life do you say, 'I want to live properly'?

For Anne, it was having a mini stroke.

"When are you back in work?" asked Anne.

"I'm due back on the twenty-eighth of October."

"Is that not a bit soon?"

"No, I'll be okay."

She didn't seem convinced and started to probe about how I was affected mentally. I had to tell her that the only thing making me mental was the Zoladex and my shrivelled ovaries. She suggested that we both take our shrivelled ovaries on a play date in a few days to a new place in town that does meditation.

I'm looking forward to it.

Tuesday, 9th October 2019

I met Amara today during her lunch hour to discuss my return to work. She doesn't think I'm ready to come back either and enquired if Occupational Health had been in touch.

"They're calling me on the fifteenth of October."

"Well, let's wait until we hear what they say and see if there are adjustments we need to make."

"Like what? I haven't lost a leg or anything."

"You complain about the pain on your left side."

"Yeah, but that's nothing."

"Why are you rushing back?"

I didn't think I was rushing back. I simply wanted some normality back in my life.

"I'm okay, Amara." It was all I could say.

It was then that I noticed she seemed nervous, and not thirty seconds later, she dropped the bombshell.

"I'm leaving the paper."

I'm not sure if it was lack of estrogen or the impending lack of her, but I spontaneously burst into tears. She pulled me to her, and I sobbed and sobbed. She held me like I was her baby and kept smoothing my hair while I snotted over her Hobb's silk blouse.

"What am I going to do without you?"

"You don't need a manager, Jo. You look after yourself!"

"I don't mean that!"

"And this is why I don't think you're ready to come back. If you don't think you can deal with work without me, then you definitely aren't emotionally ready."

"It's just a shock. Where are you going?"

"I don't know yet. But I've done all I can here. I want a new challenge. A man called Harry will be taking over my role."

I was surprised and pulled away from her.

"Who the fuck is Harry?! Where did he come from?"

"He's worked at *The Northern Journal* for over ten years."

"He's had an interview?!"

"Of course."

"When?"

She looked awkward. "I didn't want to tell you until you'd recovered."

"Well, according to you, I'm still recovering! Hang on, when are you leaving?"

"This Friday," she whispered.

I sat there, stunned, and quietly wished my latte was wine. I felt like a child. Not because I was crying but because she hadn't told me. Is this what it feels like when a child is told their parents are getting divorced? I realised I was overreacting. This woman was my boss, my friend. She was not my carer, my mother or anything else that suggested she should be there to hold my hand until I said it was okay to let go.

"Sorry for whinging," I sniffed.

"You'll be fine, sweetheart. Let's not forget you're the one who keeps saying you're going to leave one day."

"But that's to do my pottery."

"Well, you have Mark living with you now, which will help with the bills."

"What are you suggesting?"

"All I'm saying is you do what you want. Cancer has a funny way of making you take stock and realise what's important."

Was dancing in the Mardi Gras or spitting in Paris important? It didn't seem so as I drank from a cup with my name scrawled on it, but when I thought of a future me lying in my bed and waiting to die...yes, it was important. I looked at Amara; she smiled, and her eyes welled up. She knew where my mind had gone.

"Promise me we'll always be friends," I sniffed.

"Always. I love you very much, Jo."

As I drove home, I wondered if it was Amara's cancer that had made her want to leave. Did she have her own Tracey who constantly reminded her that life was delicate, precarious and sometimes desperately frail? Did someone visit her in the night and creep into the darkness of her bed and the shadows in her mind? Or am I the only one who wakes in the navy night and watches someone play with my discarded bra? I'm not sure Tracey knows I'm awake, observing, peeping over the covers. She's not always there. It happens less and less these days as I get used to the strange feeling of the implant in my body. But there are nights when I've been lying on my tummy, and I wake and I see her. Those are the nights I'm grateful to cuddle my sleeping Mark.

Monday, 14th October 2019

I called the GP's today for my bone scan results. I will admit, dear Diary, I thought they would say everything was normal and then I could carry on watching season seven of *Ru Paul's Drag Race*.

"The results show you are osteopoenic. Can you come into the surgery and discuss with the doctor?"

I was a little shocked. How can I be? I'm not old.

The surgery has late-night opening most nights now, and they made an appointment for me this evening. I didn't see my usual doctor, but the lady I did see was very nice. She explained that there are signs of bone thinning in my hips, and due to my cancer and Zoladex injections, she felt it best to refer me to a rheumatologist. I now have to wait for a letter from the hospital, but in the meantime, she advised me to walk more and run more.

"Maybe dance for ten minutes a day."

This woman has no idea how close I am to buying a ghetto blaster and a large piece of cardboard for the floor as I'm dancing that much.

Something else I now need to deal with.

Tuesday, 15th October 2019

A lady called Vicky from Occupational Health called today. I was slightly sceptical as to how the call would be handled. I honestly thought she would read from a tick-box list and the computer would tell her what to say. But she actually talked to me like a human being. She asked all about my surgeries and knew all the technical terms when I tried to dumb things down for her.

"So are you finished with everything now?"

"Treatment wise?"

"Yes, and visits to the hospital."

"No, I'm still under the oncologist, who I will see in a few weeks. Then I have my weekly appointments with the physiotherapist."

I went on to explain my cording, and she corrected me when she noted axillary web syndrome. I was impressed.

"I'm also under the cancer clinic to receive ovarian suppression injections into my tummy."

"Zoladex?"

"Yes."

"Any other tablets?"

"I'm on daily Tamoxifen."

"Anything else?"

"I take a monthly dose of twenty thousand units of Vitamin D. I've been taking them for around three months."

"Anything else?"

"Yes, I'm also being referred to a rheumatologist as I have been told I am osteopoenic. But it's just in my hips." I'm not sure that made any difference.

She summarised what I'd told her, what I was currently taking and ongoing appointments, and what was happening in the near future.

"I'm going to send a report to your manager, which is Harry Hudson." I didn't know that was Harry's surname. He sounded like a lighthouse owner from an Enid Blyton book. "Unfortunately, I can't sign you off as fit for work for at least eight to ten weeks."

I was stunned and remained quiet while she explained why she couldn't sign me off as fit and suggested I go to my GP and get another sick note to cover the period of absence she recommended. There was no negotiation about it; I could not go back to work.

Mark was working from home today and listened to the call, as I had it on the loudspeaker.

"Can you believe that?" I asked when I hung up.

"I agree with her, Jo. Even I didn't realise how much you're still recovering until I just listened to all of that. You're under so many doctors—Christ, you're still being referred and being diagnosed with new stuff. Even Amara said the other day you weren't ready to go back."

"She was talking emotionally, though."

"Which is another thing. That woman on the phone didn't even ask questions about how your head is."

"I'm fine."

"You're not fine! You were crying the other day when you missed the bin man and then ripped my head off when I turned the heating up."

"I can't help it! My body temperature keeps going up and down. I feel like a well-fiddled hotel toaster." He came over and hugged me. "Am I a nightmare?" I moaned.

"Yep, but it's okay. You need to realise that just because you feel better doesn't mean you are better."

Even though she has now left work, I called Amara and told her, and she seemed relieved. Everyone seems to think this is for the best. But is it? I'm the one who's left at home with only Tracey for company.

Friday, 18th October 2019

I'm not sure Mark wants to marry me anymore. We went out this evening for a meal, which was lovely, but whenever I broached the subject about dates, he kept saying we'd sort it out in the New Year. I can't even get a rough timeline out of him. Maybe the thought of being with someone with one boob, of constantly being reminded of cancer with hospital visits is too much for him to take on for the rest of his life. I tried to push it.

"Just a general time of year?" I asked.

"Maybe in the summer."

"Next year?"

"Maybe."

"Well, when were you thinking?"

"I hadn't really thought about it much. What do you think of these curry bombs?"

And that is how most of the conversation went. The only thing he would commit to was his opinion of the naan bread. A glowing review of, "I could just eat this and not bother with the rest." I wish he'd said that sooner. It could have saved us at least £50 in unnecessary accompaniments like chicken tikka masala and lamb sagwalla, to say the least.

I didn't push anymore about the date. I feel a little sick about it. Surely he wouldn't have moved in if he was going off me. I might leave raising it again until nearer Christmas, or when we next go to IKEA. He'll be in a good mood then.

Wednesday, 23rd October 2019

Anne and I ventured to town today to check out the new meditation sessions at the 'Recently Refurbished Old Soup Factory', according to the website.

"Still got a smell of mulligatawny about it, if you ask me," sniffed a not-impressed Anne as she walked in.

After getting changed in what was the old changing room for the long-gone factory workers, we were signposted to a room that was too large for the crowd that came. I say crowd: there were six of us. Seven if you include the woman who was teaching the class.

Resplendent in a pink leotard and black legging combo, she set herself up in the middle of the old factory floor, and like a flock of lambs, we found a space within earshot of her. The room was drab, grey and cold. A lot of the windows were rattling with the wind, and at various points, huge chunks of plaster were missing from the walls.

"Dragging out the old canning machines does not constitute refurbishment," Anne whispered as she settled onto the old lino floor. I sat next to her and waited for the instructor to start.

"Hi, all. My name is Joan, and I'll be guiding you through a wonderful meditation experience."

"We'll be the judge of that," muttered Anne. Joan didn't hear her.

"But before we start, let me tell you a little about me. I'm married to a wonderful, wonderful man. I live in a wonderful house in Cheshire with our two dogs and two cats. I wasn't blessed with children, but I live a very full and wonderful life. I organise events, offer mentoring services and also create wonderful vlogs about accessorising your home, called Style over Shop." She looked at us all expectantly, but the half dozen blinking faces confirmed to her that we had yet to stumble on her digital show.

"What does your wonderful husband do?" shouted Anne.

"He's in banking," she said with pride.

"That's wonderful," boomed a sarcastic Anne.

Joan looked a little perturbed as to why Anne was not suitably impressed. When I glanced at Anne, she rolled her eyes and shook her head.

Joan, who had clearly learned how to meditate via YouTube, started the session lecturing us about the benefits of breathing. She didn't go as far as explaining anything wider than 'breathing in and out is essential'. While I was trying to get through the session, which was undoubtedly going to be our only one, I concentrated on ignoring Anne's swearing next to me.

"Now, I want you to find a point on the wall behind me, and when it gets a bit blurry, close your eyes."

"What? Like that growing damp patch over there?" shouted Anne.

Some of the girls began to snigger. I closed my eyes and hoped Joan would continue. My bum was starting to get numb from the cold, lino-covered, concrete floor.

"Keep breathing, girls."

Joan began to talk of a light. It wasn't like when Anne talks of a light that envelops you and makes you feel warm and fuzzy. Joan just said I could see a light, and in my head, a forty-watt bulb appeared. She kept saying to look at the light, as it was supposed to help me relax, but all I kept wondering was if it was one of those economy bulbs and what was the difference in electricity costs between the light bulb in my head and the energy-saving ones Mark buys in IKEA.

Soon after, Joan decreed we should be in a perfectly relaxed state, but I wasn't. I was wishing I had kept my coat on and was desperate to rub my upturned hands together. After about fifteen minutes, I became aware of someone moving next to me, and when I squinted to see what was happening, I saw the lady on my left tiptoeing out of the room. I look to my right to see if Anne had noticed only to discover she wasn't there! I decided there was only one thing for it, and that was to do a runner if my stiff frozen legs would uncurl beneath me.

If Joan did see me leave, she never said. I crept out with her behind me telling people to listen to the gentle music and, of course, to keep breathing. Maybe Joan didn't think her CPR skills were up to much and that's why she felt it necessary to keep telling people to huff and puff.

When I got to the changing room, there was no sign of Anne or her belongings. I went into my bag, and sure enough, she had texted me.

In the horses over the road

Within five minutes, I was in the Coach & Horses pub, where a glass of wine was waiting for me.

"What a crock of shit that was!" Anne said as she passed me my drink.

"When did you go?!"

"Somewhere between her telling me to listen to my lungs and me praying for a happy death!"

"How bad was that?" I started to laugh.

"Fifteen pounds! She's got a bloody cheek. I wouldn't have minded listening to all that nonsense if I was warm. My Aunty Nelly worked in that building years ago. She always had blue hands, and I thought it was from the ink on the fish soup labels. She always did have trouble opening a jar of Branston pickle in her later years."

"Just Branston, yeah?" I laughed.

"Well, she didn't like any other brand," sniffed Anne. "So, I think up until the end of the year, we'll stick with my front room, eh? While I may not prompt you to *breathe in and out*, I do offer a wide selection of pastries and the occasional glass of fizz."

"We never have fizz!"

"That's because you don't bleeding bring any!" I made a mental note to take some next time I went.

We stayed for another small wine, and then I dropped Anne back at her house before I came home and ran a bath to warm me back up.

Tracey watched me as I undressed, but we didn't speak.

Saturday, 26th October 2019

Mark and I had a huge fight today. It started because I said I wanted to go to a ceramic gallery, which he said he couldn't. He could, he just didn't want to. It then escalated to all the dumb places he drags me around without complaint and how he never wants to do any of my stuff. I also pointed out that it was a long way and I needed him to drive. I know I could have said it a bit more tactfully, but after an hour of dodging his protruding bottom lip, I couldn't be arsed trying to make it sound good. It got to the point where I didn't want to go anyway, and when I said this, he started muttering about me doing more meditation as the tablets were making me a crank.

I went apeshit!

He's been gone for four hours.

It's not the tablets, it's him.

I'm convinced he doesn't love me anymore.

Sunday, 27th October 2019

Mark came back late last night. He went to his mate's until he figured I'd calmed down. We had a good talk about blaming the tablets and agreed that while I may get emotional at times, I tend to be weepy, not angry.

"To be honest, you were a bitch before you got cancer," he joked.

"Exactly! So don't blame my hormones. It's all me coming at you."

I did toy with the idea of addressing his lack of commitment when it came to setting a wedding date, but I bottled it. Maybe he just wants us to stay living together and not get married. A year ago, I'd have been happy with that. But since then, I have had a proposal.

I apologised for making him feel like a glorified taxi driver, which he said he wouldn't have minded if he got paid.

I paid him later in kisses and more.

Friday, 1st November 2019

We went to a Halloween party tonight. There was a huge crowd of us in Archie's Wine Bar, including my mates and some of Mark's. It was fancy dress, so I went as Maleficent while Mark went as a Ghostbuster, complete with pipes robbed from the Henry hoover.

The girls all looked great, especially Lucy and Andy, who came as a gangster and his moll. We watched them all loved up on the dance floor.

"There are certain points in a relationship when you know you've crossed the next line. The comfortable line," began Charlotte. "It starts with no make-up, then you skip a shower hoping he doesn't notice. Then you start farting, shitting in front of him while he brushes his teeth, and then you ask him to buy you tampons. Finally, you go to a fancy-dress shop and walk out with your matching rent-an-outfit, clutching your shared ticket."

"Well, she's crammed a lot in a short space of time, I'll give her that," quipped Anne, watching the dancing couple.

"Do you shit in front of Mark?" Charlotte asked me.

"Mark and I have made some very important decisions while defecating," I said.

"I hope one of them was not to refer to it as defecating! What are you? Ninety?"

"Okay! Pooping then!"

"What are you? Nine?"

Mark came over with a round of drinks, and soon all of his mates were joining in the poo debate about whether it was acceptable and at what point in a relationship it was okay to do it in front of each other. Most people thought three months of a steady relationship was an appropriate time to introduce 'shitting in an open gallery', as Rob called it.

The conversation moved to the weird places we had all taken a dump. Anne won when she told us of stumbling into an Amish community on her travels years ago.

"It was either ask them or take a shit in their neighbouring woods. So they pointed to a shack that was no bigger than two feet by two. I thought to myself, beggars can't be choosers, but when I went in, there was only a hole in the mud floor. I was going to leave, but then I noticed a man standing outside, keeping guard."

"Did you go?"

"I didn't feel like it anymore. When he let me out, I told him he should watch the film *Witness* and see how Harrison Ford built a barn because their toilet facilities were shocking."

"So technically, you didn't take a dump," said Mark.

"I went back to the woods and took my chances with the poison ivy instead. What do I win?"

"Our deepest respect and admiration!" Andy shouted.

The rest of the night followed a similar vein of talking rubbish, drinking lots and sweaty dancing.

And not once did I think of cancer!

Tuesday, 5th November 2019

Had my monthly injection today, which went fine. Even driving home didn't hurt as much, probably because I remembered to take some painkillers beforehand.

When I got home, Tracey was waiting for me on the bed. She watched me while I changed into a pair of pants with a more comfortable waistband.

"You don't complain about the pain in your boob anymore."

"It's not a boob. But for your information, it hurts much less now."

"You still don't like touching it, do you?"

"I don't need to."

"I've seen you in the shower. You practically grimace when you cover it with soap."

"And who's to blame for that?"

"Again? Seriously? Aren't you bored of this?"

"Aren't you bored of me?"

"I wish I had that luxury, sweetheart. I wish I could up and leave here, but you won't let me!"

"What?"

"You're the one keeping me here!"

"I'm doing no such thing!"

"Every time you look in the mirror or when you have a shower or when you put a bloody bra on or even if you see Mark glance at your chest, you see me over his shoulder, don't you?" She jumped off the bed and walked towards me, while I backed myself to the wall. "I can't go anywhere. Me and you? We're stuck together for life, love." She pointed her finger in my face.

"But I don't have cancer anymore!" I shouted.

"No, but you still have me. So get used to it."

I ran downstairs, threw my shoes on and dived into the car and drove. I cried all the way to the next county and only came to my senses when I realised I had no money and wasn't sure if I had enough petrol to get home. Surely, she was wrong. Surely, there was some way of getting her out of my life. But how? I wondered if there was a tablet I could take to suppress her. Or maybe I needed therapy to get rid of her. But the only thing that will make me forget her is forgetting I ever had cancer, and how is that going to happen when every time I look at my body the scars are there to remind me that Tracey and her disgusting brood were part of me?

How does anyone get over this? How does anyone carry on with their day-to-day life with the constant creep of a diseased shadow somewhere in the midst?

I made it home in time to go to the local firework display. Mark didn't notice I was quiet or the fact that Tracey stood beside me throughout the whole spectacle.

Thursday, 7th November 2019

I went to Anne's house this morning. More furniture has disappeared as well as pictures off the wall and various ornaments that covered windowsills and high shelves. As soon as she saw me, she knew I wasn't feeling okay. I felt as empty as her disappearing home.

I admitted to her through a torrent of tears that sometimes I still feel like I have cancer. That sometimes I can't accept I am well, and I feel exhausted all the time.

"But you're not well. You're still recovering. Oh, yes, you might think you're okay, but we all know that you get tired and try and hide it. We know that the injections give you ongoing pain, but you never complain. And we know that even though you smiled every day from the day they told you up until today, you've been terrified. All that fear would exhaust anyone, I'm sure. I was watching your Mark at the party last week—I think he could do with a holiday."

"I don't think he wants to marry me anymore."

She looked shocked. "Why on earth would you think that?!"

"He won't give me a date. I ask him, and he changes the subject."

"Of course he wants to marry you."

"Why would he want to marry me now? I'm so ugly. I'm practically deformed, and I won't let him touch me anywhere near there. What if it's all affecting him and he doesn't want to say, and that's why he won't commit?" I was blubbing so much I was surprised Anne could understand a word I was saying.

"The only thing men can commit to is finishing a beer and watching *Match of the Day*. Why do you think I became a lesbian?" she joked. "Jo, that man loves you for you and not simply because of what's in your bra. I've never heard a man turn around and say, 'I fell in love with her because she had a matching pair of tits.' And so what if you won't let him near the new one? There's still plenty of other things to play with in the park. Has he stopped having sex with you?"

"No."

"Well, there you go then."

"Yeah, but men…well, you know."

"What? Will shag anything? I might bat for the other side, but I'm quite sure most men grow out of that." She put her arm around me. "Humans want love more than sex." I pulled a face. "Which would you pick? A lifetime of love and no sex or a lifetime of sex and no love?" She didn't wait for my answer. "Most people pick love, Jo. It's love that gives us smiles and laughter and healing and support, and as far as I know, Mark has been providing you with all of that daily, with or without cancer, but especially since."

She was right. My relationship with Mark was much deeper than sex, and when I thought about the times we had made love since the operations, he had been very gentle, caring and more loving than ever.

"You could just sort the date out yourself, you know?"

I hadn't thought of that. How would he react if I said I had booked the reception without consulting him?

Anne continued, "The only thing I would suggest, though, is to wait until the New Year. Sort Christmas out first. This is your first one living together, and after the year you've had, you can go all out and make it extra special. Then, once you say goodbye to me and the missus, you can crack on and sort the wedding. How does that sound?"

"Will you be here for the wedding?"

"Wherever we are in the world, we'll be flying back. We've discussed it already."

I couldn't imagine getting married without Kelly and Anne.

"Now, let's get out of this house. It's starting to depress me."

We went shopping for shorts, which was no easy task in November, and then we had lunch in a country pub.

Monday, 11th November 2019

I woke up this morning feeling stiff in my arm. I think the cold might be affecting it. I can't win, though. Half of the night I'm lying on top of the bed due to the hot flushes, and I eventually go to sleep, but then I wake because I'm too cold and my arm is sore. Unless I go to bed with lard on one arm like a Channel swimmer, I'm not sure how I can regulate my temperature.

Tracey sat in silence as I did my exercises to loosen it up. She was still quiet while I walked around the shops. I've started my Christmas shopping, and taking Anne's advice, I want to make it extra special. I usually have a plastic tree, but I've decided to get a real one this year. This was met with applause from Mark, who always hated my old one from British Home Stores. My decorations are already tasteful and include several tree ornaments from places all over the world.

The only tree bauble I covet is one from Tiffany's. I saw an old film once where the whole tree was covered in decorations from Tiffany's. I don't want the entire tree laden because quite frankly it looked over the top, but just one would be nice.

Tracey disappeared now and again but returned when I tried on new dresses for Christmas Day. I tried on a black silk dress, thinking the thin fabric would help with the flushes and the opening of the oven door all day.

"Silk and goose fat? You sure?" Tracey sat on the small stool in the changing room, biting her nails and spitting the snaggy bits onto the floor.

"You might be right."

"Put a Christmas jumper on! It's more fun."

"I don't think I'll ever wear a jumper again." I couldn't decide on the dress. It was £200, and I wasn't sure if it would stand a day of me sweating on and off, never mind spitting roast potatoes.

"Get a nice silk camisole, all sexy like, and one of them cashmere thingies. That way, you can keep warm and cool whenever you want." She had a point.

"That could work."

"See! Not just a pretty face."

"You're not pretty, Tracey, and don't let anyone tell you differently," I said as I pulled off the dress.

"Don't put any sugar on it! Just give it to me straight."

"Just like you did to me, eh?"

She sulked in the corner while I got dressed but soon cheered up when she saw me buying the camisole and cashmere wrap.

She gave me a smile as I paid for them like I was forgiven. Anything for a quiet life.

Sunday, 17th November 2019

I met Amara for lunch today. She still hasn't got a job, but as far as I could tell she isn't that bothered. She seems to fill her days better than me with family, lunches and weekends away. She doesn't have a husband, but there have been a couple in the past. Both of them sound like they gave her a hard time for different reasons, but she's surprisingly not bitter about it all. She talks of crap in her past with the same emotion as ordering a coffee. Had time done that for her, or was it simply Amara and her incredible spirit? Either way, I wondered if I would ever feel like that about my cancer. After a few wines, I broached the subject of how much cancer affected her.

"It never goes away, darling. That fear of it coming back? I'm sorry, but it never goes." I was surprised to hear that, not just because of what she said but because she looked so vulnerable. "You learn to live with it and try to ignore it as much as you can. But with the daily tablets and the side effects and the annual scans and the prodding and poking, you're always reminded that you are a cancer survivor."

It was then that I realised just how naïve I've been. What on earth made me think I could go back to being the old me? I thought the old me was left on the operating table when they took my breast away, but actually, the old me started to disappear that day in Amsterdam, when I told Mark about the lump. That was the day when it all felt a little real. That was the day when Mark started to worry, even though I said it would be fine. Even though we laughed about porridge tits and about how a new pair of boobs might not be a bad thing.

"You just have to get on with it, darling," Amara said and then promptly ordered two cocktails.

But how do I get on with it? Who is the new me?

Friday, 22nd November 2019

I spent most of today online, looking at kilns for the studio. I've decided what I want but didn't order it. I just want to get some costings sorted. Until my arm is a lot stronger, there's no point me even thinking about using a potter's wheel. Even pulling the clay can be hard work. While I spent no money, I feel better for having made a few decisions about all of my new equipment.

Later on, the girls came over for a few drinks, as Mark has gone to a stag do in Scotland for a few days. Talk turned to Kelly and Anne's leaving do.

"We want a theme," said Kelly. "The Halloween party was such a laugh."

They've booked a function room at a local country restaurant, The Lodge. The room is one of the old barns, which has been renovated and is popular for weddings and christenings in the summer and charity functions in the winter months.

We suggested several themes, including bad taste, famous film stars and *The Great Gatsby*.

"We looked at The Lodge for our wedding reception," said Mia, "but we couldn't get the date we wanted. It's very popular. I would've loved my wedding pictures to have had the backdrop of the lake there."

"Have you seen it at night?" asked Saskia. "There are fairy lights everywhere. It's stunning. I hope they put them on for your party. Hello?" Saskia waved her hand in front of Anne's blank face, and for a moment, I was afraid she was having another stroke. Thankfully, she was just lost in thought.

"I've got it! Why don't we have a bride and groom theme?" Anne looked at Kelly. "We always argue about who will have the best wedding dress if we ever get married, so why not use this occasion and have some fun with it?"

"Seriously?"

"Oh, I'd love to put my wedding dress back on!" Mia squealed.

"My cousin had the most amazing dress," mused Charlotte. "I wonder if she'd let me borrow it."

"Why not?" said Anne. "People have black-and-white themed parties. We're just taking it a step further. Men are only allowed in white or black tuxedos. It would be fun if some of the girls wore wedding dresses from bygone years. What do you think, Jo?"

I was still mulling over what a party would be like with dozens of brides—especially the toilets. When Mia got married, I walked in on her mum holding her dress above her head and telling Mia to walk backwards until she reached the pan to have her wee. Mia was cocooned in all of the fabric and did as she was told.

"It could be fun," I said.

"Right, that's settled then," beamed Anne. "Kelly, you can finally wear a wedding dress."

"Why don't you two just get married?"

"Oh, we're not arsed about getting married. I'm only arsed about being able to wear a wedding dress," said Kelly.

"Which is why so many marriages fail," added Anne.

I wondered if I knew anyone who had a wedding dress I could borrow. The only one I knew was Mia, and she was still jumping up and down, knowing she could wear it again herself.

"I'm going to look on eBay," said Saskia. "There's tons on there. Designer ones as well, costing buttons."

"Oh, this is where Saskia turns up like Carrie bleeding Bradshaw in her Vera Wang," I joked.

"Get on there, Jo. You'll be surprised. You might even see one for when you get married!" Saskia must've seen my face drop because she came over and sat next to me. "What?"

"She's being silly," said Anne. "She reckons Mark doesn't want to get married because he won't set a date."

"Set it yourself," said Mia. "I did."

“That’s what I said!” Anne grinned smugly at me.

“I know I’m being paranoid about it. I’m going to wait until the New Year and then start looking at some venues and dates and then just tell him. If he reacts badly, then I’ll know for sure.”

The girls agreed that early next year would be an excellent time to start looking and also echoed what Anne had said about men being crap at sorting things. As usual, they made me feel better.

Saturday, 23rd November 2019

I woke up slightly hungover and was glad I didn't have much to do today. With Mark being away, I don't even need to tidy up or cook for anyone. I toyed with the idea of staying in bed all day, but being an insomniac gives you the feeling you've been in bed all day anyway by eight o'clock in the morning.

Does lying on the couch with the quilt qualify as getting up?

Does opening the door to the pizza man qualify as doing something with your day?

Does buying a pair of shoes online qualify as a shopping trip?

If so, I did loads even if I was still in last night's pyjamas and I've not ventured near a shower all day.

I even turned my phone off for most of the day—a habit I am forming more and more now. I used to laugh when people said they felt liberated when they came off social media, but it's true. I find I'm leaving my phone in another room on purpose, and each time I do, I'm more reluctant to return to it. If anyone wants me, they can call me on the landline. Do I have a landline? Do I have a phone number?

And who's going to call me on it when even I'm not aware whether I have what is now classed as an antiquated contraption?

By the evening, I was suitably stuffed on pepperoni pizza and decided to watch a film. I stumbled across *Love Story*, which had only just started. I watched it years ago and had forgotten most of the story, such as Ali McGraw's character, Jenny, getting cancer. I thought about turning it off, but by the time she received her diagnosis, I was too invested in the film.

That was when Tracey joined me.

She sat at the other end of the sofa I was lying on and didn't look at me at first. She just watched the telly, as I did. She stayed like that until the credits began to roll and then turned and watched me wailing like a banshee.

"Why do you watch this stuff?" she asked, shaking her head.

"I don't know. I forgot she got cancer and died, and now he's on his own, and his dad is too late," I howled.

"It's a film! She went on to do *Dynasty*, and he…well… he nursed Farrah Fawcett through her cancer, didn't he? He might have learnt stuff while he was making that film."

"Don't be stupid!"

"Well, I don't know! I'm just trying to make you feel better."

And there it was. It was then that everything changed.

"Why do you want me to feel better?" I whispered.

"You still don't get it, do you? You still don't realise I did you a favour." She looked hurt. No, I didn't get it. I just stared at her blankly. "How long do you think Tyson and the kids and the dog were in there for?"

I hadn't thought about how long I'd had cancer before they diagnosed me. I just shrugged.

"Well, it had been a while, love, and you would never have known they were in there, growing bigger by the day. Tyson had a sneaky streak, I don't mind telling you, and the kids… they just didn't know any better. Not their fault, I suppose."

"But you?"

"Now do you get it?" She looked at me expectantly.

Tracey was the first and only one I felt. Tracey was the reason I went to the doctor in the first place. Tracey was the reason they found Tyler, Tina, the dog Sentinel and of course, Tyson—the big one. If I hadn't felt Tracey, I'd still be none the wiser, ignorantly walking around, working, overeating, drinking far more, stressing and not exercising while they festered and got bigger and spread, latching on to various parts of my body, inaccessible parts, inoperable parts. My mind went straight to the moment I first felt her upstairs in the bathroom—the moment I caught her lurking in the shadows. She was warning me. She was telling me.

I started to cry. Tracey didn't move. She just carried on looking at me.

"I get it."

"I know I'm not the best thing in your life, Jo, but I was trying to help you. Strange to think of it like that, I know, but it's true. I didn't bury myself like the others. I pushed myself right to the front." She laughed a little.

"Typical you. You're still like that now. Wanting to be noticed all the time."

For a long time, we sat in silence, except for the moments when I would cry again. To say I've had mixed emotions about my cancer is an understatement, but this was something else. I actually felt gratitude towards this creature before me. I was glad she was in my life. And for a moment, I felt a degree of comfort that she was there.

After an hour of my periodic blubbing, she gave my leg a motherly rub. "Call Mark and forget about me for a bit, eh?"

I did as she suggested. As soon as Mark picked up his phone, she went away.

Friday, 1st December 2019

Charlotte had the day off today and came to my house for lunch. I invited her over to talk about Kelly and Anne's leaving party and how we could make it more special for them. It seems everything I suggested is already in hand or would be put to the vote with the rest of the group, who, I should add, all have dresses already. I haven't even started looking.

"How have you not got something? You don't work all day!"

"I'm still running to physiotherapists and the doctors and the hospital and stuff!" I protested.

"Every day?" She saw my face drop a little. "No, I didn't think so."

"I hate shopping for normal clothes on the internet, never mind a wedding dress. How do they size them?"

"Like normal."

"What about the length?"

"You get it taken up if it's too long."

"Have you got a big puffy one?"

"It is a little. Aren't wedding dresses supposed to be like that?"

"I don't know. Why couldn't they just have a normal party?" I grumbled.

"This is Kelly and Anne we're talking about! Look, just find something you like on eBay and get it ordered."

We spent most of the afternoon looking at second-hand dresses and some of the brides who'd originally worn them. We realised we were judging the dresses on how pretty the bride was and if her new husband looked impressed. Most of them looked terrified.

"I hope Mark doesn't look that scared when he marries me."

Finding nothing second-hand that appealed, we ventured into the 'made to measure from China' area of eBay. It seems you can get a Vera Wang copy for £100.

"Can you believe that?" Charlotte was astounded. "A bride's dress can be cheaper than her accessories! Go and get a tape measure!"

The tape measure was still on the bed from my morning lymphoedema paranoia check-in. Within half an hour of being measured, a dress was ordered, and an email arrived to say the dress would be with me in fourteen days.

"They say they work fast, the Chinese," said Charlotte.

"Who says that?"

"I dunno. But that email from eBay suggests that 'they' are right." She shrugged.

We spent the rest of the day eating chocolate and watching old episodes of *Sex and the City* until Mark came home. When she left, I had the feeling that Charlotte had needed my company more than I'd needed hers today. She's extremely independent, but I know deep down she wants her 'Mark'. She wants to look after somebody, and until her Mr. Right comes along, me and the girls are her 'somebody'.

Wednesday, 11th December 2019

Today was my last physiotherapy session. While I may not be cured and never will be of axillary web syndrome, at least I can manage it myself moving forward. They've manipulated my scar tissue as much as they can. They've stretched all the cords they can reach as far as they will go. I know all the exercises and have adapted them so much that Esmé has been suggesting some of my moves to other patients.

I'll miss Esmé. Over the last few months, she has not only helped me, but I've been giving her advice on lots of things including handbags, Farrow & Ball and men, of course. While I may not be an expert, I am a lot older than her, and she took all man advice with great enthusiasm. She was only a breath away from pulling out her notepad when I advised her to talk to her man on a subconscious level.

"What do you mean?"

"Well, you can't ask a man to do something straight out. He has to procrastinate, to delay. He can't help it. He's just made that way. So you have to sow the seed in his head in other ways. Once it's in there, you just water it now and again and let it flourish. Then when it blooms, he'll suggest whatever it is to you, and all you need to do is smile."

"Like what? Give me an example."

I thought of all the things Mark had done for me. All the things he thought were his idea. I was an expert at it. This poor kid in front of me did not have a clue about men. I had to start small.

"How often does your man cook?"

"He never does. He says he can't, but he can."

"Okay, so start with something simple like getting him to cook you a meal. I bet if you asked him to cook you a meal, it would be served with a side of sulk."

She laughed. I continued.

"Getting a man to cook is a three-day lead-up. Day one, you cook him his favourite dinner. Make sure you point out that you cooked his favourite because you love him. Day two, when he's eating your dinner, ask him something like, 'Have you ever noticed when someone else makes you something to eat just how much nicer it is? Like when you make your lasagne, I enjoy it so much more than mine.' Then leave it hanging. Don't overwater it—you'll kill it. Then on day three, ask him what he would like for his tea. Say you want to go to the shops early because you feel a little tired. By the end of day three, he'll be serving you lasagne like Gino De'fucking Campo with a tea towel draped over his arm. Then he'll want sex. Just warning you!"

"He'll have to unblock the kitchen sink before he gets that."

We laughed at how much we could manipulate men with the promise of sex, food or the remote control.

So my physio is no more. I just have to keep up with my exercises every day, and if it gets really bad then I can go back to my GP and get another referral, but it won't be to go back to Esmé. It will no doubt be the one in the doctor's who doesn't actually touch you. She just sits behind a desk and gives you the appropriate leaflet. I made a mental promise that if I needed physio in future, I'd pay for one who understands this condition.

My first discharge from a clinic. It's taken nine months. I'm more patient than Winnie Mandela.

Tuesday, 17th December 2019

My party dress turned up from China today. I'm not going to lie, dear Diary, it's actually quite lovely. I'm even thinking of using these people again when I get married. The strapless, drop-waist gown has an A-line skirt covered in tiny tulle flowers. Charlotte and I picked it as it reminded us of an Oscar De La Renta dress we'd seen on Carrie Bradshaw in the finale of *Sex and the City*. A pale-silver organza sash ties around the waist in an exaggerated bow. It fits perfectly, and I took some selfies and sent them to the girls, who said it looks great and how they all can't wait to put theirs on too. The dress is long enough that you can't see my feet, so I've decided to wear my white leather brogues underneath. I'll be able to dance all night.

I'm feeling mixed about New Year's Eve, to be honest. On the one hand, I can't wait to see the year out, but on the other hand, let's not lose sight of it being a leaving do. My dearest friends are saying *Bon Voyage*, and even though Kelly and Anne say they are coming back in twelve months, I'm not so sure. Part of me hopes they stay on their adventure for as long as they can, as I have a feeling Kelly will need and feed on those memories one day.

Before I took the dress off, I checked how my boobs look with the strapless neckline. Should I change my bra?

"Put the padded satin one on," said Tracey behind me. "It'll make you feel more confident."

She's right, of course.

Tuesday, 24th December 2019

We—mainly Mark—have spent most of the day cleaning, which Mark was annoyed about, as we're not even having dinner at our house tomorrow. Anne invited us over and looked hurt when we initially declined.

"All the girls are coming. You can't be the only ones not there. Lucy is bringing Andy, and Mia and Rob are coming. You and Mark have to be there. And the house looks nice now since Andy has painted it all through. You don't have to stay all day, but I'd like to cook you all one last meal."

Did Anne have a feeling she wasn't coming back? I had no choice.

"Of course we'll come."

Mark suggested we have our own Christmas meal in between Christmas and New Year, which I said was a lovely idea. If I'm to get any help, though, I'll need to start working on his subconscious now. That's proving difficult, as he cleaned most of the house while I was wrapping presents.

"Why have you left it to the last minute, Jo?" he shouted as he vacuumed around me.

"What's Christmas without a bit of last-minute rushing?" He smiled and kissed me while he wrestled with the Henry hoover. It's not been the same since Halloween.

With the presents wrapped and the housework done, we went to our local church. I haven't been to mass for a while and felt today was a good day to end my abstinence. We sang Christmas carols; well, I say 'we'—I sang like Maria Von Trapp while Mark stood there occasionally joining in with a prolonged vowel at the end of random lines.

Then after a nightcap of Bailey's, we went to bed to wait for Father Christmas. I hope Mark likes his presents. I usually fret more than I have this year. But when I think about it, I already have my gift.

Life.

Wednesday, 25th December 2019

Mark loves his new watch. I had it engraved with *Thank You for Being My Strength* on the back. He had other presents, but that was the one that made him quiet. Always a good sign.

I was spoilt, as usual. But my favourite present was tickets for both of us to go to the New Orleans Mardi Gras next year. He remembered my bucket list.

"I looked at Paris as well," he said, "but figured we could wait until you have a chest infection and make it a good one."

I was repulsed at the thought of spitting green infected mucus off the top of the Eiffel Tower and yet found it hysterical at the same time.

"Paris isn't far. We can go anytime you want next year," Mark said.

We had breakfast, then Tracey joined me while I dressed in my camisole and cashmere wrap. She silently watched me finish my make-up and hair and smiled at me when I left the house for Kelly and Anne's.

Their house looked very different when we arrived. Mark walked in none the wiser while I took in the white walls and new grey carpet. Everything smelled shiny and new, and virtually all traces of our friends' former lives had gone. I felt a little sad when I walked into the lounge. The Wilton rugs were no more. Most of the furniture had also disappeared except for the dining table, a four-seater sofa, a TV and a Christmas tree.

"I didn't think you would bother with a tree," I said.

"We're becoming adventurers, not Jehovah's Witnesses," said Anne as she passed me a Buck's Fizz.

"So who's moving in?"

"A lovely family from Ireland. The husband has a new job in town. Something to do with maritime navigational equipment. Anyway, they have two kids and only wanted to rent to see if they settled first."

"Makes sense."

"I'm glad there's going to be kiddies in the house. We've laughed," Anne looked over at Kelly, "but kids' laughter is something special, don't you think?" She didn't wait for an answer. She made her way to the kitchen to attend to one of her bubbling pans.

We were the last to arrive, and once we did, Kelly and Anne were keen for us to be seated. The meal was lovely, far nicer than anything Mark or I could cook. The wine flowed before, during and after every course, and then the meal was polished off with brandies all around.

The rest of the afternoon, we played games, silly games like Charades, Pictionary (using Andy's leftover lining paper) and Who Am I? It felt like a proper Christmas—not like the ones from earlier years where I spent most of the day hungover and wondering why on earth I bought such a large turkey for two people. Mark and I struggle to eat a whole chicken between us, but because it's Christmas, I always end up with a bird that could feed a small African country. That, plus forty pigs in blankets, enough potatoes to threaten another famine and so much gravy it can only be served with a hose would see us swerving the Yule log until Boxing Day. Not like Anne's! Anne had given everyone a portion that took them to 'suitably stuffed' level, and she didn't have to play Jenga with the leftover food in the fridge when we'd all finished.

It was a lovely day. A special day. And I am truly grateful.

Saturday, 28th December 2019

Today was my turn at making Christmas lunch. We didn't hold out much hope of it being anything like Anne's, but as I began to make my twenty-four stuffing balls, I realised I didn't want it to. I wanted our flaws in the meal. I wanted us to be begging for our fat pants before we finished eating, and I wanted to get very, very drunk.

I started the day drinking Buck's Fizz just like Anne's except mine had less Buck and more Fizz. I was soon dancing to Michael Jackson while I prepared the veg, and I felt the implant protesting to all the frivolity when I jumped up and down.

Tracey appeared and sat on the worktop, watching me being brutal with the broccoli. "You better tell Mark to move his car so the coach can pull up outside the house," she joked.

"I know. I'm the same every year. I don't know why I buy so much. But to be fair, we don't waste it. We just get fed up of eating leftover turkey by February."

"You had a nice Christmas?" she asked.

"I did. I felt really well, and I hardly saw you—no offence."

"None taken, sweetheart."

"I hope you're not going to be hanging around me all day."

"Well, stop jumping up and down like you're in a mosh pit then."

I gave my implant a rub to make sure it was still in the right place, which it was.

She watched me while I danced to Marvin Gaye and was gone by the time I needed to make the gravy. Mark arrived in the kitchen, circling me like a vulture, asking if he could help. He only offers assistance when he catches himself licking the telly when the food adverts come on.

I didn't serve the meal in lots of china dishes like Anne did—which I don't like, by the way. The food seems to go cold really quickly, and if you're in company of more than four, you start to scrutinise everyone helping themselves and wish you were sitting at the other end of the table where all the good stuff is. No, I serve mine on the plate, and it resembles Ayers Rock. When I see that sandstone monolith rise from the IKEA plate, I know there's probably enough.

This year, we had some foresight and sat at the table with our fat pants already in situ. After four hours of cooking and thirty minutes of eating, we admitted defeat and retired to the lounge, where we promptly fell asleep in front of *Love Actually*. Sorry, Hugh Grant, but you bore the arse off me.

Wednesday, 31st December 2019

I have never been so glad to see a day like this day when I opened my eyes this morning. I know it's only a day, and 1st January doesn't usually make that much difference, but I think it will for me this year. I need a sign, a symbol, a point in time when I can say this is the start of something else. I'm not sure what it is, but I know there are things I don't want to take into the new year. I don't want to take the Jo who got wound up over the silly stuff. I've learned most of it doesn't matter. I don't want to take the Jo who is scared of speaking her mind because I've learned that most people want my advice or opinion. I've learned who my real friends are and to get rid of people who can't see beyond the end of their own front path. I want to see the Jo who dances more and shrugs more when things don't go as planned, who learns to love her new body and learns to live with Tracey.

I didn't see her all day—not even when I was getting ready for Kelly and Anne's leaving party. I forgot all about her. I thought she might have turned up to see Mark in his tuxedo. He looked so handsome, and I told him we might have to leave the party early as he looked that fit. He got quite emotional when he saw me in my fake wedding dress.

"Do you feel pretty?" he asked as he zipped me into it.

"I do. It's probably the prettiest I've felt in a very long time." I went on to tell him how the dress was a *Sex and the City* knock-off, but he just smiled at me and kissed my shoulder as I carried on looking into the mirror.

So, Diary, we turned up at The Lodge.

Instead of a leaving party being organised, it was a wedding.

My wedding.

I walked into The Lodge, and the whole place was lit with fairy lights and candles. There were white flowers hanging from the ceiling, from the backs of chairs and huge displays around the perimeter of the room, which was also swathed in huge swags of white tulle. I stood there stunned, looking at everyone bathed in the gorgeous candlelight.

I looked at Mark.

"I'm sure you've gathered by now that this is not Kelly and Anne's leaving do." He watched my face change. "Though they are still leaving," he added quickly. He looked really nervous, and I grabbed his hand. He smiled and took a breath and bent down on one knee.

"Will you marry me, Jo? Will you marry me now?"

"You still want me? Even though I'm wearing brogues." He smiled and nodded. "Well, seeing as it looks like you mugged the Chelsea Flower Show, I guess I'll have to say yes." There was a huge cheer and a round of applause, at which Mark shouted for them to calm down, as we hadn't got married yet.

A woman married us. I didn't know her, but she was lovely, and her voice was warm when she spoke to all of our friends about the love Mark and I share. Because I didn't know anything, Mark revealed that we could say our own vows or go with the traditional ones. We did both. I promised Mark that I would let him watch *Match of the Day* every week and he could get Sky Sports. I promised him that I would rinse the sink after I brushed my teeth so he wouldn't have to shout at me anymore. I promised that I would not slag off his music all of the time, only half of the time. But I also promised that I would love him more than he could ever show me. I promised to look after him as well as he has looked after me this past year, and I promised I would never stop.

So I am now Mrs. Mark Houston.

The rest of the night was a glorious haze. I danced and laughed and listened to stories of cloak-and-dagger meetings and secret conversations that had been taking place in the last couple of months without me knowing. Mark and the girls have all been very busy.

By the end of the night, which came around too soon, I realised that I hadn't said goodbye to Kelly and Anne.

"We're not flying until late tomorrow," said Anne, "so pop over tomorrow afternoon and say goodbye."

"I can't believe this is my wedding day. Today is the first proper day I can look forward."

"Oh, you should never look back." She paused for a moment. "Unless you're reversing in the Asda car park." She gave me a familiar wink. "And for God's sake, bring a bottle of fizz." I had never taken the fizz I'd always promised, but I knew tomorrow that I would.

We were the first to leave even though it was after two in the morning. We silently sat in the cab going home, and I suddenly felt overwhelmed with the enormity of the night.

"Are you okay?" Mark was concerned.

I nodded.

"Why are you crying?"

"I don't know," I said truthfully.

"Do you feel like you've made a mistake?" He shifted in the seat towards me.

"Oh, God, no! Never! I'm just so happy that after everything, you still love me, I suppose."

"I couldn't stop if I wanted to."

"Then don't."

When we reached the house, I told Mark to go straight upstairs. I told him I needed a glass of water and would follow him up. But instead of going to the sink, I went straight to the studio. In the darkness, I could still make out the glass fish on the lower shelf, and I stooped to pick it up and walked to the far side of the room.

"Are you there, Tracey?" I whispered.

"I'm here." She was sitting on the small step from the kitchen to the studio where I had just walked in. "Congratulations."

"Thank you."

"So, it'll be the three of us living here then?"

"I guess so."

She walked towards me. "You deserved today. Especially after what I put you through."

"And still do, Tracey."

"But look at you. You look lovely. You would never have thought that you could wear a strapless dress, and here you are on your wedding day, and no one can tell, and no one bleeding cares."

"If it ever comes back, will you show me again?"

"I can't promise. And anyway, who says it's coming back?"

"I'm scared."

"I know. But I'll be here to remind you in here," she pointed to my head, "that I'm not here anymore." She then pointed to my chest. "You put up a good fight,

Jo, and I'm glad to say the best woman won. You proved you are stronger than me, Tina, Tyler, Tyson and even the dog, all put together. You slayed us, bitch." She laughed.

"I did, didn't I?"

"Wear those scars with pride. Don't always hide them with your fancy bras, especially from your husband. He loves you more because of those scars."

"You think?"

"Jesus, girl. He's upstairs waiting to take that wedding dress off his wife. Ain't no think about it!"

I put the glass fish back on the shelf. I thought she would follow me, but she stayed in the shadows on the far side of the room.

"Happy New Year, Jo."

Epilogue

When he opened his eyes, it took him a moment to adjust to the dimly lit bedroom. He was facing her side of the bed and immediately noticed she wasn't there. He sat up, rubbed his face and then peeled the quilt away from his warm legs. He staggered to the en suite bathroom, and once he was finished in there, he emerged again, looking for his dressing gown. He found it, draped over her dressing table chair, and slipped it on, at the same time spying her perfume on the dressing table itself. Without thought, he reached for it and sniffed the silver tip. A smile hinted at the corner of his mouth; it was too early for a proper smile. He put the perfume back in the exact spot where he'd found it because that's where she liked it to be.

In his bare feet, he padded down the stairs which led directly into the lounge, and that was where he found her. She was surrounded by presents of various sizes and various shapes, some wrapped well and some not so much. After greeting her husband good morning, she explained how their wedding presents had arrived. Her excitement was infectious, and he was soon inspecting the labels to see who the generous giver was. She wanted to start opening them straight away, but he instructed her to hold on for a moment while he went to fetch something.

***

She watched him leave, presuming he was going to put the kettle on…until she heard him open the squeaky drawer that contained items which couldn't be grouped into 'cutlery' or 'tea towels'. The drawer that hid half-burnt birthday candles, batteries and an old Blackberry charging cable.

He soon returned clutching a small but perfectly wrapped gift. The paper was pearlescent white; a pewter-coloured ribbon made it look more beautiful still. He held the small square out to her. There was no label, but she knew it was from him. Still on her knees, she reached out and took her first present from her husband.

Carefully and slowly, she peeled the sticky tape away and unfurled each precisely folded end. As she pulled the last of the covering back, she spied it.

A diary.

And at that moment, she knew he knew. She knew he knew of the woman who lived with them. The woman and her blown-glass fish and Care Bear T-shirt. The woman who had lost Tyson, Tyler and Tina. The woman who would never go away, and whom they had both come to accept. They would talk about it one day, the contents of the pages hidden in her bedside drawer. But not today. Today was her first morning of being a wife. Today was the day when Mrs. Houston would begin another story.

Which, according to the front, would take a standard twelve months.

THE END

About the Author

Estelle Maher was born in the heart of Liverpool, England. After spending her teens in rural Dorset, she returned to the North of England and now resides in Wirral with her husband, two children and three dogs.

Her career has been varied, but in her spare time, she's quite at home with a paint brush, upcycling furniture. She also writes a blog in her spare time, The Secret Diary of a Middle Aged Woman, a humorous snapshot of random thoughts.

Estelle has been writing on and off for a number of years, and writing the blog was her first step in writing for an audience that was wider than her and her husband.

Her debut novel, *Grace & The Ghost*, won a Best Spiritual Fiction Award 2018, and her spin-off *Angel's Rebellion* also became an Amazon bestseller. Her third novel, *The Killing of Tracey Titmass*, is based on her own cancer journey. Told in diary form, it offers an alternative way of accepting cancer.

Estelle is now in recovery and still smiles every day.

Also by Estelle Maher

Grace & The Ghost

Angel's Rebellion

Find out more at:
https://estellemaher.com

Beaten Track Publishing

Printed in Great Britain
by Amazon

49377262R00222